Michael Braccia

Vision of Another Life

To Jesse

Best wishes

Michael Braccia

First published in this format 2025

© Michael Braccia

Cover image by Gabriel @ natural

All characters and events in this publication, other than those clearly in the public domain, are fictitious and any resemblance to real persons, living or dead, is purely coincidental.

All rights reserved.
No part of this publication may be reproduced, stored in a retrieval system or transmitted in any form without the prior permission of the author / publisher.

A CIP catalogue record for this book is available from the British Library.

ISBN   979-834-9-651-747

Acknowledgements

To my wife, Lesley, and my son, Philip, for their love and support.

Lesley played a significant role in helping me to produce this book. Many hours of proofreading, cover design, and giving me helpful suggestions have resulted in a novel of which I am very proud.

To Mark Jones, my friend and fellow writer, and the editor of this book through his own business, Emjay Editing. Thank you for your friendship, help and support over the years.

Also by Michael Braccia:

Could it be that way: Living with Autism (semi-autobiographical novel)

Banfield Tales (a book of short stories)

Leeford Village (co-written with Jon Markes)

All available via Amazon.co.uk

See Michael's website for details:
www.michaelbraccia.co.uk

VISION OF ANOTHER LIFE

By Michael Braccia

Part One

1: The Village

I can't see anything. Total darkness, but I know a main road is only feet away. I can hear traffic going by. The scent of trees and leaves to my left, the edge of the pavement to my right. One foot in front of the other, paving slabs beneath my feet. Stand still for a moment. Is anyone here to help me? A bird's wing flapping near a tree. I can sense the branches swaying, the wind gently brushing past. The rustle of grass, an animal, a squirrel. I'm in the middle of the pavement. Safe there. A few steps, not too far, get your bearings. I'm on the left side of the road, walking in the direction of the traffic passing close to the kerb. Perhaps they're going into a town; commuters, shoppers. A little to the left, a driveway. It's wide. Not a house, at least not an average house. Walk a few yards. It's a warm day. My hand on the ground touches the stickiness, the gritty firmness of tarmac. Oddly reassuring. Normal. At least twenty paces. This is a car park. A building to my left, a large building. Shops? A clinic? Sit down now, feeling tired, dizzy. Need to sleep.

Walking through the village, starting at the Methodist Church. Crossing the road would take me to the Swan Inn and a row of pre-war semi-detached. All teachers and accountants. Youngsters can't afford houses like that. I stay on this side. Past the church, I see the physiotherapist's, more houses (terraced), garage, optician's, baker's, undertaker's (opposite the local library). Further down, I'm not far from the main village crossroads now, only two hundred yards. It must be early morning, the aroma of freshly baked bread seeping into my senses. On the other side, past the library, the familiar sight of the newsagent's, chip shop, bank, jeweller's, down to the charity shop by The Cross. On the left, where I'm walking - the hairdresser's, chemist's, solicitor's, flower shop, right by the lights at the crossroads. The fruit stall on the market suggests the essence of the countryside and lands further afield: mangoes, passion fruit, oranges. Familiar faces pass by, acknowledge, wave. Cross the road at the lights, back up the other side, past the bank. Bus stop outside the chip shop. An old man. He's there every day. His cigarette smoke, although not pleasant, is somehow reassuring. We exchange nods as I breathe in, before encountering the small cloud he creates. Over the road, the shutters are being raised at the hairdresser's. It must be 9am. The creaking, rattling of the springs and levers, noises entering my brain, creating a train of thought. Next door, the same procedure followed by the local chemist, and, further along, the flower shop. The high street bursting into life with all the familiar noises taken for granted as the morning commuters march by. A car pulls over to allow an ambulance those crucial extra seconds that could save a life. A bus wheezes to a halt outside the chip shop to pick up a single passenger, who dispenses his cigarette in the gutter. The engine splutters in unison with the smoker as it pulls away once again.

I must have fallen asleep. I am sitting up, leaning against a wall, tarmac beneath me. Back in the car park.

The village, I suppose, was a dream. The sights and the smells are so familiar. I've been there many times before, but I'm still confused. The headache comes and goes. I sense something is changing. I can no longer hear the flapping of the bird's wing, the breeze caressing the branches, traffic going by. I can no longer smell the freshly mown grass. A dim light, like a faint dawn, touches me softly. Not a blinding light, but a realisation. My senses collide as I harvest one and squander another. A perception of movement, arriving, but I am still sitting there. Shapes appear, familiar shapes. The trees surrounding the car park. Not far from the road, maybe ten yards. I can stand and turn round, no longer dizzy. The church. Something tells me this is my starting point, or is it the end of something? Instinctively, I understand that I can't go up the road, past the church, away from the village. I must go towards the village. But not just yet.

Days pass, in and out of sleep. It must be sleep. Not sure where I slept, where I stayed, if I've eaten. This road, this area that holds me, knows me. I live near here, surely. We live here, my family. I'll remember soon. After the blackness, I can now see. The doors open. People are leaving the church. Some of them with tear-stained faces, walking to their cars. Everyone ignores me. No one challenges me, asking why I am sitting there. They are gone now, a stream of cars. The doors are closed.

I want to walk now, and I am compelled to walk towards the village, towards the crossroads. A memory appears. It's called The Cross. Maybe I dreamt it before, but as I progress down the high street (Swan Inn over the road), people are viewing a second-hand car at the garage. The baker's, undertaker's, hairdresser's, to the market by The Cross. Lights changing, people crossing in all directions except one. Haven't seen anyone cross the road *away* from the village. They seem to stay this side of The Cross. The scene gets clearer as I watch it again and again. Memories are flowing in. At least, bits of memories, linking, repairing. From darkness, I can now see every detail, and the village is everything I have. I know this place. I know the people. This is where I should be. At least for now. But it's not right. It doesn't feel right. So many questions.

No one speaks to me anymore. It's like I'm invisible. Since arriving here, I've not had a single conversation with anyone, even to exchange the odd pleasantry, the occasional 'hello, how are you'. I prefer the quiet life, but now I am disconnected, alone. There is no longer an email address - I used to check it at least six times a day. In those days an hour couldn't go by without a compulsion to check Hotmail and texts 'just in case'. There's no mobile phone now.

I'm in the local library. Not sure why. Browsing the fiction section - always good to find an author you recognise. Must get round to reading that, one of the days. He sounds good, just my kind of author. Won't bother with a coffee. They installed the machine last week. Strange having a coffee machine and Wi-Fi in a public library. How times change. Must renew my ticket sometime - sure it's out of date. That one who does the afternoon shift is a bit surly. She was quite rude to that old man the other day. I've not taken any books yet. I don't have my library ticket with me. I'll pop in one of the mornings and sort it out. Just seen my Uncle Graham. He must be busy. He didn't notice me.

The sounds and the smells of the village have changed. I remember the aroma from the bakery, first thing in the morning. That wonderful smell of freshly baked bread evoking memories of home, childhood - good memories. I remember the smell of fruit from the market. I remember the old man's cigarette smoke and the sounds of shutters rattling and creaking as shops open, ready for business. Ready to start another day. I recall an ambulance rushing by, cars pulling over. Now, there is no sumptuous aroma of freshly baked bread, no tangy taste of exotic fruit, and no cigarette smoke. No creaking shutters. Cars glide soundlessly past. Ambulance sirens set to silent.

No smells, no sounds, nothing. The sounds, smells, tastes, all the senses in my dream, if it was a dream, have left me with a strange reality.

The move here must have happened suddenly, and there was no time to think, no time to be aware, given no choice in the matter. I know that much. Who decides these things? It seems such a long way from where I used to live and such a strange environment. Not even sure who my landlord is. Don't think I've paid any rent yet. I don't recall the journey. Perhaps I fell asleep on the way, became ill, bumped my head. Did someone give me a lift in a car? Or was it train, or coach? Wish I could remember. Thing is, everything has changed. Someone must have told me to move here. Someone decided for me.

At Leeford Park now, by the lake. Beautiful here. I love to watch the boats sailing by. Reminds me of those early dates with Joanna. We loved to stroll by the shore, the peace of the lakes or the immense power of the sea. Never mind, it's a beautiful day. Have I brought any lunch? No. Maybe I'll get something later. Not so hungry these days. Let's walk up to the golf course. I used to play there. Cheapest nine holes in town. Council-run, so it's subsidised. The greens are not brilliant, but the views around the course are stunning. From the fourteenth tee, you can see the counties of Shropshire, Staffordshire and Worcestershire; countryside that belies the Midlands' industrial image. Relaxing. Doesn't matter if you're not playing well, if there's no one behind you complaining about slow play. Don't worry, you don't play now.

Back in the village now. Don't remember walking back from the park. I don't know any of these people, and they certainly don't know me. Perhaps just as well. They all seem so busy, dashing about. Sometimes I notice people walking towards The Cross. Look at that woman! She virtually ran into the bank - bet she'll jump the queue. No, it's just the cash machine. Fifty pounds for a special night out I expect. Haven't done that for a while. She's off again, scurrying into the supermarket. No time to live, everything an emergency. I have no recollection of walking from the village to the park and golf course, and now I'm back. Check my wallet - no cash or credit cards. My watch has stopped. It's broken. The glass is cracked, but I can still make out the time. Twenty-five past seven.

Alan, that's his name. And Peter. Joanna and I were very happy and so proud of our two boys. Alan is at Manchester studying graphic design, and Peter is a fitness instructor, always into sport. Peter was the first one, just twenty-four years ago. We were so young. Not sure how we coped, but we did. I'm an accountant. Good career. We had a nice life. Shame that it had to stop. A pleasure going home at the end of the day. Joanna would, without fail, say 'nice to be home love?' and tell me what we would have for tea. I miss that.

What did I do wrong? It's horrible to feel like a criminal, but that's how it is. Even my family don't talk to me anymore. Friends and ex-work colleagues ignore me. Funny that, at first, I thought I didn't know anyone in the village, and then I saw Joe and Teresa. I used to work with them - wasn't aware they lived here. Another memory stabs at me, but the fog in my mind won't clear. They walked straight past me. I have the impression that I am a long way from home, an outcast serving a life sentence. It's not a just punishment. I only wish that someone, anyone, would explain where I am and why I'm here.

Is someone controlling my situation? I'm getting a sense of two options – the village with its silence and isolation, or the beauty and serenity of the park. Is there a choice? I want to get back to the life I had before, but something is nagging away at me. It's not going to be an option. No idea why. There's no one to ask for help, but I perceive a sense of consciousness within me. Questions that may be answered, hopefully clarifying what has happened to me and what will happen next. My past is falling away, and nothing is certain.

Keep thinking I remember something, then it's gone. Yes, we were happy at home. Few arguments. We loved each other so much. I have a feeling that she still loves me and misses me. There goes that thought again. What is it? If I concentrate, the image in my mind becomes stronger. I need to understand. Instinct tells me that remembering what happened will bring everything to a conclusion.

I suddenly remember my childhood. On holiday in America with Mom and Dad. No older than thirteen, maybe fourteen. I was at the hotel with Dad's brother and his wife. The police told us that they didn't stand a chance when their car left the road. We used to go to church. Not after that, not for me. Not after Mom and Dad were taken from me. I wouldn't say that I don't believe as such, but I have no faith. They are different to me, belief and faith. Faith implies trust, and confidence that you will be cared for. I was angry, and that never really left me. Joanna says I'm agnostic. She likes labels.

There is a voice, maybe my own thoughts. It's all I have now. Something, someone, is telling me I'll never go back. Where is this coming from? There is a threshold, a window of time. One day. I don't want to walk towards The Cross. I've never seen anyone return from there. He is imploring me to move on, cross the threshold. Do I know this voice or is it my imagination? I am consumed with grief, panic, grieving the loss of my family. I sense they are well, but they can't reach me.

2: Ben and Joanna

'Hope you're not making a fuss tonight.'
'What about?'
Ben lowered his chin, but raised his eyes – the look that Joanna knew was a precursor to his making a point.
'Joanna, I'm forty-six today. I'm a boring old accountant who's had the day off to celebrate, and I hate parties. Remember now?'
'Oh, that. No, nothing happening. Honestly.'
'If it does, I'm off to the range. I've not played in three weeks and the monthly medal is next Saturday.'
'Now you realise why Mother calls me a golf widow.'
Joanna smiled, but Ben knew that look only too well.
'That's rubbish and you know it. I've got my golf, you have church, gardening and *Corrie*.'
'We both have our work, Ben.'
'I know that. I mean hobbies, if you can call *Corrie* a hobby.'
'What the hell are you arguing about now?' said Alan, shuffling towards the fridge.

On the generous work surface to the left of the fridge – his favourite spot – the rack on the wall invited selection of his Wallace & Gromit mug for yet another coffee. Joanna's Leeford Parish glossy calendar reflected the light forcing its way through from the garden, striking the Manchester United magnet that Alan had strategically placed at eye level.

'If you've always been like this, how on earth did me and Peter get born?'

'My child, it's the making up that's the thing,' Ben replied, smiling at his son.

'Ben Stone!' exclaimed Joanna.

'Love, he's twenty, and knows more about the birds and the bees than we ever will.'

'All the same.'

'Mom, I'm on your side,' Alan said, throwing a sideways glance at his father, deciding against a coffee, and grabbing a cold drink instead.

'Typical,' said Ben. 'Never mind the birds and the bees. Anyway, aren't you due in Manchester soon?'

'Whatever.' Alan ignored the question as he slumped back to his room, can of Coke in hand.

The occasion of his forty-sixth birthday didn't exactly depress Ben, but it gave him pause for thought. Two boys - Alan was twenty, Peter was twenty-four, and it seemed only yesterday that he was collecting them on those two occasions from the General, along with their mother. Joanna, it had to be admitted, made much less fuss about either pregnancy than Ben. His concern was not simply that of a nervous father-to-be. From the moment he first met Joanna at the local David Lloyd gym, he knew that he wanted her and always would. His first sight of her was in a bikini, climbing out of the pool. With his three student friends about to dive in, his eyes turned towards her. It was not just his immediate assessment that she had a fantastic body, but also the realisation that she looked back at him, only him. He could never understand why, as he assumed that his college friends were each, in their own way, a 'better catch'.

'You should have more confidence in yourself,' she said to him after their second date.

'I'm just grateful you picked me,' he said.

For someone so bright, intelligent and well-qualified, Ben suffered a surprising lack of confidence. Joanna managed to prop up that self-confidence with constant reassurance. In his work as finance director for a large flooring wholesaler, the mask he wears for the outside world is firmly fixed into place. No apparent lack of confidence there. Decisive, thorough, ruthless if necessary. Fools are not suffered 'at the coalface' as he puts it.

'I'd love to see you digging coal,' Alan often says.

Firm jaw, deep-set dark eyes and prominent forehead give Ben the appearance of a prop forward rather than a member of his chosen profession. His broad muscular shoulders and somewhat overweight 5' 10" frame provide him with the means to live out his son's wish. He was better suited to business, mathematics and computing being particular strengths - specialities within the accountancy degree. At first glance, a full head of dark, slightly curly hair belies his forty-six years. However, as Joanna often reminds him, the small thinning crown seen only from above is a reminder of impending senior middle age.

Though he presented as a self-assured, confident man, Ben was more sensitive and self-conscious than other people realised. Before Joanna, as a youth, he was never confident about getting a girlfriend (unlike his friends), and would never describe himself as attractive. He could not understand what Joanna saw in him but was, nevertheless, eternally grateful. Through all their years together his passion for her had not subsided. Circumstances other than age changed the nature of their physical relationship. Bringing up two growing boys curtailed some of the playfulness in which they would engage.

One summer, before Peter was born, Ben dared Joanna to sunbathe in the nude.
'We've got twelve-foot conifers all round the garden,' he said.
'I will if you will.'
Meant to be a private occasion, it was only the twitching curtains from the rear bedroom of number fifty-six that caused a suspension of activities. Joanna was unable to face Mrs Granger for a considerable number of weeks.
'She wasn't looking when I..?'
'Think so, Ben.'
'Oh, God! You couldn't blame me. You've got a lovely body, Joanna.'
'And I love you too, Ben.'
'Speaks volumes that. Does wonders for a bloke's self-esteem. Hoped you would reciprocate, you know, about my body and stuff,' he said, giving her a knowing look.

'Different for girls, and you know I fancy you. Your stuff is fine. Come here you daft lump.'

'I suppose we'll be confined to barracks from now on unless we want to give Mrs Granger a coronary.'

~

Monday morning. Ben was back at his desk, third coffee in the first hour and an ample supply of chocolate digestives provided by Samantha.

'Nice day off, Ben?'

'Lovely, Sam. One more year gone. Any messages?'

'Board meeting, Thursday, 10am. Jim wants to discuss the new warehouse plans.'

'Fine. Get me the accounts for London, Bristol and Nottingham please. Auditors next week. I'll review the other branches tomorrow and Wednesday. Should give me enough time.'

Ben did enjoy his birthday, even though Joanna had arranged a party, meaning Ben did not escape to the safe confines of the driving range. When it happens, he loves the attention but doesn't like to think about any celebrations in advance. Even Alan seemed to enjoy the occasion. To Ben, he was still a teenage grump who saw his parents as ancient. Overhearing a conversation when the last guest had left caused Alan to call out 'gross' and feign putting his fingers down his throat.

'Thanks love. I did enjoy it. Sorry I threatened to go off and practise my swing.'

'All I want now is for you to take me upstairs and make love to me, Mr Stone. Is that okay?'

'Is it okay? Are you kidding? Give me two minutes.'

Not a conversation intended for their son's ears, but seeing the expression on Alan's face, Ben simply raised his shoulders in a mock-teenage 'whatever' pose. Joanna squirmed slightly, mouthed an apology to her son then squeezed her husband's hand as confirmation of the agreement, whatever the initial embarrassment. Ben is always grateful for the variety of ways in which he is loved by his wife. Not just physically, but emotionally with the support he needs. He loves the way she tells him something in a straightforward way. 'No messing' as the lads would say. To Ben, she is the perfect woman. Clear, sparkling blue eyes that connect with him, engage him, a smile that dazzles the room and lips he wants to kiss every time he sees her. What he calls her 'mop' of blond hair (actually an expensive trip to her stylist belying that description) surrounds her slim, pale face, accentuating high cheekbones. As a teacher, she does not dress provocatively but always smart. He thinks she looks sexy in anything. More 'yuks' from Alan if he reminds her of this. Others have commented that they can't believe she is forty-six and has borne two strapping lads.

Deep affection for each other does not preclude arguments, but those disagreements tend to be over relatively trivial matters. Certain subjects set them off, notably gardening, takeaways and *Coronation Street*. It's not that Ben doesn't like a tidy garden, but his limit is cutting the three lawns – one at the front and two at the back. Five years ago, they had the back garden landscaped (at immense cost) to minimise maintenance. A central path leading from a large patio area is straddled by the two lawns. Just right for practising putting, even to the extent of a single four-inch diameter hole housing a stick with a red flag, much to the chagrin of Joanna. The shed, Ben's pride and joy, is situated at the bottom-right of the garden. All Joanna's 'gardening stuff' is in there, but it is primarily the home for Ben's ladders, DIY equipment and two sets of golf clubs.

Then there is Ben and his takeaways. He loves fish and chips, and loves nothing better (easier when the lads are both in) than to pop down to the chippy in Leeford and indulge in salt-encrusted, vinegar-soaked cod and chips. Possibly HP sauce on top. Joanna hates fast food, and although she agrees that the traditional fare of fish and chips does not plumb the depths of the modern cheeseburger, it should nonetheless be restricted to a monthly billing.

'It's good for you,' argued Ben.
'Not the way they cook it,' she said.
'Well, it's not every day, and the lads love it as well.'
'Home-cooked food is better for you. Don't forget, even Doctor Evans said you could do with losing a few pounds.'
'He said I was perfectly fit at my last annual check-up.'

Ben placed both hands on his stomach.

'For a man of fifty-six,' said Joanna.

'Cheeky.'

Coronation Street. The Nation's favourite. Ben can't stand the programme and Joanna loves it. Never misses. He just can't see the point of it.

'Why can't you watch the Brian Cox science programme with me, Jo? Or maybe the latest costume drama? Charles Dickens. Can't beat it.'

'Why don't you watch *Corrie* with *me*?'

'You're always doing marking at the same time. Don't know how you can do it.'

'Women are better at multitasking. It's a fact.'

Ben would never win an argument, and he didn't mind one bit.

3: Enright

There are many facets to Joanna Stone's life, but her priority is always family. The three men in her life, Ben, Peter, and Alan, define who she is and how she runs her life. Ben was the first (and only) man with whom she had fallen in love. Physically attracted to him, but, even more important, she has always felt safe with him. She is proud to have provided Ben with two sons who are strong, awkward, independently-minded and intelligent. She has the family she dreamt of. Petty squabbles erupt, as in all families, but she is assured of their love and support. She is, after all, Mom.

Joanna's Christian beliefs are not just important to her way of life, but give it meaning and substance. Sunday mornings are important, but it is the rest of the week when she demonstrates her faith. As a teacher at the local comprehensive, she is seen as 'tough but fair'. As head of English, she has seen young trainee teachers come and go (a high proportion eventually leaving the education sector). Twelve to sixteen-year-olds can be difficult to deal with. The experience of two feisty young men at home probably gives Joanna a head start on other, usually younger, members of staff. Last year she turned down the chance of a headship at a school in the neighbouring authority. She wants to teach, not be stuck with the issues of management, budgets and local authority politics, although management of people is invariably part of the day-to-day running of a school for any teacher.

In Ben's opinion, being a Christian does not simply mean wearing your Sunday best and smiling sweetly at the vicar, then forgetting it until the following Sunday. Part of Ben's scepticism concerning religion (at least organised religion, not so much about faith – he calls them the 'big hat brigade') is that if you're going to be religious, you should 'damn well practise it seven days a week, not just one'. Needless to say, Joanna keeps her better half well clear of her friends at church. She does, however, have some sympathy with his views, being at times very frustrated by regular churchgoers who would cheerfully close a local children's park because the kids made too much noise, too much mess and too much whatever else irritated the old dears. The parish council has much to answer for when dealing with anything built on church-owned land. She regularly speaks out, telling the council members that the land should be used for the well-being of the community, not the Church of England.

'Go get 'em, Jo,' Ben will say if she attends a meeting. He offers to accompany her, but she, sensibly, will always politely refuse.

In Joanna's opinion, kids need to let their hair down, and she is aware, after twenty years of teaching experience, that allowing freedom for young people will occasionally backfire. At school, she has witnessed bullying, drinking, smoking, even drugs. For minor misdemeanours, she has fought for leniency (sometimes the sole voice of reason in the head's study), but repeat offenders will find her a very capable and resilient foe.

James Enright could be assessed by many of the teachers at Joanna's school in two words – a pain. James, if there was any real justice, would, without doubt, be found guilty of at least three of the offences previously mentioned, all carried out at school. And Joanna had her suspicions that the fourth activity had a chance of being included on his calling card. One day, Joanna brought James into the headmaster's office.

'Why do you always pick on me?' James said.

'That's rich coming from you, James,' snapped Joanna.

'Let's all calm down and talk this through.'

'I agree, Headmaster. Let's hear what James has to say.'

'Andrew started it. I just pushed him, and he tripped.'

'That's not how two members of staff saw it, James. Bullying is not clever. What has Andrew ever done to you? He's half your size.'

'He's a sneak. Nobody likes him.'

'All the more reason for you to give him a chance. Headmaster, would you leave it with me to deal with this?'

'Of course, Mrs Stone. James, we'll be watching you. I will ask Mrs Stone for a report on your behaviour at half-term. If I hear any more about you before then, I will consider exclusion. Do I make myself clear?'

'Sir.'

'Get out now and think about what I've said.'

A glare from Enright in the corridor did not deter Joanna.

'Get your act together, James Enright.'

He muttered something, which to Joanna sounded like 'you'll be sorry one day.'

'What, Enright?'

'Nothing.'

She let it go but made a mental note to keep an eye on the young man.

~

'Ben can be infuriating,' Joanna told two friends in the village coffee shop. 'He will moan if I ask him to help with the weeding or planting bulbs, but he's quite happy to sit in his deck chair and admire the flowers and shrubs in the garden. That's when he's not retrieving golf balls from the flower beds after over-exuberant chipping practice on the back lawn.'

'Likes his golf, doesn't he?' asked Liz.

Joanna glanced at the menu as the waitress brought their usual coffee order.

'He used to play twice a week. Fourteen handicap, if you know what that is. Mind you, he works so hard, particularly at the moment. Even his beloved golf has taken a back seat. I shouldn't complain, he's been marvellous with the lads.'

'You're lucky,' said Gloria. 'My George spends most evenings with his precious darts team at The Bull. I wouldn't mind if it was every other Sunday. But no, it's "well we've got a big match coming up". He thinks I'm happy to stay at home with my knitting.'

Joanna agonised for a second, then dropped a saccharin tablet into her coffee.

'I am lucky, Gloria. Incredibly lucky. I must admit, most of our arguments are over silly things. *Corrie*, for example. If he sits in the room while it's on, he will tut-tut and snigger, while I'm trying to lose myself in the storyline. For me, it's that little bit of escapism after doing battle with a bunch of hormone-infused teenagers. Particularly 5C. I try my best to forget 5C whenever I can.'

She reached for the plate of Café Noir biscuits.

'I'm more for *Emmerdale*,' said Liz.

Joanna nodded her head.

'Yes, I watch that as well, and *'Enders*, but it's *Corrie* for me, whatever Ben says.'

'What about church? Does he really not mind you going?'

'Not at all. He's agnostic – hopefully, he understands what that means – but he has respect for other people's views, as long as they don't try to force them down his throat, as he puts it. Woe betide one of those amateur doorstep preachers trying to tell him what to believe. I have to drag him away. Some of the things he says…'

Liz caught Joanna's eye.

'I saw him in the post office last week. He looked a bit fed up.'

'Yes, his Uncle Graham has passed away. Only sixty-four. His dad's younger brother. Cancer, and it was quick.'

~

Joanna would love Peter to settle down. It seems to her that he has a different girlfriend every week, and trouble is never far behind.
'I do worry about you,' she said one day as Peter went to the fridge to claim a bite of last night's leftovers.
'Hang on, have you got a black eye?'
'Sort of, but it's nothing, Mom,' smiled Peter, kissing her gently on the forehead.
The fine lines on her face widened slightly as she pursed her lips.
'How did it happen?'
'Sure you want me to tell you?'
She glared at him.
'Peter, just put your old mom out of her misery.'
'Okay. You know that gig we did at the Old Bell? Well, the fans were doing what they do. Mainly girls standing at the front by the stage, flirting. You know the sort of thing?'
'Flaunting, I suppose, rather than flirting. Carry on.'
'Well, after the first half, we have twenty minutes for a drink, and we like to chat to the crowd.'
'You chatted with one of these girls.'
'Yes, and one thing led to another. We sort of, well, started snogging.'

Joanna's eyes widened.

'Did anyone see you?'

Peter sighed. Joanna knew that he wanted the parental interview to draw to a conclusion.

'We were standing in front of the drum kit at the time,' he continued.

'How old is she, Peter?' Joanna asked, giving him a stare that only a mother can produce.

'Oh, it's not that. She's nearly twenty. It's just that her boyfriend didn't take kindly to it. Nor did his biker mates.'

'What happened?'

'It was all sorted after a few minutes. The rest of the band, and some of the crowd, joined in. I managed to throw a few punches of my own. A couple landed.'

'Peter!'

'Honestly, Mom, it's alright. I bought him a drink later and promised to leave his girl alone in future, no matter how much she flirted.'

'Glad to hear it.'

Joanna constantly worries about Peter, a fitness instructor and personal trainer at the local gym (in addition to his role as part-time lead guitarist in The Tragic Monkeys). Not too surprising that most of his 'personal' clients are young ladies. He's not ready to settle down, unlike his younger brother, Alan, who has been with the same girl, Cheryl, for the last three years. Studying graphic design at Manchester University doesn't stop him from seeing her. Ben says that it's the only reason he comes home at all. Just somewhere to stay at weekends (bringing his washing for his mother) while he spends time with Cheryl. How different the brothers are.

~

Joanna is not without her admirers. She keeps in shape by swimming every morning before school. Men have been known to make approaches and are politely rebuffed. She smiles to herself, remembering the way she met Ben. She has been tempted, particularly on a couple of occasions when the marriage hit a rough patch after Peter was born. Ben was being so unreasonable, she thought, but her relationships with other men never went beyond a coffee and chat at the leisure complex bar. Joanna is very aware that she can still attract men, and often feels guilty if she enjoys the attention. She was having lunch with Liz one day when she revealed she had been for coffee with one of the men.

'What was he like?' asked Liz.
'Muscles on muscles and a gorgeous smile.'
'Will you see him again?' Liz drew breath, hoping for an answer that would suit a tabloid headline.
'Shouldn't think so,' said Joanna. 'He's married, I'm married. One coffee, lovely chat, nothing to it.'
'I'd be tempted,' said Liz with a smile.
'Liz, you'd always be tempted.'
'Anyway, Jo, there's something I wanted to ask you. You know Dawn, who lost her husband a few months ago?'

'Only in passing.'
'Well, she's organised a séance. I wondered if we should go along for moral support.'
'Don't think so.'
Liz playfully nudged Joanna's elbow.
'Go on, might be a giggle.'
'It can be dangerous playing with people's emotions. Think I'll give it a miss.'
If I did go, a giggle would be the last thing I'd expect, she thought.
'If you're sure, but I'm going. Let me know if you change your mind.'

~

Temptation can show its face in many guises. At school, Joanna was at the point of taking a risk. Not a relationship, but in the way she dealt with an unruly student. James Enright was still the bane of many teachers' lives and had been since year one. In the final years of GCSEs, a high proportion of the marks are assessment-based. Overall, James averaged grade B, and he was expected to perform to a similar level in the exams in the summer, with maybe a few A grades. James was also a bully, picking on two particularly vulnerable boys in Joanna's class.

'Have they shopped me again, Mrs Stone?'
'No, James, they don't need to.'
'If they snitch on me, they'd better watch out.'

'Listen, James, despite your behaviour, you're a good student. You don't need to behave like this. Couldn't you calm down for your final year and concentrate on assignments and revision for exams?'

'I could walk the exams without even trying,' James said, with a sneer.

'Not sure about that, and bullying other lads will not help.'

'Whatever.'

He looked down at the floor, dismissing her gaze.

'I've just about had enough of your cheek young man. Think about what I've said. Think on.'

'Think on miss, whatever.'

'Just get out, James. Get out.'

He would deserve it if I dropped his grade, she thought. *That'll show him. A bare pass, C minus. Yes, that's it.* Anger welling up inside, she stayed on that path for the rest of the day. Back at home, she soon changed direction.

'Nice day at school love?' asked Ben.

'No, I don't like one of the kids.'

'Only one? Sorry, kidding. You don't often talk like that.'

Ben placed his hands around her middle, pulled her towards him and kissed her, softly.

'They can't be that bad.'

'When I'm with you, everything's okay. I wobbled today. I considered breaking all the rules, but I think it's out of my system. I'll be fine,' she said, pouring herself another glass of Don Cayetano.

4: Manchester

'Sure you've got everything?'

'Don't fuss, Mom.'

'It's a big moment for me. First day at university. I'm so proud. So is your dad.'

'He hasn't said much,' said Alan, giving his trademark scowl.

'He's like you, doesn't like a fuss.'

'He wanted me to do accountancy, like him.'

'Only to start with love, but when he realised how passionate you are about computer art, he accepted it.'

'How many times, Mom? *Graphic design*, and I'm specialising in product branding, logos, that sort of thing.'

'Sorry, Alan, I'm a mere English teacher.'

'No probs. Anyway, see you next weekend.'

'Hug for your mom?'

Alan reluctantly let his mother put her arms around him, and she gave him her customary kiss on both cheeks.

'That felt embarrassing when I was six, outside the school gates. Glad we're inside the house where no one can see us.'

'If a mom can't kiss her little boy, who can she kiss?'

'Don't get me started on you and Dad.'

'We're just affectionate, us oldies, as you call us,' Joanna said, smiling.

Alan had arranged to collect Cheryl, who was finishing early that day. Working three days a week at Boots chemist's in Leeford gave her the flexibility she enjoyed. If she worked twenty hours a week between

Monday and Sunday (usually spread over three days), she was able to swap shifts with colleagues and negotiate consecutive days off. Alan and Cheryl planned to stay together in his room in Manchester. They shared a car (financed by Ben), so she could travel back after a few days - back to work. Alan planned to go home every weekend (on the train, if Cheryl had the car in Leeford).

Ben and Joanna were very 'modern' about Cheryl sleeping in Alan's room. He constantly reminded his parents not to embarrass him in front of her. Now, travelling seventy miles up the M6, he just had his studies and Cheryl to concentrate on.

'Do you like Manchester?' Alan asked.
'Went to Old Trafford with my dad before I met you. We beat Liverpool three-nil.'
'We've never talked about football before.'
'Alan, we're usually busy doing other stuff,' Cheryl replied, giving him that look, 'and you never complain.'
'What would I do without you?' he said.
'Couldn't put it better myself.'
'We're here. I promised to ring Mom. That makes me sound twelve, but you know what she's like.'
'Don't worry, I've got to ring Mom and Dad anyway. They don't like me driving on the motorway.'
'We'll get a drink and settle in. I've got my uni induction in the morning. Can you amuse yourself for a few hours?'
'Shops,' said Cheryl.

~

From the age of sixteen, Alan argued with his father. As a child, probably closer to Ben than Joanna, they'd go everywhere together: local football matches, ten-pin bowling, country walks, and they loved to set off in the car on Sunday mornings. Supplied with biscuits, chocolate and a flask of tea, Ben would ask Alan to pick a point on a map and the adventure would begin. They talked about anything and everything, including any problems at school that Alan was going through. He would look to Ben first, whether it was an issue with maths homework, disputes with teachers (Alan was famous for it) or even girlfriend trouble. Dad was always there. For some reason, when Alan started A-levels, their relationship changed. Love and respect still there, but no longer as close.

'I do wish you'd consider maths as one of your options, Alan. Art and history are all very well, and I know you want to do graphic design at uni, but it would give you another avenue, whatever career you choose.'
'Not again, Dad. I don't want to be an accountant.'
'You're so good with figures. A good solid career.'
'Just because *you* did it. I want to do my own thing. Why can't you be more like Mom?'

It became clear as Alan moved through his teenage years that the more he was pushed in one direction the more he rebelled. Ben moaned about his 'living in Facebook and Twitter'. Joanna admitted that she never saw him without his phone and could not understand the fascination it held for young people.

'At least we bought the all-in phone package for him, Ben. He's got unlimited access.'
'Don't we know it!'

After A-levels, Alan took over a year out, travelling around the UK, those Sunday morning map-reading sessions not wasted. He met Cheryl at school during A-levels. She decided that university was not for her, but the signs were that they would stay together. When he applied for the place at Manchester, they wanted to see as much of each other as possible. Ben never said it openly, but he was immensely proud of his son. A precocious teenager maybe (even beyond his twentieth birthday), but he had a stable relationship with a girl, he was intelligent, hard-working and ambitious. Not a bad combination.

Slight in build, taller than Ben at five feet eleven, his pinched cheeks and pale complexion could, in a certain light, give him a gaunt expression. Around the house, he had a reputation for scowling. Narrowed eyes and pursed lips accompanied the glare indicating that 'the oldies' had once again infuriated, and invariably embarrassed him. His trademark outfit around the house, when going out or to college, was his favourite dark blue denim (he had three pairs), slightly too long, hanging over the non-designer black and white trainers. No one accused him of being pretentious. Tee shirts, sweatshirts, never collar and tie (except perhaps for the rare interview), covered by a grey cotton hoody. His mop of unkempt auburn hair gave him a permanent seventeen-year-old look.

Amongst his peers, with three years ahead of him doing what he wanted to do, you would see a different side to Alan, the shackles of home now removed, although he was quietly grateful for his parents' support. He had told Joanna, the night before his first day at uni, how much the car meant to him. Neither he nor Cheryl could afford to buy one, and he realised that it was Ben's way of saying how much Alan meant to them. It was easier for Joanna to show her feelings. She realised how, in some ways, Alan and Ben were so alike – sensitive, occasionally grouchy, deep-thinking and essentially decent. Chatting with everyone he met in the hall where the inductions were being carried out, he met the man who would be his main lecturer. Don Gil, a quiet man, tall, slim with short dark hair and a thin face. He appeared to look through the person he was addressing, into their eyes, and had an air of authority that made one pause when it was evident he had something to say.

Alan, however, warmed to him immediately. This man knew his stuff. They had statutory forms to complete, but they still had time to discuss the details of the course. *Mr Gil knows graphic design*, he thought. *I can learn a lot from Mr Gil.*

~

After the inductions, Alan and Cheryl sat chatting in his room.

'When would you have time to do that?' she asked.

'I've only got lectures four days a week, and sometimes I'm free a morning or an afternoon each week on the other days. There's always the evenings...'

'Alan, I thought we were trying to spend time together when you're not studying.'

'No problem. We'll work it that I'll go to The Meadows when you're back in Leeford.'

'Well, we'll see how it works out. Anyway, why voluntary work?'

'Much as I go on about Dad, he's been really helpful, but don't tell him I said. Apart from the car and a tank of petrol each week, mainly for you, he's subbed me fifty pounds a week for spending. If I can avoid bar work, I will. Everyone I know is either serving in a restaurant or doing bar work.'

'What do they do at The Meadows?'

'It's a care home for the elderly. Most of them are so lonely. They need people to pop in for an hour a couple of times a week.'

'What will you do there?'

'No personal care or anything like that. Make the tea, read to them. They like Scrabble, dominoes, cards. I don't mind.'

'Come here, Alan,' Cheryl said, kissing him.

'What was that for?'

'People don't get the real Alan Stone. I love you so much because I know the real Alan. The only other person who understands you is your mom.'

'You'll have me in tears in a minute, Cheryl. Anyway, you're always helping people in the shop.'

'That's different - it's my job.'

'You help them to their cars with shopping and stuff, and you've stayed over if anyone's got a problem. You don't have to.'

'We were talking about you, Mr Stone. My hero.'

'Shut up and kiss me again. We've got an hour to spare.'

~

Later, Alan visited Don Gil in his office.

'Tell me about your family.'

'Not much to tell, Mr Gil.'

'Don, please. No, it's just interesting to get backgrounds. It helps us to sort out any problems.'

'I tend to be self-sufficient. Don't ask my parents for much.'

'You've got your car. From your father?'

'How did you know about that?'

'You mentioned it at the induction.'

'Oh, yes. When I say I'm self-sufficient, I mean I don't go running to them every five minutes. They've been great, you know, but parents can smother you, can't they.'

'Of course, but they want the best for you. What does your father do?'

'Accountant – financial director for a flooring company.'

'Successful?'

'Very.'

The student supervision continued, moving on to the first assignment that Alan was to complete. Don Gil couldn't have been more helpful. Alan now had his email address, mobile number and was told to contact him, whatever the issue.

'I've noticed that you share an office, Don.'

'Yes, Geoff Hawkins is in here much more than me. It's his room really. I told the faculty I don't need an office. I do most of my work at home.'

'How many days are you here?'

'Usually, three half days a week. The rest of the time, I'm writing my book.'

'What's it about?'

'Designing systems for marketing analysis. I know that sounds a bit dry, but I tie in graphic design - all the stuff you're interested in.'

'So you're not a full-time lecturer.'

'Let's say they have allowed me a flexible contract.'

'When's my next supervision?'

'I'll text you. Probably every other week?'

'Sounds great. Thanks, Don.'

5:   Jodie

Peter Stone could not be more different from his brother. His manner is casual, and he is described by Alan (on a good day) as a 'laid-back dude', though their father would challenge the logic of this phrase. Words not necessary - Alan and Peter seem capable of reading Ben's mind. The laid-back dude has an enviable lifestyle. The role of personal trainer at the local leisure complex has opened many doors. Most of them result in Peter walking through each open door straight into the affections of yet another in the stream of young ladies that he attracts. Out of earshot of her younger son, Joanna claims that her elder son is 'the most handsome man in Leeford, and probably the country.' Her husband is not surprised by being excluded from that contest. Peter wears glasses, but they serve to accentuate his dark brown eyes, and the frames are, in any case, the most expensive designer frames he could find. Short-cropped, dark hair supplemented by what appears to be a permanent five-day growth of beard give him what the female members of the gym call the 'Hollywood look'. In complete contrast to his kid brother, even at work, he doesn't settle for casual; jacket, shirt and tie to travel into work, then changing into designer tracksuit and trainers. Unlike his father, who rather overfills gym wear, and Alan, whose slim frame might under-fill the same garments, he has the knack of getting it exactly right. Not over muscular, but lean and fit. Not one woman at the gym is likely to construct an argument against that. The resulting physical specimen, nonetheless, copes with the attention. Not that a queue has formed, as such, but his parents have given up trying to remember the name of his current date at any particular point in time.

'Suzie, Barbara, or Ellen is it?'

'Hannah,' said Peter, casually.

'How many women do you have on the go at the moment?' enquired Ben.

'Only one at a time, Dad, one at a time.'

Peter enjoys life. His main job at the gym does not quite finance the lifestyle he craves, but as part-time lead guitarist of the *Tragic Monkeys,* he can supplement that income. The band can take £800 on a good night. Divided four ways, Peter can earn, after expenses, over £175 for two hours' work. He doesn't think of it as work. Keeping fit, spending time with the ladies and playing his guitar are the three points of his 'personal life triangle'. He found that in *Psychology for the Under-Thirties*, becoming as much a bible for him as Dale Carnegie's *How to Win Friends and Influence People* was for his father, twenty years before. A confirmed atheist, not even sharing Ben's doubts, Peter has the confidence to find answers wherever he can. His mother's acceptance of his attitude and lack of faith has enabled his healthy respect for the faith (or lack of it) in any individual.

The facts about the incident at the Old Bell were not quite as described to Joanna. Peter already knew the girl in question. She had pursued him relentlessly at the gym over the previous three months. She was a little young for him, at seventeen (three years younger than he had admitted to his mother), and the incident involved slightly more than flirting. According to the girl, Barbara, she had supposedly become the 'property' of local bike gang leader, Terry Hickens. He was known for being possessive. Barbara had made excuses to Terry, enabling her to attend three of Peter's gigs, and, to date, their relationship had involved no more than a kiss.

This night was different. At the break she climbed onto the stage and kissed him, holding him close to her. Within minutes they were back-stage in a dimly lit corridor leading to a storeroom. Their timing could be described as unfortunate. It hadn't taken long for Barbara to encourage Peter to divest himself of his jeans when, of all people, Terry Hickens appeared. She had been followed to the other gigs by his associates and this time he wanted to see for himself.

'What do we have here then?'

'Terry...'

'Get out, Barbara. Just need a chat with your new friend.'

Negotiation not possible. Terry was joined by two fellow bikers as Peter quickly dressed. Barbara was pushed down the corridor as Terry laid into Peter. Most of the punches, to the back, stomach and groin, were not likely to display obvious bruises, but the black eye attested, at the very least, to Terry's flexibility and an array of attacking techniques. Peter hadn't admitted to Joanna that he had been unable to re-join the band that night. Their first abandoned performance. He tried to mitigate the situation with Terry.

'Nothing happened.'

'Okay, Mr Clever-Rock-Star. Something was about to happen. Just as well we turned up. If you know what's good for you, keep away from Barbara.'

Terry, standing over Peter, aimed one last kick at Peter's midriff. Not badly hurt, but winded, he lay there for ten minutes before searching out the rest of the band.

'I'll have to go lads. Sorry I messed up.'

'Will you never learn, mate? You need to settle down.'

'Not just yet.'

~

They never talk about it - the day that everything changed for Peter. The day that changed him, made him the man he is today. He was a bright student, concentrating on sport but, like his father, a good mathematician. Even extended guitar sessions with the fledgeling band (no name at that stage), football matches, and swimming events, could not adversely affect the levels he attained.

Attending the local grammar school gave him access to the best-qualified teachers in the borough. After eight GCSEs (including six grade As) he selected maths and the classics for A-levels. A strange combination, but he had enjoyed Latin and loved history and mythology. The head teacher assured Ben and Joanna that Oxford was not beyond his reach.

In his first year in the sixth form, he shared classes with girls for the first time. The grammar school was boys only, and the equivalent single-gender school, the Girls' High, merged at sixth form level. Peter had met girls at the weekly 'Friday Club', the combined disco for the two schools but had not experienced a serious relationship. Jodie changed that and changed his life.

'You know, son, she could be a model, and she's extremely bright,' said Ben.
'I saw her first,' joked Peter.

Joanna could not help dreaming about the beautiful grandchildren she might have in a few years' time. Ben was also happy that someone could match Peter's intellect. Jodie was taking English Literature and European languages at sixth form, and the couple somehow managed to concentrate when sharing his room most evenings to study. She was bright enough to understand his maths studies, and his flair for Latin could easily have been the basis for his studying Spanish and Italian, had he chosen that path.

This must have been considered the high point for the Stone family. Alan, still at the stage when he was happy spending time with his parents (particularly Ben), had just started his GCSEs. Peter was very supportive and tutored Alan through his mathematical difficulties as they occurred, and the relationship between the brothers was important to both of them. Alan had experienced a phase of being bullied in his early years at senior school. When his brother heard about this, no words were exchanged, but Peter regularly turned up at the school gates, keeping a discreet distance. Only on one occasion was an intervention necessary.

'Oi, Stone-face!' Frank Carter shouted.

'For Christ sake, Carter, leave it.'

Alan was in no mood for a confrontation. He never was, but Frank Carter would not leave it alone. He had never liked Alan, the boy from the large, detached house, his mother a teacher and his father a company director.

'Rich boy, how much does your dad earn?'

'Jealousy will get you nowhere,' said Alan.

'We'll see about that Stoney.'

Frank did not realise that Peter was leaning back against the wall, not far from the zebra crossing linking the school with the park on the other side of the road. Frank followed Alan towards the crossing and tripped him. Fortunately, Alan fell onto his school bag, avoiding a face-first collision with the pavement. It was over in less than a minute, Peter pinning Carter against the wall.

'Right! It stops here! Now! Don't bother to tell me you've got a brother, or that your dad is bigger than me, or indeed bigger than my dad. Whatever. This is a final warning. You will not believe the grief you will suffer if you so much as breathe on my brother. You will now apologise, walk away and put this behind you. Final and only warning. Got it?'

Carter had held his breath throughout the lecture from Peter. Irrelevant details about his having a brother (he didn't) or whether his dad was bigger than Ben (he wasn't) did not have the opportunity to zap across his synapses.

'Right, okay.'

'Apologise, Carter! Now!'

'Sorry, Alan.'

'Thank you. Remember what I said.'

No words exchanged between the two brothers. Not required. They shared a bond, and it never occurred to Alan that Peter was interfering or making it worse. It was sorted, and they moved on.

~

Jodie became ill that summer. During a break from studying, she and Peter travelled to the coast for the day. Peter couldn't remember where. Probably Aberystwyth or Borth, on the west coast of Wales. Maybe Weston, Blackpool, wherever. It hardly mattered. He thought she had fainted, but she was having a seizure. They had both attended first aid courses, but the training mattered little when it happened. Looking out to sea, they had been holding hands seconds before, quietly, contemplating. Not like a teenage couple, passionate, giggly, constantly making an effort, but comfortable, loving, mature. Jodie was in Peter's thoughts every minute of every day, and now she was lying on the ground, her face cut, a bruise around her left eye already forming. He shouted for help. Someone phoned for an ambulance.

Later, much later, thinking back to that time, he thought it must have been Weston-Super-Mare. His parents came down to Bristol Infirmary. They brought Jodie's parents. They were in no fit state to drive, but they had to face the consultant.

'Has Jodie been experiencing any headaches, nausea, episodes of fainting, visual disturbances?'

'No, not that we're aware of. Peter, have you noticed anything?'

Jodie's mother turned to him, imploring, but he could not help her. No words could do that. The consultant placed his hand on her arm.

'We took Jodie straight in for an MRI scan when she arrived. We thought possibly epilepsy, but there were other signs. We needed to be sure.'

'What do you mean?'

'I'm so sorry. She has a tumour, on the brain. She needs an emergency operation to relieve the swelling. She is very sick.'

Jodie passed away five days later. Nothing would console her parents, or Peter. The loss was deeper than he could bear. Nothing existed with the ability to fix it, and the only emotion capable of matching the feeling of loss was the guilt he would carry. He had been with her, felt he could have done more - felt that he should have spotted the signs, somehow. Irrational, understandable guilt. From that day he changed. He completed his A-levels but had no intention of going to university, focussing instead on sport. The local college provided the training he needed to progress in the career he now wanted. Maths and the classics took a back seat to personal training. The gym he attended offered him an apprenticeship, funding his two-year course.

Only on the anniversary of Jodie's death is her name mentioned at home. Alan, Ben and Joanna felt the pain, but not like Jodie's parents, not like Peter. They expected a reaction, depression even, but he just launched himself into his career, continued to develop his band, and loved and left every girl he met from the day he had to let her go. He didn't tell anyone. They didn't need to know, but no one would ever get close to him again. Not like that.

6:   Cheryl

Cheryl didn't mind walking into work. After all, the car was Alan's, paid for by his father. She looked forward to the days in Manchester with Alan. She loved the shops there and the nightlife. Her pattern of work and her twenty-hour (three-day) contract at Boots meant she would need to be back in Leeford four days a week to allow for travelling. Once Alan was settled at university, she had at least one day with him in Manchester each week.

She loves Leeford Village. It has only one charity shop, unlike many large town centres where most of the traditional shops have moved to out-of-town shopping centres. A ten-minute walk to reach the church, over the road from the pub where they have spent many hours including their first proper date. The optician's, then the garage where Ben had bought the Fiat Punto. Cheryl has been known to stop at the baker's for a treat. Freshly baked bread is a temptation she struggles to resist, and she will occasionally give way to a banoffee pie. She crosses the road to view the latest literary releases, making a mental note to pop back at lunchtime to reserve the latest Tóibín offering that will transport her to another world for an hour before sleep.

A mere glance into the hair stylist's window after crossing back. He was still there. He was always there, and she avoided his stare. Three months after meeting Alan, she had succumbed to the debatable charms, once again, of an older man. She doesn't think that his wife ever discovered the truth, and she didn't tell Alan. It only lasted for three weeks, and she still regrets every minute.

The initial excitement was exhilarating, but essentially pointless. Aged seventeen, she first saw Alan at the Friday Club held by the joint efforts of the boys' grammar school and the girls' high. For some, it was the first chance to forge relationships with the opposite sex. She was the first girl that Alan had kissed. A full-on kiss, not just a peck on the cheek, the girl to whom he lost his virginity. He didn't know that six months before, Cheryl had flirted with her history teacher, a young man barely out of college himself. She was experienced, and Alan never once questioned the source of that experience. As if satisfying the stereotypical 'teenage boys at disco', Alan and his mates stood nervously on the fringe of the club's activity. It took Cheryl's bravado to take the lead.

'Come on, I'm going to show you how to dance.'
'I can dance.'
'Sure. I've been watching you for weeks, hoping that you'd ask me.'
'Well, I'm glad you did. End of term would come round before I got round to it.'
Cheryl and Alan were inseparable within days. Joanna took to her straight away, with Ben putting the brakes on before she considered popping down the local milliner's to place an order.

'It's his first proper girlfriend. Don't interfere Jo, just let them enjoy themselves. Like we did.'

'Hopefully not exactly like we did.'

Cheryl has never mentioned her risky relationship with Roger Timmings, history department. That was before she met Alan anyway, and she had protected the teacher's career. Neither did she, nor could she, divulge either the three weeks of madness with Trevor Knight, hairstylist, or one day of passion with Ralph Clements, senior pharmacist.

'What are we doing for you today, Cheryl?'

'Just a trim.'

'Can't I tempt you?' he said, gently brushing her shoulder with his hand. She smiled.

'Just a trim for now, Trevor.'

If she thought about anything during every waking moment, if she wasn't at work, and not being pursued, or engaging in flirting, those thoughts involved Alan. But she justified her feelings for other men by telling herself that she was not yet ready to make a commitment. *Why not have some fun*, she thought, while at the same time struggling to push the guilt from her mind. The struggle did not last for long.

'Glad you could come.'

'Alan's away. I'm at a loose end, not travelling up until Thursday because of work. What have you told your wife?'

'Freemasons.'

'Funny handshakes, that sort of thing?'

'Small businesses supporting each other and raising money for local charities.'

'Like I say, funny handshakes.'

Trevor kissed her, and she didn't resist.

'We'll drive over to the Common for a bit of privacy.'

'You old romantic,' said Cheryl.

The irony of Cheryl's situation was that the affair ended after only three weeks, not because of Alan, or Trevor's wife, but because of another man. She attended a three-day course funded by a number of the major pharmaceutical manufacturers: *Recognising over-indulgence in over-the-counter medicines.*

The company she worked for would of course wish to maximise sales and profits, but there was an ethical side to their operations. Two places were available on the course, allocated to senior pharmacist Ralph Clements and Cheryl. If, at thirty-seven, almost twice her age, Trevor qualified for the description of 'the older man', then Ralph Clements, fifty-two, certainly did. Married, with two teenage girls, he was old enough to have been Cheryl's father.

Not discreet enough on the second day of the course, they elicited glances from both the hotel staff and fellow delegates.

The hand on her knee, intimate whispering, and the looks she gave him were not hidden, with the only care being taken on the late-night transfer from her room to Ralph's. 'Regret' the wrong word to use, or at least not the emotion felt by Cheryl when waking up in his bed the next morning. She enjoyed sex with older men, but she also knew that one day she would have to commit, and she convinced herself that when the day arrived, it should be with Alan.

Cheryl had grown to love Joanna and Ben. They not only made her welcome, but it also became apparent that they saw her as a future daughter-in-law. Joanna made no attempt at subtlety.
'I can't wait for the day when Ben has to buy me a nice new dress.'
'Leave her be, Jo - you've got loads of dresses,' said Ben.
'It's alright, Mrs Stone,' laughed Cheryl, 'I'm looking forward to that day as well, but we've got plenty of time.'
'Do I have to buy a big hat too?' enquired Ben, cheekily.

The looks from both women said, 'shut up Ben.' He knew his place, and he also felt that this girl was right for his younger son. *If only*, he thought, *if only Peter could find true happiness. He's never really moved on, but Alan seems so happy. We've been badly hurt more than once. This family deserves some luck.* Ben recognised in Cheryl the freshness and vitality he had seen when first meeting Joanna. Similar height and the same small, almost petite, but muscular frame. Could be an athlete or gymnast - someone who works out. Long auburn hair caressing her shoulders and surrounding the perfectly symmetrical features of her face. Dark blue eyes below sloping eyebrows, and a mouth providing perfect white teeth and the brightest smile. *Alan is a lucky boy*, Ben thought, *but then so am I.*

Alan's room at the university digs could be described as basic, yet adequate and functional. Two single beds provided – allowing for visitors – a desk, two office chairs and a two-seater settee. Also, an adjoining bathroom including built-in shower. Their first job on arrival was to push the beds together. Then Cheryl decided what she would leave in the room when she travelled back to Leeford: basic cosmetics, toothbrush, underwear, a couple of nighties, to save her having to pack every time she came back to Manchester. There was a communal washing / drying area in the basement, so although Alan planned to take his washing home, Cheryl preferred to get it done during the week.

Cheryl was so proud of Alan. He was confident that after his degree he would secure a good job, enough to give them a solid basis for their future, if they were to have a future together. Her relationships with other men did not detract from her love for him. Alan the only man she ever loved. She had a vague understanding of graphic design but felt that all she needed to know was that he had important skills relevant to the modern world. Global companies were crying out for fresh young talent – people who could innovate, bring new ideas to give their products a facelift. She was particularly proud of his commitment to helping people.

Never making a fuss or engaging in self-promotion, he prioritised Cheryl and himself, then would give whatever spare time he had to other people. She often thought that he could have developed a career in the voluntary or care sectors, albeit at a fraction of the salary he expected to receive in marketing and design.

She was aware of Alan's senior lecturer, Don Gil, considering him to be attractive, in a thin, angular sort of way. On meeting him, she found Mr Gil to be the epitome of politeness, but she felt that his eyes bored through her, searching. She was intrigued. *Alan likes him*, she thought, *and that's good enough for me. We'll get to know him better as Alan's course progresses.* It was important to Cheryl that she got on well with all of Alan's acquaintances.

7: Hamlin

Ben has many memories of the year 1984. His parents gave him a copy of the novel by George Orwell on New Year's Day.

'My favourite book at school. Published in 1949. Only been out a few years when I first read it,' said Jack. 'This would have been one of your Christmas presents, but we thought it appropriate to give it to you on the first day of the year.'
'What's it about, Dad?'
'The way government suppressed ordinary people. "Big Brother" spying on everyone through cameras on every street and in every building.'
'Science fiction?'
'Yes, but it's considered to be very political. Makes you think. Thank goodness it's not quite like that yet.'
'Jack, are you filling that boy's head with nonsense again?' asked Lucy.
'He's got to learn, love. It's like our holiday this summer. Very educational. Talking of which, Ben, have you done your maths homework?'
'No problem. I've done the optional questions as well.'

Ben excelled at maths but also enjoyed music, books, films and sport. Their planned holiday for two weeks in July took them to New York, but not Los Angeles, the location for the Olympics. He would watch some of the events in his room. Everyone would remember different things about that year. For Lucy, it might have been 'The Bill', launched around that time. She loved television cop shows. She would also have followed the pregnancy of Princess Diana, resulting in the birth of Prince Harry on 15th September. Lucy missed that event. She no doubt followed the marriage of Elton John and Renate Blauel in Sydney on Valentine's Day, seemingly dominating the news.

Jack, like Ben, loved his sport. Jack might have remembered the LA Raiders winning the Super Bowl in February at Tampa, Ben Crenshaw taking the Masters title in April, Fuzzy Zoeller the US Open in June, and McEnroe the Wimbledon Championship in July. Jack's favourite moment would have been Seve Ballesteros winning the British Open on 22nd July. It should have been a special memory for Jack, but it will only exist for his son, Ben. That was the day they flew back to the UK, cutting short the holiday they had planned for so long, and Ben would have an all-consuming memory of July 1984.

Ben's uncle and aunt collected them from Leeford. They drove to Heathrow in Graham's BMW 3-series. Ben loved travelling in that car and enjoyed listening to his uncle talking about the engine size, power ratios and acceleration. Aunt Carol and Ben's mother, Lucy, were not quite so impressed, but they needed something to pass the three-hour drive to London. Graham had booked a parking lot for sixteen days to allow for the two-week holiday, and extra days for the inevitable flight delays that haunted the early 1980s.

The British Airways flight to New York took just over seven hours including the usual customs checks.
'It's called the Algonquin Hotel,' said Graham. 'Ben helped me with researching the hotel.'
'On West 44th Street, near Times Square,' Ben added.
Lucy smiled at Carol.
'You boys. Everything down to the last detail. Nothing left to chance.'

Ben's first time out of the country, and he was with his favourite people. He loved his mother and father but also liked to spend time with his aunt and uncle. Carol was so kind to him, and Graham was the stereotypical interesting uncle. After checking in and a night's rest, breakfast was dominated by a family meeting to confirm the agenda for the day.
'Right folks,' announced Jack. 'There are five main attractions in New York itself, according to Ben's detailed research, and then there's the other interesting stuff further afield. Over to you, Ben.'
'Can we start at the American Museum, Dad?'
'No problem.'
'The rest of the week I'd like to go to the Bronx Zoo, the Brooklyn Children's Museum, and I can't wait to see the Wollman Rink at Central Park.'
'See what you mean,' Carol whispered to Lucy.
'Let's start at the American Museum of Natural History,' Graham agreed.

The next few days they worked through Ben's list, and they found plenty of other attractions. They visited the ever-popular Statue of Liberty, and Graham and Carol took in a Broadway show while Ben and Jack spent a few hours in the hotel's sports room. Ben won all the games of table tennis. Jack dominated the pool table. Lucy caught up with her paperbacks. At the start of the second week, Ben still hadn't seen the Bronx Zoo. Jack and Lucy wanted to see Niagara Falls.

'I'm not bothered about Niagara Falls,' said Ben.
'You'll like it when you get there,' said Lucy.
'We've got so much to get through, and I want to go to the zoo.'
The waiter, overhearing this, chipped in.
'Sir, you must see the Falls. It's one of the wonders of the world.'
'I'd rather stay in New York,' replied Ben.
'Tell you what, said Graham, 'you can go to the zoo with me and Aunt Carol. Your mom and dad can have a romantic trip up to Buffalo and take the helicopter ride over the Falls.'
The waiter, a tall, thin, serious-looking man, took a close interest in the discussion, and the family didn't mind. They had been taking advice from the staff since they arrived.
'You'll regret it if you don't go, young man. You should be with your parents.'
'Up to you Ben,' said Lucy.

'No, I'll go to the Bronx with Aunt and Uncle. Is that alright?'

The waiter retreated, his advice to Ben not heeded.

'That's decided then,' said Jack. 'Niagara Falls for us, Bronx Zoo for you lot.'

New York State suffered a downpour the following day, so the trip was delayed, but on Tuesday of the second week, Jack and Lucy set off to the north of the state. A 370-mile trip meant they would stay overnight in Buffalo, and they planned to travel to Rochester the following day. Jack was looking forward to seeing the aqueduct of the Erie Canal incorporating the Broad Street Bridge. Lucy was happy to be with Jack wherever they went, looking forward in particular to the helicopter ride over the Falls, and she knew that Graham and Carol would take care of Ben.

During the walk round the zoo, Ben told his uncle he was curious about the waiter's insistence that he go with his parents to Buffalo.

'Ben, he was just trying to help. You must come back to New York one day and see the Falls. Your mom and dad will have the trip of a lifetime.'

'Have you been?'

'Five years ago. Me and your aunt had a romantic trip to the States for our tenth wedding anniversary, didn't we love?'

'From what I remember, Graham Stone, it coincided with the Super Bowl. We had to fly down to Florida to see the game.'

'Yes, but you enjoyed the trip two days later to the Falls.'

'You're right, it was worth sitting through an American football game. That was for you, Graham. I wouldn't have missed Niagara Falls for anything.'

'Auntie, maybe the waiter was right after all.'

'No love, and it's nice for your mom and dad to spend some time on their own. Don't listen to us. You'll still have a lovely holiday. You can come back again, maybe when you have children of your own.'

Ben smiled at Carol. *She's so nice*, he thought. He did enjoy his time with Graham and Carol, and he was old enough to understand that all couples like time to themselves. *Hope they enjoy the Falls*, he thought.

The weather much brighter, Jack and Lucy had a relaxing drive to Buffalo. Lucy had picked up a leaflet from tourist information, which she read to Jack.

'Jaw-dropping beauty. Thundering roars. Shimmering rainbows, and the raw power of six million cubic feet of water rushing over the edge every minute of the day. Comprising of the American Falls, Bridal Veil Falls and Horseshoe Falls, Niagara is a true natural wonder that plays Cupid to lovers, a muse to artists and a Pied Piper to millions of visitors each year.'

'You should go on the radio reading that stuff out. Mind you, not sure we need Cupid.'

'Nor the Pied Piper of Hamlin.'

'Shall we go on the *Maid of the Mist* first, then the helicopter ride?'

'Yes, it's forty dollars each, but well worth it.'

'I've never been on a helicopter before, Jack. Is it safe?'

'Let's put it this way. You've flown 3,500 miles to get here. I think we can manage twenty minutes in a helicopter.'

The view was spectacular. After getting soaking wet on the *Maid of the Mist*, Jack and Lucy spent an exciting twenty minutes admiring one of the most popular attractions in North America, but not before the surprise Jack had in store for Lucy.

'Didn't expect a wine-tasting session as well.'

'I paid for the session and lunch in advance, but what the hell,' said Jack.

'I wish Ben were here. He'd have enjoyed this. Helicopter parked next to a posh hotel, sun shining, food and wine on the terrace.'

'Think he'd prefer the zoo, and he loves being with Graham and Carol. There'll be other opportunities for him. Just enjoy it and try not to worry.'

'Jack, look at that man carrying the wine to the tables.'

'What, the tall guy?'

'Yes, isn't he like the waiter in New York?'

'Can't be. Suppose he might have a brother.'

As they boarded the helicopter to take them across the front of the Falls, Lucy looked again. He was there, and just for a second, caught her eye. A smile, of sorts. Jack held her arm as she climbed in. As she glanced back towards the hotel, he was gone.

After a comfortable overnight stay, they took the coast road towards Rochester through Niagara-on-the-Lake and drove nearly half the length of Lake Ontario. No more than an hour's drive from Rochester, Lucy chatted about the interesting place names.
'This is a lovely road, Jack, Lake Ontario State Parkway. Fascinating road names and villages. Bald Eagle Drive, Norway Heights, The Cottages of Troutburg.'
'A lot of American places are based on British and European towns and famous people, usually nobility.'
'Hang on, we were talking about the Pied Piper earlier on. You know, the leaflet. Hamlin Beach State Park,' continued Lucy.
'Sounds nice,' replied Jack. 'We'll stop off for an hour if you like.'
'According to the map, there's a headland just before. Devil's Nose.'

Jack was not speeding, just on the fifty-five limit. Approaching the turn-off for the Hamlin Beach Park, Lucy pointed out the Devil's Nose headland. They reached the right-hand bend and Jack didn't have time to respond. He would never respond. They say that a front tyre burst as the car approached the bend. It left the road, hitting the kerb. The car tipped over and landed on the marshland separating the two carriageways. Silence.

The emergency services arrived within fifteen minutes. Four cars had stopped on the highway, all of them trying to call it in. Fire crews worked to free them, but it was a salvage operation, not a rescue. Both suffered serious head injuries, and Lucy's neck was broken. She died instantly as the main impact was on her side, but Jack's rib cage was crushed, and he died minutes after the paramedics arrived. Nothing could be done except treat the deceased with dignity.

Graham could not hold back tears when told the news. Carol held him as the sobs shook his body.
'How are we going to tell young Ben?'
'I know darling, it's not fair. The family don't deserve this.'
'They were so happy, Carol. Where is Ben?'
'I sent him to his room when the police turned up at the hotel. Don't think he realised anything. Jack had the contact details in his wallet. They could have phoned other members of the family in England, but this was for the best.'
'When do we tell him?'
'We should go and do it now,' said Carol.
'Hang on, we should phone George and Mary. That can't wait. The family need to know. Between us, we've got to keep an eye on Ben. Me and Jack lost our mom and dad when we were in our twenties, so they're the only grandparents Ben has. They need to be told about Lucy, and it might help them to focus on Ben. I don't know what else to think.'

'I know love, it's hard to get it straight in your mind, isn't it?'

Graham phoned Lucy's parents, the most difficult telephone conversation of his life. George had not been well, and he idolised his daughter. Even though distraught, Mary had enough control over her emotions to be concerned for her husband's welfare.

'Graham, this must be very difficult for you,' she said. 'I know you will look after Ben while you're out there. I'm going to phone the doctor. It's shaken us both, but I'm really worried about George.'

'I'm so sorry, Mary. Please tell George we'll bring young Ben back safe and sound. He can stay at our house for a few weeks while we sort things out.'

'Thank you, Graham. We'll see you in a few days, I suppose?'

'Yes, the police have already said that emergency post-mortems were carried out. They've contacted the police in England. Jack and Lucy can be taken home in a couple of days. We've just got to tell Ben.'

'Where is he now?'

'In his hotel room watching telly. We haven't told him yet, and we're not looking forward to the next few hours.'

'Give him a hug from his nan and grandad.'

'I will Mary, I will.'

Lucy's parents waited at Heathrow. The protocol had been explained to them, and a British Airways stewardess specially trained for these circumstances sat with them. Losing any member of the family is bad enough, a daughter and her husband even worse. A fatal accident on holiday for a couple in the prime of their lives is not only unexpected but also devastating for those left behind. They loved Jack, who had made their daughter so happy, and he had given George and Mary their only grandson.

'You're being so kind my dear,' said Mary to the stewardess.

'It's no trouble. We want to do the best for your daughter and son-in-law.'

'Do we have to wait here in the lounge?'

'When the plane arrives, all the other passengers will go to the customs area as usual. Your grandson and his aunt and uncle will be allowed to stand on the tarmac, and you can then join them.'

'What happens next?'

'Jack and Lucy will be brought down a ramp by British Airways staff and a policeman. We thought you would like to put these on their coffins.'

Mary cried as the stewardess gave her two yellow and white posies. George gripped Mary's hand. She could see that life had drained from his face.

'We must be strong for our Ben.'

'I know love, I know.'

Carol held Ben as they stepped down onto the tarmac. Graham hugged Mary and George, neither of them able to speak. Then Mary took Ben into her arms.

'I've stopped crying now, Nan. Uncle Graham says I've got to be a man. Mom and Dad would be proud of me.'

As Ben said those words, the image of his parents' coffins being brought out of the plane was engraved on his mind. Even the images of the funeral at Leeford church, his parents being buried together, did not surpass the grief etched into his soul as he witnessed the end of their journey; a holiday that took away the two most important people in his life.

Of course, he would never forget them, but the experience shaped him, guided him. His mother, more than his father, had been a regular churchgoer, and she believed in heaven. Ben could no longer trust a God that would carry out such a despicable act or allow someone else to carry it out.

George and Mary moved into the Stone family home, the house that Jack and Graham had inherited from their parents more than twenty years before. Jack had bought out Graham's share, so Ben was the sole beneficiary. They spent a couple of days a week at the bungalow, only a few streets away, to keep things tidy and make sure it was secure (Graham organised an alarm system), but two things were certain: Ben needed someone to stay with him, and he had insisted that he stay in the house where he was born. His uncle and aunt offered a room at their house, but he was adamant.

George had been showing signs of the early onset of Alzheimer's, and within three years he was taken into a local care home. Mary concentrated on looking after Ben. Her daily routine consisted of getting him off to school and then visiting George for a couple of hours. Two months before Ben's seventeenth birthday, George passed away and Ben insisted that after his birthday he would manage in the house on his own. After much debate, his grandmother moved back into her bungalow. Graham and Carol visited Ben at least twice a week, making sure he was taking care of himself.

Ben wasn't being selfish. He realised that Mary was struggling to cope, managing the house and keeping an eye on her own home. It made sense, and Ben showed great maturity by recognising his grandmother's needs as well as his own. He was to live alone for two years until the day he met Joanna at the leisure centre. After the sudden death of his parents, meeting Joanna was the single most significant event in his life. They lived together within six months of meeting and were married within a year.

8:   The Seance

'Tuesday night, eight o'clock.'
'Not sure, Liz.'
'Go on, I know you're tempted.'
'Alright then, just to shut you up.'

Joanna's reluctance to attend the séance with Liz was not entirely due to a disturbing experience ten years before, but it troubled her enough to fend off requests from a friend hoping for 'a bit of a giggle'. Strangely, she didn't mind at the time (*a bit of fun*, she thought), but events a few years later made her wary of interfering with the spirit world. In her eyes, most spiritualists are frauds, but Joanna is a Christian, and by definition, she believes in spirits and has a natural fear of evil.

Peter was at school, the first year of GCSEs, and Alan was about ten. Ben's career was going well and Joanna was becoming established at the local school, popular with both staff and children. A friend at school asked her if she was interested in attending a séance.
'No, Jill, don't think it's for me.'
'I've never considered going to one myself, but my grandmother died last year, and Grandad has been very depressed. He won't go himself, but he keeps asking me to talk to Nan. He's seen an advert in the local free paper. I know, I know, but I'd do anything for him.'
'Trouble is, Jill, the medium is either a fraud or at the very least they are meddling in things that should be left alone.'

'You do believe in the next life, don't you Joanna?'

'Of course, I do, but that doesn't mean I have a need or desire to talk to the dead. I don't necessarily think it's possible anyway.'

'But you believe in the Resurrection, all that stuff.'

'Yes, but we are mere humans. Just because I accept that Jesus rose doesn't mean that we all can. Heaven is a strange concept for any of us to grasp, even committed Christians. Surely it's not right to meddle.'

'Would you go there - just to support me?'

'If you insist. But any funny business and we're out of there.'

An ordinary street, but Joanna feared that this would be no ordinary occasion. Neither of them had been to a séance before, and Jill's excitement exceeded Joanna's uncertainty, if not trepidation. Jill was excited by the prospect of hearing from her late grandmother, and it wasn't until she stepped into the house that Joanna's words hit home.

'What if she's not a fraud?' she whispered.

'Too late now, Jill, but if she's genuine, maybe you'll get something out of it.'

The medium, a short, plump woman in her mid-forties, greeted them.

'I'm Andrea, lovely to see you. We have six people here tonight. I do hope you will find the occasion worth it.'

'Ten pounds each. Is that right?' asked Jill.

'That's right. Hope that's okay.'

The other four attendees were already in position at the table. Curtains closed, light on but candles positioned around the room. Andrea was prepared.

'Please sit down and we'll start in about ten minutes. I will light the candles and as we start, my daughter will turn off the main light.'

'Do we hold hands,' asked a balding, middle-aged man sitting to Jill's right.

'Not yet, Mr Jenkins. I will give you instructions as we go along.'

On one side of the table, Joanna sat to Jill's left. Opposite, an old lady smiled at Joanna. Next, her daughter, no doubt the driver of the BMW 5-series parked outside and some sort of businesswoman or other professional, surmised Joanna. Power-dressed, with facial expression to match. To her left, opposite the man next to Jill was a girl, or appeared to be a girl. Probably late teens or early twenties. *So hard to tell these days*, she reflected. The scene was set, the cast ready.

'Lydia, if you could switch off the light and close the door, we'll get started.'

Six candles distributed around the room, one for each attendee, and one large candle in the centre of the table, gave enough light for each person to see the outline of Andrea's face. She instructed them to join hands, making a closed circle of seven people.

'Please don't break the circle at any time, until I say. If something does go wrong, which is rare, call out for Lydia, my daughter, who is in the next room. She will know what to do.'

Andrea's instructions created a sense of tension in the room. Joanna wasn't sure if the other people had been to a séance before, but they seemed familiar with the procedure. Andrea started by bowing her head, almost touching the table. The candles flickered.

From the corner of her eye, Joanna noticed the door creep open. No lights on in the rest of the house. *Lydia supports her mother*, she assumed. She glanced across at Jill. She was staring forwards, not at anyone in particular, concentrating. Joanna had not seen her friend like this before. A classroom assistant at school, she presented as a bubbly, vivacious young woman. Single, late twenties, a string of boyfriends, she wasn't the type to take this seriously. If there is a type. Jill tightened her grip on Joanna's right hand. Not painful, nor reassuring, but somehow preparatory for what lay ahead. Andrea used the stereotypical opening lines to establish contact, and, as she seemed to engage in a stilted conversation with a group of the departed, Joanna was more convinced that it was clever stage work. Jill straightened up when Andrea talked about a grandmother joining them, wanting to contact a young lady, asking about 'Dad'. Joanna considered even Jill capable of seeing through that. Too vague and general.

'A girl trying to speak. Jackie, Julie, no... Jodie. That's right, Jodie.'

No one knew anyone called Jodie.

'I am confused, I will admit,' said Andrea. 'This might be someone speaking on behalf of Jodie. An uncle perhaps, or grandfather?'

No one in the room reacted. A connection expected to elicit a sigh, a gasp.

'She wants to be with Peter. They won't be together for long, but they will be in love.'

At that, Joanna glanced at Jill. In the half-light, Jill stared back.

'Peter,' she mouthed.

~

Joanna hadn't thought of the séance she attended with Jill in 2006 for some time, but after agreeing to go along with Liz, she made the connection. *Peter and Jodie*, she said to herself. *Liz says it's in Langstone Road. Could it still be, what was her name, Agnes, no, Andrea?* Joanna didn't question it at the time, but, five years after that first séance, Peter had met and lost Jodie. A coincidence, surely. Maybe she'd ask Andrea if she remembered, but it was a long time ago.

'So, it's the same place as your last séance?' asked Liz.

'You make me sound like a regular, a professional. I've only been to one.'

'Think she's the only medium in the area. The only one that advertises, anyway,' said Liz.

'Real shame about Dawn's husband.'

'Yes, they thought he had a chance. Only thirty-five, six months of chemo.'

'She's definitely going?' Joanna enquired.

'Phoned her last night. She sounds fine, quite positive.'

The ten years disappeared in seconds as they walked up to the front door. A young woman ushered them in with hardly a word, simply a gesture directing them to the front room.

'I recognise her,' whispered Joanna. 'It's Andrea's daughter. She must be twenty-seven now.'

Dawn was already sitting at the table, an elderly lady to her left. Liz sat opposite Dawn, Joanna next to her.

'Hi Liz, glad you could come.'

'How have you been?' Liz replied, also introducing Joanna.

'Okay. I'm trying not to expect too much.'

The door opened. Expecting Andrea, Joanna was surprised when Lydia entered holding five candles and closed the door.

'Is your mother here tonight?'

'She's out. She doesn't do this anymore. We can start in a few minutes. There are five of us tonight.'

She told them what to do, lit the candles and turned off the light. Lydia struggled to find any meaningful connections after ten minutes of intense concentration. Dawn asked her if there was someone called Keith. No, but a message from George meant to reassure somebody. The lady opposite Joanna had lost a brother called George in the war. Not who she was looking for. Suddenly, Lydia went pale and bowed her head, not moving for a full minute. Everyone gripped their neighbour's hand tighter, sensing a breakthrough. Lydia's voice changed, weakened, and she appeared visibly shaken. Joanna was convinced she was preparing to end the session.

'I have something, a message. A couple, John and Lucy. They have both spoken, repeating the same phrase, a foreign language. I don't understand.'

John and Lucy, thought Joanna. *The name Lucy could be a coincidence.*

'Unus dies vos cognoscetis,' Lydia mumbled.

'Italian?' whispered Liz.

'Latin,' said Joanna.

'No, it's not John and Lucy, the message is from Jack and Lucy; unus dies vos cognoscetis,' said Lydia.

Joanna felt her heart miss a beat. The correction of the name, but a Latin phrase? *Not sure what it means*, she pondered. *But 'cognos'? Is that 'mind' or 'knowledge', perhaps?*
Ben would know, but I'm not going to mention this to him, she decided. *Stir up too many memories, and weird Latin phrases won't help.*

Outside in the car, Liz asked Joanna what she thought, not aware of the significance of the names.

'Nothing, a load of rubbish really, and Dawn got no help, did she?'

Joanna would leave it for now but entered the phrase in her diary.

'Damn!'

'What's wrong?' asked Liz, as they pulled away.

'Forgot to ask Lydia about the name Jodie. Possibly her mother would remember. Perhaps I'll leave it.'

'Probably for the best.'

~

'Not sure how best to advise you, love.'

'Sorry to bother you with this, Dad, and I appreciate you brought me up as a Christian. We shouldn't be meddling with things like this.'

'I'm not going to criticise you for helping a friend. You went along in good faith. Mind you, I agree it's best not to tell Ben.'

Joanna's parents, Harry and Jennifer, moved to Edinburgh through his work. Now retired, still living in Scotland, Harry had been promoted to area manager for the pensions company he worked for, at the age of fifty. Previously working in Birmingham as branch manager, the opportunity was too good to miss. They loved Scotland, and Joanna remembered many happy summers travelling around the Highlands. Ironically, Edinburgh was a favourite haunt for both Jennifer and Harry. She missed them, and her weekly call usually entailed family and work stories - Alan's studies, Peter's latest girlfriend, Ben's business and the kids in her classroom. This was different, and her father was always a good listener.

Jennifer tended to panic and fluster if Joanna had a problem, but Harry had a cool head. A committed Christian, he didn't hold with interfering in the paranormal but held such respect for his daughter that he immediately understood her motives for attending the séance. However, he was still worried.

'If I were you, Jo, I'd leave it. There's nothing you can do to bring back Jodie, or Ben's parents. It was a long time ago that he lost them. Don't rake it up.'
'You always were the sensible one in the family. Love you, Dad. Speak to you next week.'
'Tell Ben he owes me a game of golf next time we're visiting.'

~

'Hi Jo, you haven't called me since the séance.'
'To be honest Liz, I've been trying not to think about it.'
Joanna ordered a latté for Liz and an espresso for herself.
'As I understand it, ten years ago Andrea mentioned Jodie and Peter. He didn't meet her for another five years. Sorry, are you okay?'
'No, it's alright Liz, carry on.'
'Three weeks ago, Lydia talked about Jack and Lucy, quoting some Latin stuff.'
'Talked to my dad last week. He advised me not to tell Ben - bad memories, you know, best left alone.'

'Fair enough Jo, but doesn't he have a right to be told?'

'How do you mean?'

'Of course, it could be a lot of nonsense, but what if his parents are sending a message?'

'Do you really believe that?'

'Not necessarily, but you've said yourself there may be something in it. When they crashed near Rochester it left him as an orphan. He never understood, did he? He's a grown man now. Perhaps it's time.'

'Not sure. See what you mean though. So, it will be better in the long run?'

'If it were me, I'd tell him. Oh, did I tell you we're off to Mexico soon for two weeks?'

'That was sudden. How are you and this new bloke getting on? Mind you, if you're going to Mexico with him, it can't be that bad...'

'He's wonderful, Jo. I've never been so happy.'

'When am I going to meet him?'

'He travels a lot in his work, so it's awkward. But one day soon, I'm sure. He'd love to meet you, and your family. Anyway, why don't we catch up for a coffee when I get back and you can tell me what you decided?'

Joanna was closer to Liz than any other friend. She could tell her anything and not be judged. They advised each other, not expecting their advice to be taken automatically. Liz had changed her job recently, and was now working part-time in the local library. *Maybe she met him there*, Joanna thought. Something occurred to her, bringing her up short. Apart from talking about boyfriends and the new job, Joanna knew little about her. She realised that Liz let her do most of the talking. She was a good listener, and most conversations centred on her teaching job and the Stone family. *Something strange*, she thought. *I can't remember ever mentioning that the car crash was near Rochester. How could she possibly know that? Perhaps I said something and forgot.* Joanna quickly put it out of her mind.

9: The Saint Christopher

'How was the séance? You never mentioned it.'
'Oh, nothing really happened.'
'Did she forecast my score for today?'
'Lydia's not that good.'

Ben lay back, arms behind his head, contemplating the growing cobweb in the corner of the ceiling over Joanna's dressing table. He considered himself lucky to have the ability to switch off. Some of his managers and co-directors lived on overdrive. Adrenaline junkies. *Life's too short*, he mused. This was the stage in his life where contentment, although not a given, was natural and welcoming. A middle-aged, successful businessman, how could he not be happy, lying beside this beautiful woman? Made a note to tell her that. She had given him two sons - quite different - but he was immensely proud of them both. A family that had risen above serious problems and come through. Joanna scanned his face, attempting to read the next thought, awaiting the next comment. *You can be predictable, Ben Stone*, she thought, as she slid her hand into his.

'Fancy a lie-in?'
'I know your lie-ins, Mr Stone. Thought you had a game today?'
'Yes, but five minutes won't hurt.'
'We'll have to get up. You've got a day off, but you did promise to pop in and see Carol. Been nearly five weeks now.'

'You're right. Anything else Herr Commandant?'

'Somebody has to give you instructions, Benjamin. Have you forgotten about the farm shop? After Carol's, get two pounds of parsnips and a bag of potatoes.'

'My life is full of excitement.'

'What time is John picking you up?'

'Eleven. We're only doing nine holes. Back nine.'

Joanna held his chin in her right hand, placing her left around his neck. Gently, she drew him towards her. *A kiss won't hurt*, she thought, *he deserves that at least*, as a knock on the bedroom door disturbed the moment. Peter waited a few seconds and popped his head round the door. In his usual rush, last-minute collection of keys, wallet, employee gym-pass, he became the second person to remind his father that Aunt Carol was expecting him. A groan from Ben. Joanna waved to her son, smiled, kissed her husband on the tip of his nose and threw back the bedclothes. The start of another day.

In the car, approaching Leeford Village, Ben listed his daily moans, realising he had little to complain about. If he had been able to plan his life through to his late forties when at college, his current circumstances would have appeared perfectly acceptable on paper. *More than acceptable*, he thought, Joanna invading his mind as he passed the church where they married, the pub almost opposite where they often sat and shared their dreams and, later, kissed in the car park under the shadow of the trees. Past the library, and a quick glance at the chemist's where Cheryl works (*Alan could do a lot worse*, he thought), and towards The Cross.

How many times he's been over that crossroads he had no idea, but it was an iconic meeting place. In his teenage years, meeting his ex-school mates, turning left to the Summerhill Hotel for the Monday night disco. Turn right towards the park and his favourite course (looking forward to his game with John Greggs. Directors versus sales management challenge. Needle, friendly, but still needle). Straight over now, The Cross pub on the right-hand side, then the local police station. On the left, yet another building society and a doctor's surgery. As he passed the traffic lights, he sensed something - a jolt, a shudder, as a car from the opposite direction trying to turn right towards The Summerhill inched forwards. 'Impatient pillock!' he bellowed. No one to hear him over his 1980s compilation CD. David Bowie assisted the closed windows, engine noise and the fact that he was thirty yards past the other car before there was any chance of the errant driver hearing Ben's insults. Not really a near miss, but he had a thing about drivers in so much of a hurry they felt it necessary to pull across oncoming traffic. No doubt tailgated as well. *Life's too short*, he thought, *you're not perfect*. Another shiver as he pulled away from the lights. Unable to account for that one.

Only a mile past The Cross, a left turn and Carol's house could be seen a hundred yards on the left. He missed Graham, his father's older brother. Carol, now in her early sixties, would easily pass for fifty, but nonetheless, she appeared to have aged in the last few weeks.

'How are you, Auntie?'

'Better for seeing you, Ben,' she said, kissing him on the left cheek.

'Can't stop for long. Jobs to do for Jo, and I'm playing John from work later.'

'You and your golf. I wanted to see you anyway, Ben. Graham left something for you. Your dad bought it for Graham's twenty-first. Your uncle left a note that it should be passed to you.'

Carol placed a small grey box in his hand. The sort of box you might expect would contain a ring or Saint Christopher. As he opened it, he remembered the close bond between his father and uncle. Jack had always looked up to his older brother. Ben was surprised to see an old coin in the box. A farthing, 1923. A small inscription in Latin read 'Vos autem sedate in terminis.'

'You must finish something?' enquired Ben.

'I didn't know the meaning at first, but it must have been significant to them. It translates as "you must stay within the boundaries". Mean anything to you?'

'Appropriate to my game today, I suppose. Wouldn't make sense for cricket, not if I were batting. Any ideas, Auntie Carol?'

'I didn't get the impression it was anything to do with sport. More a philosophical thing. They were always debating, but rarely fell out.'

'Was Uncle Graham religious? He went to church with you occasionally, but you know...'

Carol interrupted him.

'He had some faith, but it changed, and he believed in family and sticking together.'

'I understand, Auntie.'

Ben gazed at her, touched her shoulder, seeing the tears in her eyes.

'Thank you for this. You know how much I loved Uncle Graham. Both of you did so much for me. I wanted to say that.'

'Go on, do your chores and get off to your golf,' Carol said, smiling.

John Greggs had worked for National Flooring as sales manager for the last seven years. During that period of rapid growth in the company, John became an integral part of the organisation, considered a natural successor to the current sales director, Ralph Briars, due for retirement in 2018. John and Ben started the works golf society together and forged a strong friendship. The society, ever democratic, included anyone who worked for the firm. Two of the warehousemen showed great promise, with sub-eighteen handicap scores this year. With Ben playing off fourteen, and John off twelve, it made for great competition. Both of their wives felt a combination of abandonment during the season and relief that they had most Sunday mornings to themselves.

'Straight on or right at the lights?' asked John.

'Turn right, then straight up the hill for about a mile, and the park is on the left. As we drive through the park, the course entrance is on the right.'

'No problem with dogs, I hope.'

'No, the course is fenced off,' replied Ben. 'Never been an issue.'

With John two shots ahead, they paused for a drink at the fourteenth. Ben loved to take in the view. The walk towards the fifteenth tee sees the land rise about thirty feet, above the treeline of the eleventh and twelfth fairways. The club, realising the popularity of this spot, had a bench installed.

'I could sit here all day,' said Ben. 'You can see three counties from this spot.'

'Beautiful countryside,' said John.

Ben, not taking any shots from his playing partner, pulled back the deficit, both finishing a creditable five over par.

'Forty for the back nine. Not bad. I needed that birdie at the last.'

'How are things at home Ben? You haven't really talked about it. What is it now, five years since, you know, Peter's girlfriend?'

'Five years this October 4th. We don't talk about it at home, only on that day when we go up to the grave. Just once a year. He's happy now, sees lots of girls. The current one is Hannah. She's great.'

'Joanna? Alan?'

'Alan's settled in college now, lives up there during the week. Cheryl stays up there one or two nights a week depending on her shifts at Boots.'

'Suppose flexi-time helps.'

'I couldn't manage without Joanna. She knows everything about me, knows what I'm thinking. That's love, isn't it?'

'You romantic old git.'

'Thanks, pal. Anyway, how's your family?'

'Ruth is fine. Simon's at Exeter - history, second year.'

'We are lucky.'

'You were today - that last putt...'

'Bugger off, John, I can read the greens like Faldo.'

Back at the house, John told Ben that he'd seen Joe and Teresa Mason. Joe was warehouse manager until his retirement, and his wife Teresa worked in the stock office.

'Of course, Teresa left when Joe retired last year. I remember the presentation. We collected eighty pounds for his leaving present. New fishing rod, wasn't it?'

'Teresa told us the one he wanted. He was thrilled. Mentioned it last week. They both seem well.'

'I must give them a ring sometime,' said Ben.

10: You will soon be four

Cheryl had the car on one of the days she was working in Leeford, so Alan travelled to The Meadows on the 263. Past the car park at Old Trafford, down Village Way onto the Ashburton Road, a twenty-minute ride from his college digs. The interview had been comfortable for Alan - as a volunteer, he felt no pressure, and the care home manager, Dorothy Woodcourt, gave him the impression that everyone would be kind to both Alan and the other workers. In general, this proved to be the case but Melanie Crowther, his supervisor, put him on edge.

'Don't think you're here for an easy ride just because you're a volunteer.'

'I don't, Melanie.'

'Mrs Crowther to you, Alan.'

'Sorry, Mrs Crowther; I must have given you the wrong impression. I'm just here to help.'

Getting off on the wrong foot uneased him, but he was determined to make a success of this venture. Fortunately, his shifts seldom coincided with those of Mrs Crowther, but she followed him round for the first two nights, introducing him to each of the residents. Alan was not alone in his feelings about Mrs Crowther. One old gentleman, ex-naval officer George Bradley, insisted on calling the supervisor 'Melanie' (or 'Mel' if in a particularly devilish mood) and ignored any stiff retort.

'Ignore her, son. Had one like her on HMS Southampton in thirty-nine. We soon sorted him out, lieutenant or not.'

Alan smiled, and after the end of his first week realised that only one resident was fond of Melanie Crowther. At first, he struggled to engage Mrs Armitage in conversation - a lady who refused to give her date of birth to anyone but who was estimated to be in her mid-nineties. She remembered her days as a young girl in post-First World War England.

'My mother and father met a few months after the war, married very quickly, as they did in those days, and I came along soon after.'

Over a period of five or six weeks, Mrs Armitage opened up and insisted that Alan teach her some card games. They also played dominoes, Alan making sure she won most of the games. She asked about his family and took a close interest in his relationship with Cheryl. However, one night she refused to speak at all. He reported it to Mrs Crowther, who dismissed it out of hand.

'You're getting too close to the service users.'

'What do you mean?' said Alan, reflecting that, yes, they provided a service, and the residents used the service, but Crowther saw them as records on a database.

'Too personal, dragging up old memories of their past relationships. It can upset them.'

'But Mrs Armitage asks a lot of questions. What am I supposed to do?'

He didn't see much of Melanie Crowther for the next week but sat with Mrs Armitage each time he visited The Meadows. For three consecutive nights she said nothing, then one night she stared at him and grabbed his left hand.

'Mrs Armitage, what is it?'

'Be careful. You will soon be four.'

'What do you mean?' said Alan.

From that moment, she never spoke again. Three days later, she passed away peacefully in her sleep. As Alan walked through reception the following day, Mrs Crowther took him to one side.

'She left you an envelope. If it's money or anything of value, you must declare it to the manager.'

Alan didn't open the envelope until he and Cheryl were relaxing after a meal that evening. She had three days off work and was able to stay with him in Manchester.

'She's written something, but not in English. Probably Latin.'

'What does it say?'

'There are two phrases - *nuntiate patri tuo* and *mihi est in utraque parte.*'

'Why does an old lady give you something like this?'

'No idea. I'll ask Peter when we get back home at the weekend. He's the Latin expert, and if it's some other language, he'll know.'

'What was it she said to you when you last saw her?'

'She said "you will soon be four", the last thing she said before she died.'

'Alan, this is a bit scary. "You will soon be four". That could mean anything.'

Cheryl did battle with the M6 for the journey back to the Stone residence. A bag full of Alan's clothes in the boot, laptop, textbooks. She didn't mind. Alan looked tired, and his brow betrayed the tracks in his mind after the connection he had made with the old lady. At Sandbach, she picked up a quick-read paperback for those hours she preferred to spend alone. Although fond of Joanna and Ben, not for her the traditional family habit of surrounding the TV in a semi-circle. She liked her own space. She could be social, but in moderation.

His father was likely to say Alan was in 'one of his moods', but Cheryl knew otherwise. Deep in contemplation, he recalled each conversation with Mrs Armitage (Greta), although he had not been allowed to use her first name. Doesn't matter now. A week before she died, he found Greta asleep in the armchair by the window, muttering to herself.
'She'll let you down, you know. She'll let you down.'
He thought nothing of it at the time and didn't attribute the comment to his personal circumstances. Now, halfway on the journey home, he wavered between sleep and internal discussion. He considered the significance of her words, as a voice from the past surfaced.
'Stone face!'
'Carter, leave it will you,' said Alan.
'You steaming great prat, Stone. I've never liked you, and your precious brother isn't here to bail you out.'
'What do you want?'
'I could take anything from you I wanted, brother or no brother. But that's too easy.'

'You're not making any sense.'

Frank Carter's face stiffened and his eyes darkened. Alan tried to hide his fear. He had been bullied by a few of the older boys, but Carter was different. Something about his eyes, a familiarity, a deepness. Alan repeated the phrase a dozen times that night, trying to get to sleep. The phrase that Carter uttered as he walked away.

'She'll let you down, you know. She'll let you down.'

The only female in his life at that time, apart from his GP and teachers, was his mother. A couple of casual flings and teenage break-ups, meaning little to him, but nothing to justify a sentence uttered by a school bully that included the pronoun 'she'. Who was *she*?

It was only now, sitting in the shared Punto, fifty miles from home, that he finally realised who 'she' was. His only serious girlfriend, Cheryl - apart from his mother, the only woman he had ever loved. He mulled it over. *Why should she let me down?* The bigger question for him filled his waking thoughts. *Why should a fifteen-year-old school bully say such a thing, and then a good five years later an old lady repeat the phrase, verbatim, in the final days of her life?*

~

'Hi Dad, Mom.'

Joanna embraced her son while Ben gave Cheryl a peck on her left cheek. She smiled.

'Hello Mr Stone, how are you?'

'Oh, Ben, please. We're not formal round here.'
'Give me a hug, Cheryl,' said Joanna.

Peter was in the living room watching a Channel Four documentary about a TT racer attempting the Wall of Death.
'Hiya mate, how's Manchester.'
'What are you watching?' asked Alan.
'Guy Martin. Yet another world record attempt.'
'Peter, could we see you in the morning? Out of earshot from Mom and Dad. Particularly Dad.'
'Sure. No trouble at mill is there?'
'Don't think so. Just something we need to talk through,' said Alan.

Ben was due to meet the competition committee at the club, and Joanna had the usual Saturday morning shopping. With no shifts due until Monday, Peter's lie-in extended even beyond the record that Alan and Cheryl appeared keen to break, according to Ben.
'Young people today, when I was a lad, and so on,' he jokingly lectured.
'Just ignore him, he remembers the war,' was Joanna's usual retort.

Peter finally surfaced, awaited patiently by Alan and Cheryl at the breakfast table. He needed coffee urgently before being capable of digesting anything, especially complicated information. Finally, they had their moment as he crunched into toast and marmalade.

'You say that this old lady told you something three days before she died?' enquired Peter.

'"Be careful, you will soon be four".'

'Any ideas, Alan?'

'We can't think of anything. What about you Pete?' asked Alan.

'Beats me. Maybe you meet another couple and go out as a foursome?'

'When she died, she left me a piece of paper with something written in Latin,' said Alan. 'Could you translate it for us?'

'Let's see,' said Peter. *'Nuntiate patri tuo. Mihi est in utraque parte.'*

'I'll leave you lads to it,' offered Cheryl. 'Alan, I'll sort your washing out while you discuss Latin phrases with your big brother.'

As she closed the door, Alan told Peter to put the paper to one side for a minute. He had something else to tell him.

'I didn't want to talk about this other thing in front of Cheryl. Might upset her.'

'What is it mate?' said Peter 'You look worried.'

'A week before Greta died, she muttered something in her sleep when I went into her room. At least, I think she was asleep.'

'Go on.'

'She said "she'll let you down, you know, she'll let you down". Exact words.'

'Might be anything mate, and it doesn't mean that Cheryl is involved. She's been the best thing that ever happened to you.'

'I agree,' replied Alan. 'But do you remember that kid at school, the strange one, Frank Carter? This made me remember. He said the same to me five years ago, never repeated it, and I didn't think much about it at the time.'

'I'd told that little runt to leave you alone.'

'Leave that now Peter, it's not what I'm saying. Doesn't it strike you as a bit spooky?'

They heard Cheryl's steps on the stairs and agreed to leave that matter for now in order to concentrate on the Latin issue.

'The first part means "tell your father".'

'Tell Dad what?'

'*Mihi est in utraque parte* means "I was on both sides".'

'On both sides?' asked Alan.

'When I studied mythology, that may well have been interpreted in a different, very specific way.'

'What was that?'

'Meet me on the other side.'

Cheryl had come back into the room. She didn't speak but looked concerned and pale. Alan and Peter spent the next ten minutes going through what the phrase could mean, and if it applied to Ben. They reached no conclusions, except one; that Ben should not be told. For the time being, they would also avoid discussing it with Joanna. As Cheryl went back upstairs, Peter touched his brother's shoulder.

'Try not to worry. We'll talk about the other matter when we get chance.'

'Mom's back. Should we tell her?'

'Leave it now, Alan. I might have a quiet word next week when Dad's at work.'

Within an hour, Ben returned from his committee meeting. Alan took Peter's advice to push it to the back of his mind and try to enjoy the weekend. The family back together, and Cheryl being accepted as part of that family, they managed to put it behind them. For now.

~

Back in Manchester, Cheryl agreed to accompany Alan to Greta's funeral. It was to be a small affair, with Greta not having a large family. They were told she had a daughter, a younger sister and two cousins who lived locally. The care home would be represented by management, in addition to Alan and Cheryl. The clocks had moved forward, Easter had come and gone, but the dreary weather showed no sign of abating. A fine drizzle peppered them as they moved from the car to the church, Cheryl gripping Alan's hand tighter than he thought necessary.

They recognised Melanie Crowther three rows in front of them, standing next to a young man. 'Early twenties,' Cheryl whispered, but from behind, Alan had no idea who he was. Dorothy Woodcourt also attended, a row in front of Melanie, behind Greta's family. No eulogy being delivered, the service was swift and quiet. Alan and Cheryl waited for everyone to leave the church before following at the rear. Greta's coffin, carried by four bearers from the local funeral directors, was taken around the back of the church down to a secluded corner shaded by a huge oak. Alan and Cheryl stood away from the graveside, with a good view of the mourners.

Alan had not attended many funerals in his young life, the most recent being his great-uncle Graham in February. For him, the only disturbing moment was when he saw his father cry for the first time. Joanna held him as he remembered his beloved uncle. Ben had coped with the entire service but broke down as they moved the coffin to the hearse. They travelled to the crematorium in silence. It was a few weeks later when Joanna explained to her younger son the close bond Ben forged with his uncle.

'You were told about the events in America when your nan and grandad, who you never knew, were killed. Your dad was only fourteen, so you can imagine how hard it was for him. Uncle Graham and Aunt Carol helped to take care of him. They were very close.'

'I understand, Mom. I've never seen Dad so upset.'

'It brought it all back for him. Best not to mention it, he's been fine otherwise.'

'There's that bloke with your Mrs Crowther,' said Cheryl, her words refocussing Alan's attention on Greta's funeral.

'I'm glad she's *not* my Mrs Crowther. Hang on, he looks familiar. If I didn't know any better, I'd say that was Frank Carter.'

'The boy from school you've told me about?'

'I can't be sure, but if it's not him he's got a double. Obviously, he's five years older, but I'd recognise that snarl anywhere.'

'Has he seen you?' asked Cheryl.

'Don't think so, but what the hell's he doing with Melanie Crowther? I've never believed in coincidences.'

Cheryl scanned the small gathering. Standing behind the vicar, just to the left of Melanie Crowther, a man stood with his head bowed. Tall, with a grey, gaunt face, his trilby pushed over his forehead. She felt a lurch in her stomach. Recognition of someone else they knew, someone unexpected at this gathering.

'Alan, can you see that man standing between the vicar and Mrs Crowther? Hang on, he's moved back a bit.'

'Yes, what of it?'

'Isn't he like Don Gil?'

As Alan turned for another look, the man had moved away, standing by a large gravestone just beyond the oak tree. *Just a man*, he thought.

'No, he could be anyone. Anyway, why would Gil come here? He's got nothing to do with Greta.'

Cheryl turned again. The man had gone, and she was left with her own thoughts. Disturbing thoughts.

11: The Stone family will pay

'James, did you finish the essay on the Brontë sisters?'

'Girls' rubbish,' he muttered.

'If you are not able to enunciate, perhaps we should send you for elocution lessons.'

'What was that?'

'Thought that would wake you up. Brontë sisters?'

'Mom wanted some help with my kid brother last night.'

'You've had a whole week to complete the work. Other people help their families, and they manage it.'

'Bully for them.'

'Appropriate word for you Mr Enright. See me at the end of school.'

More than a scowl, James's eyes bored into Joanna's face. The heat of his anger surged towards her from the back of the classroom. She imagined his face reddening and then swelling like a dying supernova. She admitted to herself that she hated this boy, and the shame struck home. Difficult students come and go, but James Enright was different.

When he arrived at the form room, on time for a change, perhaps hoping his trip home would not be delayed, his mood had not subsided to any great degree.

'What have I done now?' he asked.

'If you were behaving like a normal student, James, you would join in the two-hundredth anniversary of the birth of Charlotte Brontë. Anyone studying English might have a slight interest in that occasion.'

'Means nothing to me.'

'Right, you've got two more days to finish the six hundred words I asked you to do. In addition, I want you to go to the library and list all the books by the Brontë sisters. If the task isn't carried out to the letter, you'll be seeing the head. Get that?'

James stood up, nodding, feigning agreement with the head of English. Joanna waved her hand towards the door to signal that the conclusion of the meeting had been reached. He turned round and took three steps. Opening the door, he glared at Joanna. She didn't have the energy to reply when he uttered the threat. James was down the corridor and out of the school before she moved.

'The Stone family will pay for this.'

~

'Your company's logo is its visual signature. It can be used on business cards, website homepage, and vehicle livery – anything that promotes the name of the company. Remember, in conclusion, the logo must also try to describe the brand or the main product. Okay, folks, see you next week.'

Don Gil concluded the lecture with every student aiming for the double doors like Exocets. Lunchtime - catching up with Facebook and emails. *The internet takes a hit this time of day*, he mused. Only one student remained in his seat.

'You didn't ask any awkward questions today, Alan. Is everything alright?'

'Fine, Don. Lot on my mind, but I wanted to ask you about programming.'

'Fire away.'

'What's the best language to learn for our assignments?'

'We've already touched on HTML, and, of course, most of the work we do is web-based. Tell you what, I've got the study today for an hour this afternoon. Pop along about three. I have a book on introducing JavaScript you can borrow. We'll be moving onto that later in the year, but it will give you a head start.'

Alan was unaware that at the mid-morning break Gil met Cheryl in the cafeteria. Her planned shopping trip was abandoned when realising she'd left her credit card at home, but she had enough cash for cake and coffee. Gil was keen to learn more about Alan, and Cheryl was happy to provide the information.

'How long have you known him?'

'Almost three years.'

'Do you get on with his family?'

'They're lovely. Not sure I deserve the kindness they show me.'

Cheryl found herself opening up to a man she barely knew. Gil had a way of getting people to talk. Not only that, but they felt a compulsion to talk. Nothing was held back. Later, she was shocked that even the brief sortie with her boss had been revealed.

'This is all in confidence, Cheryl. You have nothing to worry about. It's up to you when you tell Alan.'

'Don't you mean "if"?'

'He will find out eventually, so you might as well prepare yourself for complete honesty.'

The affairs with Ralph and Trevor were over, but recent. Cheryl couldn't bring herself to tell Alan - not yet. As she returned to the room they shared, her emotions were confused. Angry with Don for getting her to open her soul, and yet strangely grateful. She needed someone to talk to, but had no friends in Manchester. When she thought about it, she had few friends in Leeford. Only Andrea and Julie from school, and she hadn't seen them in six months. Her life now revolved around Alan, and as she sat on the bed, kicking off her shoes, a sudden resentment towards Don Gil swept through her. *Who does he think he is*, she thought. She lay on her back, his face burnt onto her retinas, permanently on the horizon - his eyes, the way they drill down, searching. As she fell asleep, her concerns ebbed away but she found herself saying 'he knows more than we realise.'

~

'Hello, young Alan. Prompt as usual.'

'Hi Don, thank you for seeing me.'

'Here's the book I promised. You can keep it. I found two copies.'

'That's great, if you're sure. Very kind.'

'I saw Cheryl today. Had a coffee. You're a lucky man.'

'She didn't mention it. Mind you, she was very tired. Asleep when I got back to the room.'

'All the travelling, I expect. She's very dedicated to looking after you. On a different subject, how is your brother?'

'Peter? Why do you ask?'

'You told me last time that he had some bother with a thug. Biker, wasn't he?'

'Don't remember talking about Peter.'

'Could have been Cheryl, but no matter. How is he?'

'Fine. Staying well away from that girl.'

'Anyway Alan, your next assignment.'

~

Peter had walked home from the gym before. Not a fitness thing – he was fit enough – but his car was not the most reliable vehicle on the road. Ben often asked him why he didn't have an 'ordinary car', one that would at least start every day and go in the driver's intended direction. The steering had been playing up on his old TR4 for months. Not that he couldn't afford the repairs - he had more important things on his mind. He'd been seeing Hannah for three months. The only effort involved fending off his parents for an update on the 'serious' scale of the relationship.

Only two miles from the gym to the outskirts of Leeford, earphones in, iPod set to 'random'. The hour had moved forward into BST but, by eight, it was still getting dark. As he entered the alleyway, a shortcut taking a few hundred yards off the main road route, he sensed trouble. There were four of them.

'Here we are again, Stone.'

'Hickens. What's your problem? I've not seen Barbara.'

'Couldn't care less, Mr Rock Star. Maybe I just don't like you.'

Hickens's three henchmen grabbed Peter, holding him against the wall.

'I'm in no hurry. I'm going to enjoy this,' snarled Hickens.

He stared at Peter for over a minute. Sweat poured down Peter's face. He knew he was in for a beating. The first punch arrived low, taking his breath away. Hickens kicked both of his shins. Peter flinched as a boot connected with his knee. One moment of pleasure was stolen by the victim as Hickens came towards him, lining up a right hook. Peter struggled free long enough to aim a boot at a sensitive part of Hickens's anatomy. He crumpled to the ground, clutching himself between the legs. The three thugs regained control as Hickens recovered. This time his fist connected with Peter's face. Blood spurted from the gums of two loosened teeth, and he cried out in agony.

'Let him go - nearly finished with him.'

As he fell to the ground, Peter felt a boot strike his right kidney and then a punch to the back of his head. He fainted, but came to within a minute. His vision was blurred, but his eyes followed the assailants out of the alleyway. As he sat there, he saw Hickens with a smaller, probably younger, man. He was in no doubt that money was exchanged, and then they left.

'Dad, it's me. Do you mind coming to pick me up?'

'Tell me where you are, son. I'll come right over.'

Ben found Peter slumped against the wall of a butcher's shop at the top of the alleyway. Peter did not protest when Ben put his arms around his waist, hauled him up and put him into the passenger seat. Refusing any medical treatment, he also pleaded with his father regarding the nature and cause of the injuries.

'I've been straight with you, Dad. Please do as I say and tell Mom that I fell. A few too many at The Vine with my mates and I fell over the wall.'

'Not sure, Peter, but there's one thing for certain. I'm going to the police in the morning.'

'No way, Dad. Please. No police.'

'We'll talk again later. Let's get you home first. I could do with a drink myself.'

Ben reluctantly agreed to go along with Peter's way of dealing with the incident. No police. Joanna wouldn't be told the truth (for now), but he would go to the dentist for an emergency appointment in the morning. He had a strong emotional bond with his father and mutual affection, much of it unspoken. More than ever they wanted to be honest with each other, father and son. However, there was still to be no mention of Alan's situation in Manchester and the strange messages from Greta. Joanna, upset at seeing Peter in such a state, but forever practical, cleaned him up and finally accepted the 'fall' story after a fifteen-minute grilling.

'There's always trouble with your friends. It wasn't that gang again, was it?'

'Told you, Mom. Too much drink and I fell.'

'I'll leave you and your dad to it then.'

'Thanks, Mom,' he said, kissing her on the cheek.

Peter sat in the leather armchair in Ben's study. They didn't speak for over ten minutes.

'Do you believe in life after death, Dad?'

'Is this about Jodie, son?'

'I suppose so.'

'Well, your mom calls me agnostic. Suppose that means I have no faith, but I don't have the certainty of an atheist. Not sure that's the correct definition, but it sort of describes how I see things.'

'Another life?'

'I think when you're gone, you're gone, but I respect your mom's views about heaven. It's a nice thought. If it does exist, one day you'll see Jodie again.'

'I never know what to believe,' said Peter.

'Son, Jodie was beautiful, and we all loved her. Tell you what, why wait until October? Let's take some flowers up to the churchyard tomorrow. I can work from home, pop you up to the dentist as well. I'm paying for your treatment and he's a golfing mate of mine. He'll fit you in.'

'Thanks, Dad, I'd like that. The flowers I mean. I'll tolerate the dentist - nothing personal.'

Ben smiled, leaned over and squeezed his son's shoulder. They sat in silence for half an hour.

~

James Enright had missed his deadline for the Brontë essay. More than that, he was once again absent. Joanna consulted with the headmaster, explaining that she had no lessons that morning and requested that she use her admin time to visit the Enright house.

'It's time to visit his mother,' said Joanna. 'I've written to her. No doubt James didn't pass on the letter. Everything we've done so far has been built on trust. He has betrayed that frequently.'

'I agree, Jo,' said the headmaster. 'It's time for action. You have my authority to put forward the sanction of suspension. He's leaving later this year anyway.'

'It seems that I failed with this one, but let's see what his mother says.'

'You haven't failed, Jo. You've done great work with all the other kids. This one is down to James and his family background.'

Joanna pulled up outside the house, a badly maintained council property with a garden resembling the local tip. She smiled, not being able to avoid the image of Onslow, the brother-in-law of the sitcom battle-axe Hyacinth Bucket. No dog hiding in a wrecked car, but a broken pram with one wheel missing, old plastic toys, even pieces of rusty railway track from a set no longer in use.

A five-year-old BMW parked outside belied the atmosphere of the place. *Can't be his mom's car*, she thought, *and dad hasn't been seen for two years. At least their visitors look after their property. Very smart.*

'Can I help you?'

'Hello, Mrs Enright. Joanna Stone, English teacher at your son's school. Could I come in for a chat?'

'You can say what you want to say on the doorstep.'

'Please, Mrs Enright. This is important.'

Joanna spotted James in the hallway. He slid upstairs like an adder. Joanna felt angry again, clearly seeing how he'd developed his nature.

'If you must.'

No tea or coffee offered, she sat down without being asked, moving a stained copy of Woman's Own from the fireside chair, and made a mental note to brush off the cat-hairs when she got home.

'I've been concerned about James, his behaviour, the bullying, and no commitment to his work. Is he ill today?'

'Bit of a cold. Why are you always on at him, Mrs Stone?'

The conversation continued in that vein, and Mrs Enright called her son into the room. He was followed by a man, smartly dressed but with both hands covered in rings, and a face displaying two battle scars. He stood at the back of the room while James sat by his mother.

'We've decided, James won't be going back to school,' said Mrs Enright. 'He leaves in the summer anyway, and he's been offered a job working for his cousin. He's come round today to discuss the details. Don't think you've met.'

He walked towards Joanna, offering his hand.

'I've heard a lot about you, Mrs Stone. I'm James's cousin, Terry Hickens. It's lovely to meet you at last.'

12: Visiting Don Gil

'Cheryl, have you seen my phone?' asked Alan.
'When did you last see it?'
'I remember switching it off going into Don's lecture. Can't remember if I had it when I collected the book from his room.'
'It'll turn up. I'll ring your number now in case it's under the bed or something,' as she selected his name from the list and pressed *Call*.
'No. Nothing. Never mind.'

~

The dentist managed to save one of Peter's damaged teeth. One crown to be fitted, but the third tooth was consigned to history. Ben thought that his son would use it to convince girls that, amongst his other strengths, he played rugby. 'Tough sport, rugger', he'd say. Peter was fortunate to get an appointment so quickly, thanks to the private family account Ben had arranged with his friend, Adrian Tonks. Peter called in sick and was glad to spend time with his father. As agreed, they made their way to the churchyard, stopping off at the roadside florist to buy an additional flower arrangement for Graham's grave. Peter bought a single rose to place by Jodie's headstone. They drove in silence to the church, and as they parked, Peter smiled as if to say, 'thanks for this, Dad.'

Jodie's grave could be spotted from a distance. Although never discussing it, Peter tended the grave every six or eight weeks and had covered the ground on both sides with gravel, reducing the problem of weeds and making it more distinctive. Most of the plots around there were overgrown to the extent that weeds and bramble covered the lower wording on the headstones. He placed the rose below the words he had chosen. *She left us too soon, but we will never forget her.* Jodie's parents had been happy for him to arrange the funeral and select the headstone wording. He was virtually an adopted son. Ben stood beside him, holding the flowers intended for his uncle's grave, situated towards the bottom of the churchyard thirty yards away. As he turned, Ben noticed a couple near there and realised they were standing by Graham's grave. The woman placed some flowers, bowing her head. For an instant, she looked up towards Ben and Peter.

'Any idea who they are, Dad?'
'No, but they must have known Uncle Graham. Wait here, Peter, I'll have a word.'

The path towards that part of the churchyard curved to the right, bending round two huge oaks. Ben lost sight of the couple as he passed the first tree, and as he reached the grave, they had gone. Four red roses left by the headstone, with a card. He picked it up. *Vos autem sedate in terminis.*

~

'What are you doing today?' asked Alan.

'Going into the centre - you know I like clothes shopping.'

'Arndale?'

'Yes, I love it. Not as big as Merry Hill or Birmingham, but they have all my favourite shops.'

'I like to see you happy. I've got lectures most of the day. Don's not been in for a couple of days, but he left me a note to collect my last two assignments from his study.'

Cheryl had been advised to get any of the 'big blue magic buses' to the Arndale Centre. The number 41 took her to Piccadilly Gardens. She passed Primark and Debenhams, avoiding the trams, into Market Street. *I'll check out Urban Outfitters*, she decided. Cheryl was capable of spending all day and a week's wages in the Centre. She smiled, recalling Alan claiming that she fitted the stereotype of the woman born to shop. She desperately wanted to be happy and to share that with Alan. She had made too many mistakes, recent mistakes, and just had to put it right. The family he had, where she now belonged, deserved better. No more slip-ups.

A text came through. *This'll be Alan,* she thought. *No, it's not.*

```
Sorry to bother you, Cheryl. Can't get
hold of Alan, but I've got his phone. He
left it in my study and it's in my
briefcase. I'm here all day if you'd like
to collect it. 54 Carnival Way, near the
David Lewis Sports Ground. Don.
```

It was unexpected, but somehow reassuring, that Alan's favourite lecturer trusted her. They were a couple, and she could deal with any of Alan's problems. *But go to his house? Yes, why not?* She replied that she had some shopping to do. `Eleven-thirty okay?` He immediately came back with `Look forward to seeing you.`

~

After Alan's first lecture, he asked Geoff Hawkins if he could collect his assignments from the study that Geoff shared with Don.

'Meet me there in ten minutes,' said Hawkins. 'Just collecting my post from the admin office.'

Alan nodded his agreement and made his way to the library to find the textbook Hawkins had recommended during the lecture. He then made his way to the study, finding the door open and Geoff Hawkins sitting at Don's desk.

'Is Mr Gil alright, Mr Hawkins?'

'Hardly ever see him, but I believe he's working from home this week. Just a couple of lectures on Friday on the rota. Here are your assignments. Wish *my* students submitted their work on time.'

'Thanks, Mr Hawkins.'

Alan had an hour to spare, time for a quick sandwich then his afternoon marketing lecture. Opening the first folder gave him cause for celebration. B-plus, his best mark yet. In the comments field, Don had written three words: *Aequum, ipsum, optimum. Can't be bad comments,* Alan thought, *not with a B-plus. Why didn't he write it in English?* The second assignment. *It gets better. A-minus.* Comments field: *Well done Alan, excellent work. Thoughtful and provoking. Okay, English this time.* As he closed the folder, a small piece of paper floated to the floor: *Somnium cras; credere, qui in propinquo sunt.* Not concerned, but puzzled, and his first thought was that his classics expert brother was going to be busy later today. No time to research it for himself but he considered *optimum* to be a positive word in line with improved marks. No idea about the second phrase. Alan sat on his bed and reflected. *There was a Latin phrase from Greta. Why is everyone into Latin suddenly?*

~

As the Irwell rounded The Meadow, Cheryl was reminded of Greta at the home, the funeral, talking to Peter and everyone keeping things from Alan's father. Past the sports ground, a follow-up text from Don Gil informed her that Carnival Way was over the river Irwell near Green Grosvenor Park. She had been to the park once with Alan. Everything she did, all her waking thoughts, revolved around the young man she loved. She found Carnival Way, a traditional suburban street populated with 1930s semi-detached houses, the type where doctors and college lecturers live. Number thirty-four, even numbers this side of the street, forty-six. She could see it: number fifty-four. Two birch trees straddled the driveway, a row of earthenware pots lined up beside a neatly trimmed lawn. *What am I doing here*, she wondered. *Just for a phone?* Don Gil opened the door almost as soon as her finger had depressed the bellpush.

'Cheryl, how nice to see you. Come in.'

He took her coat, hanging it on the bannister. She surveyed the hallway as he led her through to a dimly lit lounge at the back of the house.

'This is where I come to relax. Coffee, Cheryl?'

'Please, Mr Gil.'

'Don. Remember, I said last time at college.'

'Don - sorry. I'm a little nervous.'

'No need to be nervous. I'm sure we can be friends. It's on the bookcase by the window.'

'Bookcase?'

'Alan's phone - that's why you're here isn't it?'

'Of course. Thanks.'

She sat in a large armchair bedecked with Victorian-style cushions. *Not a family home*, she said to herself.

'Here we go. Sugar in the bowl, put your own milk in.'

She had almost forgotten about the phone, now safely in her bag. His voice possessed a certain quality, a rhythm. The coffee soothed her throat and within minutes she relaxed. He continued to talk as she drifted away, and the dream began.

In what looked like a hotel room, she had just finished a shower and covered herself in a towel. The two men stood on the other side of the bed, near the window. Without hesitation, she was naked, returning the lust in their eyes. The door opened and a third man entered, gesturing to her to lie on the bed. She didn't recognise him at first as he kissed her and held her down. Breathing became difficult as his body pressed down, and she took what breaths she could.

'Cheryl, are you alright?'

As she woke, Don was standing over her. The top two buttons of her blouse were undone.

'Sorry, you seemed to be choking. I loosened your clothes. Here's a glass of water.'

'I must have dozed off. I feel peculiar. How long have I been here?'

'About an hour. I couldn't wake you at first. I've called Geoff Hawkins and he has asked Alan to collect you. He'll be here soon. I do hope you'll be alright, Cheryl.'

'Thanks, Don. Don't know what came over me.'

She was still drowsy when the bell rang, and Don let Alan in. Don explained about the phone, the text and what happened to Cheryl.

'Sorry to have bothered you with this, Don. I hope we haven't caused you too much trouble. You've been very kind.'

'It was nothing, Alan. It's a pleasure to help.'

~

'Nuntiate patri tuo; mihi est in utraque parte.'
'Latin?' enquired Joanna.

'Yep. Apparently this old lady in the care home also muttered something to Alan a week before she died,' explained Peter.

'What was that?'

'"She'll let you down, you know, she'll let you down".'

'What on earth does that mean, and who was she talking about?'

'Alan thinks she might have meant Cheryl, because someone at school used the same phrase five years before and Cheryl has been Alan's only serious girlfriend. Pretty spooky, don't you think?'

'You're losing me a bit, Peter. Someone at school?' asked Joanna.

'Try to keep up, Mom,' he smiled. 'You know that lad, the bully, Frank Carter.'

'Most of that was kept from me. If I'd known everything at the time...'

'Alan didn't want the fuss,' Peter interrupted.

'Alright, Peter. But what does the Latin phrase mean?'

'Tell your father - meet me on the other side.'

'I don't like this, Peter. Your dad doesn't know, does he?'

'No, and I think we agree it should stay that way, don't we, Mom?'

'Of course. So now we have a message from this old lady to your dad and something possibly about Cheryl. Can you make sense of it?'

'Not really,' said Peter.

His phone made the drum roll he used for indicating the receipt of a text. With Ben in the room, this would have set off a fatherly, irritated eyebrow movement combined with a furrowing of his brow meaning to say, 'for pities sake, Peter, what the hell is that?' Not having to fend off his father's grimaces, he focussed on the text from his brother: two more Latin phrases - from Don Gil on his assignments.

'Got to deal with this, Mom. Catch you later.'

'Okay, love. I'm off to school anyway.'

```
Aequum, ipsum, optimum.
Somnium cras; credere, qui propinquo tuo sunt.
```

'Alan, got a minute? Your text.'

'Just caught me. Lecture in fifteen minutes.'

'Listen, mate, I've told Mom about the stuff from Greta.'

'Pete, I thought we were keeping this to ourselves.'

'No, we were keeping it from Dad. Anyway, got your text. The first comment means accurate, precise, excellent. Sounds as if he likes you. Star pupil, eh?'

'Shut up. Mind you, B-plus and those comments. Strange way of doing it, but he is a bit of an intellectual nerd. What about the second one?'

'The one that starts *somnium cras* - dream of tomorrow and trust those close to you.'

'What on earth...' gasped Alan.

'Dunno, mate, but sounds a bit weird to me. On top of that, Dad showed me a coin Auntie Carol gave him, passed from Uncle Graham. It had an inscription, again in

Latin, but translates as "you must stay within the boundaries".'

'Funny saying, but what's the problem? Old coins have all sorts of sayings, don't they?'

'Alan, I agree. But, thing is, when we went to the churchyard, that exact phrase was written on a piece of paper by Uncle's grave.'

'Christ, Pete. What's going on?'

'No idea, mate. Coincidences, spooky or not. But we'll sit tight and keep Dad in the dark.'

13: Cottages at Troutburg

'How was Mexico?'
'Fabulous, Jo.'
'Spill the beans - mainly about your new fella.'

With almost no breaths taken between sentences, Liz imparted a blow-by-blow account of her latest affair. Describing Mexico as 'heavenly', she gave Joanna the impression that it had been a difficult decision to return to Blighty, the weather and library administration. At first, Liz made no effort to turn the conversation towards the Stone family. The mood changed when she dropped the phrase 'Peter and Jodie' into the mix.

'I'd rather not discuss it, Liz.'
'Weird though, how Jodie's name was mentioned over five years before they met? Maybe it was meant to be.'
'Leave it, Liz, please.'
'Okay, but the Latin phrase passed through the medium from Jack and Lucy? Have you told Ben?'
'I'd rather not.'
'Joanna, he has a right to know. Whether or not we believe in séances, someone has mentioned his parents' names, and, what was it, "one day you will know". What's that all about?'
'Not sure, but Ben is bound to be upset. I agree with my dad - it's best left alone.'
'Fair enough, but it's not Harry's mom and dad is it? If there is something in it, maybe the message would mean something to Ben?'

'Well, for now, I'm leaving it. Ben's quite happy at the moment.'

'And the other stuff?'

'What other stuff?' asked Joanna.

'The old lady in Manchester.'

'How on earth did you find out about that?'

'I'm sure you mentioned it - the Latin phrases, Peter's translation, Alan and Cheryl...'

'Stop there Liz! I've got to go. Not your fault, but I'm running late.'

Joanna kissed Liz on both cheeks, put on her coat and closed the door without a further glance. She began to wonder if her friend knew more than she was letting on. *Did I mention the stuff in Manchester?* She liked Liz and opened up to her easily, but Liz only opened up when her love life became the topic of conversation. In some ways, too much information. *But this is different,* Joanna thought. She couldn't get out of her mind the pressure she was under from Liz to tell Ben everything, her sons so much more sensible and understanding. She was aware of the possible implications, but even Joanna could not imagine how Ben coped with the most traumatic experience of his life. He had never made sense of what happened, and the loss of his uncle made it worse. Only Carol remained who had experienced the events with him, the emotion and trauma.

Joanna drove home, not having appointments that day, the extended Easter break giving her the freedom to catch up with jobs around the house. Annoyed with Liz's insistence that Ben should be told about the séances, she still wondered how Liz knew the significance of Rochester. She was angry with herself for not bringing that up. As she pulled into the drive, she noticed Peter's TR4. *Broken again*, she thought, *or a day off?* She had lost track of his shift pattern.

'Hi, Mom.'
She put her arms around him and ruffled his hair.
'Glad you're here.'
'Everything okay, Mom?'
'I shouldn't trouble you with this, but I can't talk to your dad.'
'Come on, I'll put the kettle on.'

Unwilling to burden her son, with no intention of mentioning Jodie, she told Peter about the second séance, Jack and Lucy and the Latin phrase *unus dies vos cognoscetis*. He immediately translated ('one day you will know'), and asked his mother 'know about what?'

'This is all to do with the accident when your dad was only fourteen. Losing your parents at such a young age has a dramatic effect on a person. But the horrific circumstances...'

Peter embraced Joanna as she wept. His apparent lack of maturity when it came to female companions was not evident when faced with family trauma. He had the right words to give his mother, the appropriate reassurance. She recovered, and they compared notes on the issues surrounding Alan and Cheryl. They both agreed to listen to the couple and try to make sense of it all. They also agreed that Ben should be kept out of it. She feared the repercussions of the so-called messages at the séance and from Greta Armitage.

The telephone call altered the focus of her attention.

'Headmaster. Is anything wrong?'

'No, Joanna. You remember the learning styles course we discussed? It's come through for the second week of term. I've taken the liberty of confirming the booking. I do hope that's alright.'

'Oh, yes, I suppose so. Who will cover my classes?'

'Sorted that already. We need someone on this course, Jo. The education minister is doing the keynote speech and we should be represented. You are the ideal person to push through the changes. Some of the younger members of staff are against reform, and I believe your... seniority will help.'

'Thank you for having the confidence in me. I'll need to check with Ben, but I'm sure it will be fine.'

'Tell me on Monday morning back at school in case we need to cancel your place. Enjoy your weekend.'

'Bye.'

A week in London was not Joanna's ideal way of passing the time. She had enjoyed her time at home over the Easter holiday, and once back at school, she loved nothing more than sitting with Ben in the evenings. Even if that did mean sharing him with her usual batch of marking. Once again, her train of thought was interrupted, this time by Peter.

'Free paper's come, Mom. I'm off now - practice with the lads.'

The paper plopped onto the kitchen table as Joanna opened the biscuit tin and threw the kettle switch. Something made her sit down and flick through the pages. Mainly adverts and local councillors with dog mess and litter louts the main items on the current agenda. She was turning to the centre pages full of houses for sale when she blinked and forced herself to read the heading again:

Joe and Teresa Mason killed in car accident. Mr and Mrs Mason of Straights Road, Halesowen, no children, were killed instantly. The brakes failed on Mucklow Hill in Halesowen. The car hit the kerb and it overturned. Joe and Teresa worked together for a local flooring wholesaler. They both left when Joe retired last year.

My God, she thought, *I met them. Lovely couple. Ben will be so upset.* Unsure whether to phone him, she decided to wait until he'd finished work. The afternoon dragged, even though she found a range of jobs to do. She heard Ben's car pull up. As he walked in, it was evident that he'd been told.
'Joe and Teresa,' he said.
'It's in today's paper. I'm so sorry. Come here, love.'

His face pale, she saw in Ben's eyes the grief that poured through him, and memories that were stirred. Not the best time to mention the course. It would wait until after the weekend. Ben wanted to talk about his old friends from work and told her that the funeral had been arranged for Thursday.

John Greggs had offered to collect him from home, and a few older employees who had worked with them were given time off to attend.

'Least we can do,' said Ben. 'John said that Joe was always going on about the fishing rod we bought him. I never got round to seeing them. Always too busy.'

'They knew how you felt about them. Don't blame yourself, and there's nothing you could have done,' said Joanna.

~

'Tentationem gravem iis, qui minime falli.'
'Good pronunciation, Alan.'
'Thanks, Don, but what does it mean?'
'Have a go.'
'Well, considering the context of my essay, *gravem* probably means serious, and *minime*... minimum?'
'Go on.'
'If you're serious, always do the minimum?'
'Good try, but I'm sure that your clever brother could tell you – "those who try the hardest fail the least" – you work hard Alan, harder than most of the students.'
'Why Latin, Don? Does the name Greta Armitage mean anything to you?'

'No. New one on me. Anyway, has Peter recovered after his latest run-in with that thug?'

'How did you know about that?'

'Cheryl mentioned it. She's such a caring girl.'

'I'm lucky to have her.'

'Yes, she could easily be the female equivalent of the Pied Piper of Hamlin.'

'What?'

'You know, he led the rats away from the town, playing his tune. With the notable exception of you, I often see the male students as rats.'

'Strange thing to say. What's that got to do with Cheryl?'

'She attracts them. You can see it in their eyes as they pass by. I saw two lads watching her in the canteen...'

'Stop, Don, please. This is my girlfriend we're talking about.'

'Sorry, Alan, but I suppose you've noticed yourself. Look after her. There is a saying – "follow her to the Cottages at Troutburg, she will lead the way".'

'What does that mean?'

'Nothing significant, Alan, just a saying. Come on, give me your opinion on your essay. Bit of self-assessment didn't hurt anyone. Any chance you can improve your marketing plan?'

~

Joanna found a way of telling Ben that the course was booked, waiting for the perfect moment, the right mood. His face still betrayed his disappointment. The funeral two days away, his emotions frail and vulnerable, Ben needed her more than ever. Joanna, confident that no one else sensed his vulnerability, made light of their brief separation. 'Only a week,' she repeated, and reminded him that Alan was staying from Wednesday evening, a few days respite from study with a break for mock exams. Ben conceded that it would be nice to spend some time with him. They were so close when Alan was younger. Any opportunity to retrieve their fragile relationship was worth the effort.

'Make the most of it, Ben. A couple of days to yourself, then quality time with the baby of the family.'
'Cheryl?'
'She's staying here but working Thursday and Friday. Get the nice chess set out of the loft. You used to like playing. Can you get some time off?'
'Not really. Monthly accounts report is due, but I can work from home for a couple of days.'

~

Monday morning. Joanna had tried to insist on a taxi to the station, the Wolverhampton to Euston train due at 6.50am. Ben would hear none of it, and by 6.15 they were in Ben's car passing through a quiet Leeford Village ready to pick up the A449 into the city. At the station, he bought Joanna the Guardian and her favourite magazine.
'It's only a week, and I'll get a free Metro on the train,' she said.

'I'm going to miss you, especially at night.'
'Me too. Sorry about this course. I'm convinced I drew the short straw.'

Ben held and kissed her until the Euston train pulled alongside platform seven. Joanna waved as she boarded. Ben took one last glance and drove home.

~

'Fancy a cuppa, Dad?' asked Alan.
'Long time since you've made me a drink. Lovely, yes thanks.'
'Four sugars?'
'Funny. You know very well that your mom is watching my waistline.'
'Gross.'
'Alan, you should be on the stage – sweeping up.'
'Are you going to be like this all day?'
'Shut up. Make the tea, and it's your move.'
'Do mine for me. Pawn to queen's bishop four.'
'How can you do that from the kitchen?'
'Elementary, my dear Mr Stone.'
'I've had my move. Cheers for the tea.'

The game progressed as Ben and Alan settled down to a morning they were both enjoying - not expecting to revive the closeness they once had, but they were together, father and son, and talking. Really talking. Ben asked about Don Gil, the other students, his assignments, and Cheryl. Alan had heard about Joe and Teresa, and quickly picked up on the level of his father's grief. There was something else. Always something else.

Alan skirted round anything awkward or emotional, not bringing up the incident at the churchyard. Peter had mentioned the couple they had seen, the note, and the inscription on the coin from Uncle Graham. Alan brought the conversation back to football, golf - something he considered to be a trivial pastime.
'Danny Willet did well, didn't he?'
'You're not kidding - who would have bet on him winning the Masters? Speith had it in the bag until his ball hit the water.'
'I reckon Leicester will take the Premiership title.'
'No problem. Makes a change from the big four.'
'Dad, I've just thought of an expression someone used at college last week. Have you heard of the Cottages at Troutburg?'
'What?'
'Cottages at Troutburg.'
'Where the hell did you hear that?'

From his father's reaction, Alan decided it best not to attribute the phrase to any particular individual. If, for some peculiar reason, this was upsetting him, Alan thought it prudent to leave the conversation with Don as general as possible. He conveniently forgot who quoted it. Expediency.
'You must know who said it, Alan. It's a bit specific, a place in New York State. What's that got to do with graphic design?'

'Sorry, Dad. If I'd known it was going to upset you, I wouldn't have repeated it. What is it anyway?'

'Leave it, Alan, leave it!'

Ben had not shouted at his son since his messy bedroom teenage years and only then after Alan had pushed Joanna to the brink. After telling him to tidy his room at the age of sixteen, Joanna, already having a bad day, was in tears when Ben returned home. Having warned Alan once himself, Ben lost his temper, and the offending jeans, tee-shirts and magazines found themselves flying out of the open window in Alan's room, onto the back lawn. Although Alan's housework skills had not massively improved, there had been no recent need for Ben's throwing arm to gain any further practice. That was then. However, Alan did not need to be told how angry and upset his father had become.

'Dad, what's going on?'

'I told you, leave it.'

Alan had only seen Ben this upset at his Uncle Graham's funeral, and he sensed that one more push and his father could be in tears. He realised that Ben was not so much angry with him but reacting to a memory raked up.

'I'm going out, Alan. Clear this lot up, will you?'

Alan had sufficient maturity to leave it at that. Something had affected his father. Something to do with the phrase Don had used. It was a massive overreaction but he made no further comment. Joanna was due back in three days, and the two men appeared to have an unspoken agreement - it went as far as them hardly speaking at all. The agreement was for the matter to lie. Not to be brought up again. Ben returned to the office the next day and, unusually, spent two days at the club. He needed Joanna.

14: He did not hear her scream

They are in the car in front. Jack and Lucy. A long drive, tiredness forcing his eyelids down, his joints aching. The driver tells him to sleep if he wants to. America is such a big place, and journeys between tourist attractions take time. He can't remember why Graham and Carol haven't come with him. The driver is vaguely familiar, but he doesn't say much. His eyes, sunken deep into a grey, almost featureless face. His thin, straight nose pointing in the direction he has planned. They are following Ben's mother and father, and he watches as they park the car by the sign that says, *Maid of the Mist*. Jack locks the car and takes Lucy's hand as they walk, smiling and chatting, towards the pay booth. The driver's gone. Ben is alone now. At the stern, he finds them, in his sights but out of reach. He had never realised before how happy they were together. She's dropped a leaflet. Ben wants to pick it up for her. The wind and spray take it in their icy fingers and the scene pauses for a second as the leaflet floats high above the boat. He jumps higher and higher, touching it with his fingertips. He tries to shout to Lucy, 'I've got it, Mom, I've got it,' but no sounds leave his lips. They both turn, seem to spot the leaflet floating, spinning away, but they don't distinguish him from the background, the visual strength of the Falls. He has it now, damp, damaged, but partly legible.

'Jaw-dropping beauty. Thundering roars. Shimmering rainbows.' Something else, he's not sure, and 'Horseshoe Falls, Niagara is a true natural wonder that plays Cupid to lovers, a nurse to artists and a Pied Piper to millions of visitors.'

Piped Piper of Hamlin struck a chord, a mixed memory. Past or future? His mother says, 'is it safe, Jack?'

He's flying now - they are in the helicopter. Lucy sees someone she recognises. She turns to Jack and shouts above the noise of the rotors.

'The waiter. I'm sure it's the waiter. He wanted Ben to come with us, Jack.'

They don't know, they'll never know. He's driven Ben to join them. He's back on the road again, following them. He can't, or won't, glance to his left. He no longer wants to see the driver. Blots him from his memory. He reads every road sign, every village, every beach. Route 18 from Niagara-on-the-Lake, Roosevelt Beach, Olcott. Golden Hill State Park, Lakeside State Park. They join the Ontario State Parkway, not accessible in winter. Oak Orchard Marine Park, Oak Orchard Creek, Brighton Cliff, Norway Heights, The Cottages of Troutburg. Devil's Nose, Hamlin Beach State Park. Right-hand bend coming up. They are chatting, laughing, happy. Ben smiles. He can feel the warmth of their love.

The car veers to the left, then back to the right. Jack is fighting to control the steering. The sweat pours down his face. Lucy is screaming. 'Jack, no, no!' She stops screaming.

~

'You alright, love? How are the kids?' asks Joanna.

'They're okay, haven't seen much of Peter, Alan's his grumbly self, Cheryl's quiet but then that's Cheryl...' replies Ben.

'What about you?' she interrupts.

'I'm okay. Missing you. Why aren't you coming home until Sunday?'

'That play I wanted to see – *The Caretaker* – it's on at the Old Vic.'

'On your own?'

'With friends.'

'Do I know them?'

'No, just two or three people I trained with and they are on this course. They share a house in Barnet. I'll stay for two nights and then travelling will be easier on Sunday morning. Checking out of the hotel this afternoon.'

'Oh.'

'Sure you're alright?'

'Bit frazzled, but we can talk when you're back.'

'You don't mind?'

'No, you enjoy yourself. Sunday then.'

'See you, Ben.'

Although unable to foresee the effect this would have on him, it threatened him. Joanna, the only person capable of dragging him back to normality, stability - she was otherwise engaged. Ben didn't blame Alan for setting off a train of thought. He was not even curious about who said it in the first place - *The Cottages of Troutburg*.

People at work don't see the dark side, the weak side of his character. Not weak, but vulnerable. He questions himself. Did he ever get over the loss, and how long does grief last? Forty-six years old and he has seen grief, been crushed by grief, but the book that could be written about the fourteen-year-old boy was not yet closed and may never close. 'Keep within the boundaries.' The boundaries of what? Falling now, but guilt the only emotion he recognised. Peter had suffered grief more recently. He copes, or appears to. Ben, not able to open up to the lads, kept away from everyone. *It can wait until Sunday*, he decided. New thoughts: *who is she with? Three friends (or two), teachers,* he assumed, *got to be. Think she meant teacher training and a coincidence that they were on the same course this week. Is she seeing someone else?* He tells himself to leave it. *Wait for Joanna.*

~

As the tyre bursts, Ben is there with them. Jack doesn't hear Lucy's screams. There isn't time. From the moment he has lost control of the car, a sequence of events unfolds in five seconds. The left wheel hits the kerb. Jack's hands are off the steering wheel. Ben sees everything, all his senses absorbing everything, but he is somehow separate. He will experience the loss but not the physical pain.

The car flips over, twice, three times. It lands on Lucy's side, the seatbelt irrelevant. The edge of the pavement smashes through the roof at an angle that allows it to slam into Lucy's neck and shoulder. Ben knows she is dead. He cries out, but no one is listening. He looks across at his father. Jack is alive but barely breathing. Blood trickles from the corner of his mouth. Once they close, his eyes will never open again. By the time the emergency services arrive, Ben will have lost both parents. He is aware of this, his body shaking, tears burning his eyes.

There is a crowd now. Paramedics, police, others standing around – drivers who have stopped, he assumes – no one speaks to Ben. He stumbles through the confusion of people, inhales the stench of exhaust fumes, petrol, burning tyre rubber. He sees a policeman wave away the stretcher-bearers. Not required. At least not for survivors. Two bodies lie on the grass awaiting confirmation that this young boy will no longer hear the words of affection, no longer be surrounded and protected by their embrace. He screams at the man standing nearest to him, pleading for him to do something. But what can he do? It's too late. A tall, thin man stands by the car, the metal box that brought death. He smiles. Ben turns round to find the direction of his smile. No one else reacts. The smile is aimed at him. Ben turns, and the man has gone. He finds himself running aimlessly through the medical people, investigators, onlookers. Too many people. 'My mom and dad!' he screams again.

He lay there, sweat pouring - his bedroom door opened.
'Dad, are you okay?'
'Peter... sorry, a dream.'
'I'll get you a drink.'

Still in his dressing gown, he joined his son in the kitchen. Concern etched on Peter's face as his father slumped into his usual chair facing the garden. He placed the cup in front of him and stole a glance, with an expression that said, 'you alright, Dad?' Ben nodded, and held the cup with both hands, staring towards the window, a view into the rear garden that he treasured. When weary after a hard day, he often wondered if this was the future into old age; endless hours gazing into the garden they had created together. His mind wandered, trying to escape the dream, recalling the hours they had spent in that garden, even the time that he and Joanna were caught out by the next-door neighbour. He smiled, thinking that the neighbour got to know them quite well that day. Peter gave him another look.
'What are you thinking about, Dad?'
'Some of it I couldn't repeat, son.'
'Oh yes, pray tell.'
'You don't tell me all the stuff you get up to, do you?'
'Fair enough but tell me if there's anything you want to talk about. If it helps.'
'Thanks, but I'm missing your mom. Anyway, Peter, any more hassle from that hooligan?'

'Nothing, I'm steering clear of Barbara, and, hopefully, I can avoid Hickens.'

'Say if you need any help on that score. Police, if necessary.'

'Not now, Dad, but thanks...' Peter lowered his eyes. 'I've missed Mom as well. Only been a week.'

Saturday. Ben spent most of the day at the club, and the eighteen holes he played in the afternoon provided him with his worst score for months. Tired and depressed, he reconciled himself to a lonely bed for one more night, which would be an early one. He saw Alan and Cheryl briefly, apologising for not being the perfect host. Alan told him to forget the incident, regretting the upset he had caused and sensibly not repeating the phrase initiated by Don Gil. Ben closed the bedroom door, undressed and slid into the bed. Sleep engulfed him quickly, and he returned to the story that had dominated his life. He recalled the conversation with the waiter in New York.

'You'll regret it if you don't go, young man. You should be with your parents.'

If Ben had travelled with his parents, he would have suffered the same fate. He saw the photographs - the rear seat was crushed. The dividing line between dreams and reality is paper-thin, but even in sleep he tried to hang on to the actual events all those years ago, the difference being that he re-lived their experience. He was 370 miles away when they died, but now he felt that he had been with them. He convinced himself that he should have been with them. Maybe that was the reason for the dream, not simply the memories stirred up by Alan and thinking about his Uncle Graham.

There was a voice reminding him that somehow the plan had gone astray. He should have been with Jack and Lucy. Again, he is back on the coast road towards Rochester, south of Lake Ontario.
'This is a lovely road, Jack,' said Lucy. 'Fascinating names – Devil's Nose, Hamlin, The Cottages of Troutburg.'

Not sure if that's exactly what she said, but the names seemed significant. How could he know this? He had a sense that names and phrases were being placed into his mind, but why, or by whom, he wondered. The tyre bursts, the car flips over, smoke, fumes, the sensation of crashing to earth. Silence. In the ambulance now, or an unmarked van. He couldn't be sure. They're travelling at normal speed. Not disrespectful, but no need to attract attention. The driver chats with his partner. They've seen it all before, assuming the speed limit has yet again been broken. Later, tests will reveal that their speed was fifty-five - on the limit. The inquest would rule as accidental death. *This is not an accidental death*, he thought, as they lifted first Jack, then Lucy onto trolleys at the rear entrance of the hospital. Rochester morgue. *I'll leave you now, Mom. See you, Dad. Graham and Carol will look after me.* The voice again. *Whoever you are*, Ben pleads, *leave them in peace*. The door to his hotel room opens. Carol is holding Graham's hand as they stand in the doorway.

'Okay if we come in, Ben? There's something we need to tell you.'

Carol cannot hold back the well of tears. They sit either side of Ben on his bed. He is shaking as they tell him what happened; at least the facts as relayed to them.

Ben fills in the gaps over thirty years later. On the plane across the Atlantic, they hardly speak. Sometimes Carol reaches out and Ben takes her hand. They love him, but Carol and Graham cannot match the love of a mother and father. They step down onto the tarmac, where his grandparents are waiting.

'I've stopped crying now, Nan,' he says.

Before Ben wakes, he sees the couple at the churchyard, Graham's funeral seamlessly linked to his parents' ceremony. He watches Joanna at the hotel in London. She is with someone. In her bed. Ben tries to tell her to get away from him, but she doesn't hear. His thoughts are jumbled now. Close to waking. *Don't go to the boundaries, beyond the boundaries. Stay within the boundaries. Mom, Dad...*

10.00am, Sunday. The house is empty, no one aware if he shouted. He might have called out Joanna's name. Refreshed after a shower, breakfast, first cup of tea. She'll be back soon.

~

'You'll have to let go eventually, Ben. I'm losing the feeling in my shoulders.'

'I've missed you so much.'

'Me too,' Joanna said, kissing him again.

They were able to talk openly. Peter, Alan and Cheryl were shopping, working, whatever they had chosen to do to give Ben and Joanna some space. She held his face in her hands. Joanna could sense the hurt in his eyes.

'The nightmares again?'

'Yes.'

'I haven't seen you like this for years.'

He explained how Alan had inadvertently triggered his current state, on top of losing Graham, the strange note at the churchyard, and then Joe and Teresa. He was also worried about Peter, but he held firm and kept that from Joanna.

~

Peter was no more than twelve months old when he contracted a throat virus. The GP queried meningitis and admitted him to hospital as a precaution. Peter's temperature was dangerously high at one stage. Ben and Joanna slept in the parents' room on the second night. Peter wouldn't eat and was unable to keep down water for two days. A week before Peter was taken ill, Ben had started to read a set of documents that he had previously avoided. After the accident in 1984, his aunt and uncle had submitted a request for a copy of the inquest papers. The US authorities told them that the documents could only go to the next of kin, and, because of the special circumstances, the recipient must be over twenty-one.

Ben was able to re-submit the request himself, and they were sent a few weeks after his twenty-first birthday.

He ripped open the package but could not bring himself to open the file. He had already studied the map of New York State in fine detail; every village, every minor road, and, in particular, the route his parents took from Niagara towards Rochester. The file sat in his desk drawer for almost two years. For some reason, after his son was born, he decided that it was time to face the details of his parents' demise. His Aunt Carol had told him that Lucy, when planning the trip to the Falls, had spotted the names 'Cottages of Troutburg' and 'Hamlin', and said that they sounded like interesting places to visit.

Reading the inquest documents took him back nine years. Not that he'd forgotten the trauma of losing his parents, but he'd learned to cope. He married young, owned his own house by the age of eighteen, and was developing a career in accountancy. But there would always be a gap in his life. He felt that again, and something in him collapsed. At the age of twenty-three, his normal demeanour outgoing, Ben withdrew into the world he occupied in 1984. His internal battle raged between a renewed grief and the anger with whoever allowed the crash to happen. He lost his faith, so he considered the logic of being angry with God. *But if God exists, it's His fault,* he concluded. The dreams started.

Ben existed within the world inhabited by the two people he had loved more than anyone – the world they were about to leave.

The description of the accident in the document was graphic. He had been protected from the worst of it by Carol, Graham and his grandmother, but now he had all the information. The horrendous injuries suffered by both Lucy and Jack would not leave him, and in his dreams he was taunted by a voice, a threatening voice, reminding him that he should have been with them.

A young man having to cope with renewed trauma, when his young son is taken ill. He worked his way through it, suppressing his feelings until Peter was able to come home, then the depression was all-consuming. Ben was unable to work or study, taking over four weeks to recover. Joanna, with a baby to care for, relied on close family for support. Carol and Graham, who understood his feelings more than most, stayed at the house for a week. The dreams gradually subsided, the documents permanently locked away, and Ben returned to some sort of normality.

Peter's developing character through the toddler years, and then Alan coming along, encouraged Ben to push the past behind him. Now, twenty years on, remnants of those feelings resurfaced.
'Do you want to see the doctor?' asked Joanna.
'No, I'll be alright. Self-indulgence is selfish. I know how I was then. We must avoid it this time, Jo.'

'Will you speak to Alan about it?'

'No, I think we should move on. Whatever someone at college said to Alan must be a coincidence. I've been thinking about Graham a lot lately. Then Joe and Teresa, but imagine what their family is going through, and there's Auntie Carol.'

'I'll go and see her,' said Joanna.

'She'd like that.'

'I love you, Ben. I want to do anything I can for you, and I haven't seen Carol for a while.'

'There is something I need to confess. In my dreams you were with another man.'

'Sally and Dawn were my friends from teacher training. You met them once. Check my phone if you like.'

'No, Joanna. It was a dream, that's the end of it.'

A week passed. Joanna was confident that Ben's crisis was over, proud that he had made such an effort. He surprised her, however, with his latest suggestion.

'Early spring, beautiful now. We'll have a barbeque. Friends and family.'

'Are you sure?'

'We need it. Pull everyone together.'

'Great idea. It will do us all good. Let's make a list.'

15: Childhood holidays

'Where is Newgale?' asked Joanna.
'Pembrokeshire. St Brides Bay, near St Davids.'
'Why there, Ben?'
'Went there when I was a kid with Mom and Dad. Had an asthma attack.'
'Nice memory,' Joanna said, smiling.
'Lovely place, though. Nice and quiet.'
'You realise that camping isn't my thing. Last time you took the lads.'
'I know, love, but it would be a giggle, wouldn't it?'
'Don't blame me if you have another asthma attack,' Joanna said.
'Well, it's only for a weekend.'
Joanna nodded and smiled. If it was important to Ben, it was important to her. As she rattled the cups into the cupboard and wiped the kitchen surfaces, Ben touched the back of her neck and mouthed a 'thank you.'
'One condition, Ben.'
'What's that?'
'When we come back from camping in Newgale, you'll take me to London for a show. Just like the one we went to when Peter was a baby. Do you remember when Mom and Dad looked after Peter for us?'
'Whatever you say, love,' said Ben.

Finishing his toast and coffee, his mind wandered back to the late 1970s, when, as a young boy, he went camping with his parents. Wales, it was always Wales - their normal destination Borth, gazing out to the Irish sea. That year they ventured further south, not far from the vast port at Milford Haven. Ben loved to watch the huge oil tankers inching towards the Pembrokeshire coast like giants creeping home after a day's scavenging. They had stayed at Tenby and Saundersfoot, further round the south coast where Jack, his father, had discovered a small patch of quicksand. It had been boarded off by Saundersfoot Council, but young boys like Ben wiled away hours amusing themselves by aiming bottles and bricks at the area. To their delight, the projectiles descended to the depths in seconds. No one discovered how deep it was, but even in the days of minimal health and safety, the council was taking no chances, surrounding the offending section of the beach with barriers and warning signs.

North of Milford Haven is St Brides Bay, the home of small and (in the 1970s) secluded beaches at Little Haven, Broad Haven and Newgale. At their chosen destination, the campsite was unusual, being surrounded by the sea to the west and a small river called Brandy Brook to the north and east. On the Stone family's first visit, everything was perfect. Beautiful clear skies, ideal for the amateur astronomer when everyone else is tucked up under their canvas roof. Jack liked the position of the Duke of Edinburgh Inn, a mere fifty yards from the campsite, the small supermarket a higher priority for Lucy. The second of their three sorties to the area provided them with an all-weather experience - brilliant sunshine on the first day, then the storm blasted its way inland.

"Urracan 'Erbet, Wogan just said,' quipped Jack.

The sea hit the A487 a few yards in front of the site, and the normally sedate Brandy Brook raged and swirled. By the morning of the third day, the camp was under three feet of water. Jack, Lucy and Ben had abandoned their tent shortly after midnight. Whether it was the stress, or more likely the damp, Ben was finding it difficult to breathe.

'Here's your inhaler,' said Lucy with a concerned expression.

With hardly enough air in his lungs to draw in the powder (before the days of the modern inhaler requiring less effort), Ben panicked.

'We'll have to get him to a doctor,' Lucy said to Jack.

They were sitting in the corner of the back room of the Duke of Edinburgh, used for gigs and parties, alongside four other intrepid camping families. After a frantic discussion with the publican and campsite manager (one and the same, a Mr Elwyn Simmons), Jack returned to his family with the information that the nearest doctor was four miles along the A487 in Solva. Elwyn very kindly offered to contact the GP, via the emergency number. No locums in that part of the country in those days. If the doctor was needed, he attended, whatever the hour.

'You'll have to pay, I'm afraid.'

'No problem,' said Jack, 'thanks for your help.'

It took no more than half an hour to gather their things, get Ben into the car and pull up outside the GP's house, conveniently situated at the top of the high street as they entered Solva. He administered oxygen, helped Ben to use his inhaler and prescribed antibiotics. Ben had shown signs of a slight cold at the start of the holiday. It had now developed into a mild chest infection.

'Precautionary. He should be fine in a day or two. Keep him out of the damp.'

'Thank you, doctor, we have to get home soon anyway. The tent is ruined.'

~

When baby Peter had recovered from the throat virus, it gave Joanna and Ben a chance to relax. Her parents offered to look after Peter while they had a short break.

'Just a weekend. What about London?'

'Don't know, Mom.'

'Joanna, you and Ben need it,' her father insisted.

Joanna loved Andrew Lloyd Webber's music. She gave Ben the task of booking the theatre tickets and hotel room. They were lucky. *Sunset Boulevard* was opening in London at the Adelphi ahead of an international tour. Webber had based the musical on Billy Wilder's 1950 film of the same name. Ben, a fan of Patti Ann LuPone (who played Norma Desmond), was easily convinced. Harry and Jennifer were great with Peter, and this was the perfect opportunity for Ben to put the spectre of the inquest papers behind him. Still a very young couple with a small child, they needed time to themselves.

'I promise not to mention Mom and Dad, Rochester and all that once we're in the car.'

'Ben, you can talk to me about it any time you like, but it will do you good to relax. You'll never forget, but we all have to learn to cope.'

Ben and Joanna stayed at the Strand Palace Hotel, a few hundred yards from the Adelphi. Harry paid – he insisted. Ben tried to argue but gave in gracefully.

'Concentrate on enjoying yourself. I'll drive you to Wolverhampton. After Euston, there's one train to Charing Cross. Ten-minute walk to the Adelphi and The Strand.

'How do you know it so well?' asked Ben.

'Stayed at the Strand many times, haven't we Jen?' Harry said, winking at his wife.

'You never mentioned it before,' said Joanna.

'Long before you came along, Jo.'

~

Saturday, 10.30am. Ben and Joanna had already booked into their Strand 'standard double room.'

'What are we going to do before the show starts?' asked Ben.

'Sure we'll think of something, Mr Stone.'

~

Ben's daydreams took him back to his childhood holidays on the Welsh coast with his parents and his early years with Joanna. Also, the upcoming weekend in London distracted him from the disturbing nightmares and the memory of the death of his parents. Time spent with the woman he loved helped him to cope. One mention of the West End gave Joanna a spring in her step, but 'Newgale first' he reminded her. The tent he had used with his teenage sons might not promise his wife four-star luxury. The Strand it was not, but she was prepared to snuggle into a sleeping bag for a few nights on the condition that he buy an inner tent, complete with netting, to keep out the bugs. She was not sharing her sleeping quarters with earwigs or indeed anything that flew or crawled.

'Even me? I can crawl,' laughed Ben.

'You're sounding better already.'

These days, Peter and Alan can look after themselves. The motorway-free, four-hour journey to Pembrokeshire itself was a refreshing diversion for Ben and Joanna. On their arrival at Newgale, Ben saw that little had changed. Elwyn Simmons, now retired, had passed on the mantle to his son, John. Ben recognised him at once. John had the same mannerisms, the same sense of humour. Joanna realised this as she was introduced to him.

'Hopefully, we'll have no floods this year,' he joked.

'Let me know when it starts to rain and we're out of here,' replied Joanna.

The rain didn't sweep in across the sands, nor did they require the services of the Duke of Edinburgh. At least not the large back room. The following morning after breakfast, they walked along the beach and up to the hills stretching towards Solva.

'It's not been so bad, has it?'

'I'm with you, Ben. That's what matters. Mind you, in two weeks we'll be in London. Are you looking forward to the show?'

'Of course I am. Then we've got the barbeque.'

Joanna recalled childhood holidays with her own parents. Harry and Jennifer decided when she was still at Wollaston Infants that their daughter would be educated; that is, beyond the teaching provided by the establishment. One year, they visited the Scottish Highlands, working their way across to what is now the seat of government, Edinburgh. Life in the Scottish capital can be traced back to 8500 BC. Evidence of Bronze Age and Iron Age settlements have been discovered on Arthur's Seat and Castle Rock. Arthur's Seat is the main peak in the hills of Edinburgh. In the centre of the city, the hills form most of Holyrood Park, the site of the modern Scottish government building. Harry taught Joanna about British history and literature. She was reading Dickens and Shakespeare by the age of seven. As she developed her interest and expertise, it was not surprising that she went on to become an English teacher.

One particularly exciting excursion was their trip to Belgium. Harry drove down to Dover, onto the Calais ferry. The A16 to Ostend took them past the forts and dunes on either side of Dunkirk.

They stayed at Ostend, visiting Brussels, with stops at Bruges and Ghent on the way. Jennifer wanted to see the cathedral at Ghent, and Harry once again investigated the history of the area, discovering that humans had lived there since the Stone Age. The trip back was eventful - a journey that should have taken no more than ninety minutes eventually completed after a gruelling five hours at sea. While the weather and sea conditions even turned the stomachs of the crew, they could never have allowed for what happened halfway across the Channel. A small plane was in trouble. Joanna, her parents and the other passengers were blissfully unaware when the plane lost power and ditched into the sea.

They only became aware of a serious problem when the ferry appeared to stop and then turned, very slowly in the choppy waters and seemed to be returning to Calais. Within an hour, everyone on deck feeling more than slightly nauseous, a red speck could be seen riding the waves. This speck, a lifeboat containing the pilot and two passengers from the single-engine plane, thrown violently from side to side, crashed into the swell of the surf. Too ill to appreciate the enormity of the situation, Joanna later realised the excitement and, thankfully, the ultimate success of the rescue.

Many trips to the major cities of London, York, Portsmouth and Bristol in the following years helped Joanna understand the history and culture of the UK. She brought that into her teaching as she focussed on the structure and history of the English language. As a wife and mother, she acceded to any request from her family to pursue different types of activity. The boys liked sport, adventure holidays, roughing it under canvas – not so much culture, more the physical experiences of nature and the countryside. She tried to bring a little of her father's approach whenever possible. Castles, dungeons, artefacts in museums; the boys took an interest, but were just as likely to rush onto the next activity, invariably involving a ball, sometimes bat and ball. Joanna didn't mind one bit. She had been happy from the moment she met Ben, and even more so when Peter and Alan came along. She struck mini-deals, however, and this holiday in Newgale had a condition beyond the mandatory inner tent and netting – the London theatre. Money was no longer a problem for them, and Ben was simply happy to be with her. Very happy. For now, they gazed across the cliffs from the Pembrokeshire Coast Path, round the rocky bays as the salty air brushed their faces, walking for more than two hours, winding their way between the fields and the chalky cliffs.

The bridge over the Solva River a welcome sight, they rested over lunch, fortunately having no more than an hour's wait for the number 400 bus to return them to the campsite. For Joanna, it may not have been high culture, a Belgian cathedral or Welsh history, but it was an important time for their relationship and for Ben to place recent events into perspective.

Ben woke early on Sunday morning, the day they were to return home. The dream had returned - the one in which he saw his wife in the hotel room with a man. Again, they were asleep in her bed. She had booked a double room. She rolled over and kissed him, her hand around his waist. As if watching a movie, he paused, seconds before the man turned round to face Joanna. The man with Joanna in the dream was Ben.

16:   The Barbeque

'We've got to see *The Mouse Trap*,' announced Joanna.

'Where is it playing?'

'St Martins, in the West End.'

'Bet you've done your research.'

'You know me, Ben. Nearest hotel, St Martin's Lane near Charing Cross. We'd get the train to Euston, then switch to Leicester Square underground.'

'Thought so.'

'Do you mind?'

'Course not. Next weekend?'

'It's in the shopping basket - I've only got to confirm.'

The time they were spending together brought Ben back from a potential crisis. Joanna was able to find ways of normalising his life and help him to deal with the here and now, rather than the past. It made her more certain, if she needed confirmation, that the family should protect him from the strange comments and predictions made by the old lady in Manchester. Joanna wasn't aware of Peter's second beating by Hickens, although it would come out eventually, and she saw no reason to give Ben something else to worry about, in addition to fretting over Alan and Cheryl.

As the frosty mornings receded and the rain clouds thinned, the May flowers signalled the onset of barbeque season. The garden might have been designed for such a purpose or indeed any party - a large patio with room for two tables and eight chairs, joined by a slope leading to a second paved area. Ben calculated that they could accommodate up to thirty people. The utility room, off the kitchen at the back of the house, boasted a large working surface – perfect for laying out a buffet. Guests would be encouraged to come and go as they pleased and cool off in the lounge where Peter's DJ spot would take place. Unlike Alan, Peter was happy to allow for the visitor age range, and not immune to the odd Sinatra or Tom Jones. The front of the house boasted a drive large enough for five cars, with most of the neighbouring houses having similar facilities. The roadside, usually free of parked cars, left ample space for visitors. The guest list expanded exponentially as the boys became involved. Not content with just close family, they wanted to include friends and colleagues.

'First weekend in June,' declared Ben.

'We're all agreed then. What about this list?'

'Peter, you can't ask everyone from the gym. And, Alan, there's no way our garden would fit everyone from uni.'

'Not everyone, Dad - just selected friends.'

'Your dad's right. Family first, close friends, work and college,' said Joanna.

'Okay, Mom, but can you tell me how many will be able to stay? Some people are travelling a distance.'

'Nan and Grandad for a start, Peter. They'll sleep in the spare room. If you can sleep on the sofa, someone will have your room. We've got at least four camp beds - we'll set them up in the back room and conservatory.'

'Right - that's Aunt Carol, your mom and dad, your friend Liz...'

'And her partner.'

'Right. Peter – you and Hannah.'

'Dad, I'll keep my own room thanks. I'm not asking Hannah to rough it downstairs.'

The debate continued for the rest of the evening. Friends from school, Ben's company, the gym and Manchester University on the list, the final number approaching twenty-five. One person was not mentioned: someone whose name had been included in most of the conversations with Alan since he started college. Someone Ben would very much like to meet - Alan's main tutor, Don Gil.

'Are you sure?'

'Do you have a problem with him, Cheryl?'

'No...well, it's just that he's Alan's lecturer; not a friend. Don't you think it might be awkward for him?'

'Nonsense. Alan, ring him tomorrow, will you, and ask him. He will be most welcome.'

Alan nodded his assent as Cheryl glanced at Peter. He shook his head as if to say, 'leave it, Cheryl.'

Mary, Ben's only remaining grandparent, now in her nineties, lived in a local care home. Apart from Ben, her only visitors were Joanna, the two boys and Carol. Ben, forever guilty, told himself that he didn't go often enough.

'Gran, if it's a nice warm day, we'll bring you over on the Saturday.'

'That will be nice love.'

'You'll be able to meet everyone. The boys will be there, Joanna and her parents, Carol, and some of our friends.'

Mary held a handkerchief to her eyes. There was nothing wrong with her memory. After all these years, seeing Ben ('young Ben' as she still called him) brought back images of her husband, daughter and son-in-law. As Ben held her hand, they sat in silence, both sharing similar thoughts. She tried to change the mood. She always made an effort for her grandson.

'I don't want any of those beefburger things, and those modern spices.'

Ben smiled, kissed his grandmother on both cheeks, and assured her that Joanna had planned a range of foods to suit all tastes.

Joanna renewed her friendship with Liz. Not that they had fallen out, but she felt responsible for a cool atmosphere after preventing Liz from pushing for Ben to be told more about the séance. It was three months since Peter translated the Latin phrase Lydia quoted: *Unus dies vos cognoscetis* ('one day you will know'). Maybe not significant in itself, but Lydia, initially naming 'John and Lucy', corrected the names of the voices she heard to 'Jack and Lucy'.

Joanna's mix of emotions changed by the week. Initially disturbed by the vague possibility of Ben's parents trying to contact him, then ridiculing the idea. Anger with Lydia, 'a fraud' she said to Liz, overriding most of her emotions. Joanna possessed a strong faith and believed in the soul going to heaven but didn't hold with what she called the mumbo-jumbo of the séance. Her problem, and one reason why Ben should not be told, was the niggling doubt that scratched away in her quieter moments. Ben would be upset anyway, she decided, so why rake things up?

She was fond of Liz and enjoyed hearing about Keith, the new love in her life. Thrilled to be invited to the barbeque, Liz viewed it as vindication of their friendship, but wisely avoided the point of their minor argument. Joanna needed a friend with whom she could share her innermost thoughts, take advice but not be pressured into taking risks. There was something about Liz she couldn't straighten in her mind, something that didn't add up. Liz's knowledge of details from Ben's past provoked some discomfort for Joanna, but she wanted to trust Liz and was unable to pinpoint why she should not.

Joanna had only been to two séances. A few months before the barbeque, Liz persuaded her on the basis of 'a bit of a giggle', and it turned out to be anything but. Ten years before, she met up with Jill Smith, an old school friend, to go to the same house for the same purpose. On that occasion, it was Andrea, Lydia's mother, who ran the session. Peter was fourteen. He had not met Jodie, the girl with whom he should be spending his life. Apparently, Andrea contacted a girl called Jodie, telling the attendees gathered around her dining table 'she wants to be with Peter; they want to be together; they will be in love.'

Joanna still regretted not following it up with Andrea in 2006, and then with her daughter, Lydia, ten years later. But what would it have achieved? The only person who knew all about this was Liz, and Joanna was having doubts over her integrity. She hadn't told Ben and couldn't tell Peter. At the time of the first séance, he was a teenage boy starting his O-levels, so it wasn't relevant at the time. Now, the loss of Jodie is still a sensitive subject. It will always be so.

Joanna, justifiably proud of the beauty, design and layout of the garden, welcomed each of the guests in turn. Ben collected his grandmother from the home, offering his arm to lead her from the car, through the house to the shaded garden seat reserved for her.

Having decided to convert their spacious garden that Ben called his 'digging zone' to a low-maintenance area, they had achieved Joanna's objective of the best of both worlds: a space in which the family could relax and three separate paths leading to the bottom of the garden. One travelling around the shed and the others slicing through the manicured lawns, at the edge of which Joanna had planted an array of flowers producing colours everyone appreciated.

'I can manage, young Ben. Now, where's that beautiful wife of yours?'

'Not many people call me beautiful these days, Gran, but here I am.'

'Come and sit by me, Jo,' Mary said, as Ben wandered off with a drink in his hand.

She held Joanna's hand and kissed her cheek.

'How is he? Really.'

'Not too bad, but I keep an eye on him.'

'I never understand what sets him off. We've all tried our best over the years. Mind you, they are in my thoughts every day, and my dear George.'

'I know, Gran.'

With the lady of the house greeting friends and family as they arrived, Ben was assigned to barbeque duty. Joanna's assertion that these occasions are a 'male thing' gained credence as the guests congregated in the garden. Each couple appeared to separate, setting the tone for the day. Wives and girlfriends introduced themselves as the husbands and boyfriends helped to reinforce the male stereotype as Masters of the Barbeque, unencumbered by 21st century political correctness. There was an exception.

'Keith, I'm Liz's partner.'

'Good to meet you, Keith,' said Ben. 'How long have you been with Liz?'

'Only a few months. She says it seems like years.'

'Back-handed compliment. I get them every day. We'll soon have this up to speed. Serve yourself when it's ready.'

Keith helped himself to salad as Ben turned to his youngest son.

'Alan, where's that pretty girl of yours?'

'Chatting with the other girls. Sure you can cope with the cooking, Dad?'

'I will if you give me a hand. Peter's doing his DJ gig. Whatever you lads call it nowadays.'

The large sliding patio door opened to its fullest extent, Peter placed the speakers on a table on the patio. The neighbours were not only warned about the potential racket he might produce, they had also been invited – 'the best way of avoiding complaints', Ben had suggested. Joanna, nervous of anything that might upset Ben and spoil the day, watched Keith carefully as Ben stepped away to talk to Alan. *I wonder how much Liz has told Keith*, she thought. *Might tell Liz to have a word with him if he knows stuff that we're holding back. The last thing I want is Keith saying the wrong thing to Ben.*

Ben spotted his in-laws entering the garden through the side gate. He called to Joanna.

'Your mom and dad are here. I'll help them in with their cases.'

'Thanks, Ben.'

Ben walked down the path to greet the new arrivals.

'Harry, Jennifer, lovely to see you.'

He shook Harry's hand, exchanged their usual banter including Harry's stock phrase 'my favourite son-in-law', and hugged Jennifer.

'How are things, Ben?' she asked.

'Not too bad. We've been looking forward to your visit. Spare room's ready.'

'Room service on tap?'

'Harry, there's all weekend for your jokes,' said Jennifer. 'Let's get in the house first. Then I want to see my daughter and those handsome grandsons of ours.'

'This is what you're in for, son.'

'Already happening, Harry, but someone has to keep me in line.'

'Mom, Dad!'

Joanna couldn't help the tears staining her cheeks as she held them both. She didn't see them as often as she would like, *but at least they are here now*, she thought. Assisted by Ben, they deposited the luggage in the spare room and joined everyone in the garden. Peter's friends from work, a couple of Alan's fellow students and Ben's colleagues also arrived. After Peter and Alan greeted their grandparents, Ben sat talking to Jennifer, Harry, Cheryl and Carol. Joanna grasped the opportunity to catch up with her sons. Peter placed a Frank Sinatra CD in the drive, 'just for Harry'. His friends were warned not to jeer. There was plenty of hip hop and punk in the pile of discs he had prepared.

'What was it that Don Gil said to you?' asked Joanna.

'Cottages of Troutburg. Can't remember how it came about,' replied Alan.

'It's one of the places your grandparents were passing when the accident happened.'

'Mom, I'm sorry.'

'Not your fault, Alan. You weren't to know. On top of everything else, there was Uncle Graham earlier this year, then his friends, Joe and Teresa.'

'Mom, Peter told you what the old lady said, didn't he?'

'Greta Armitage? Yes. The name stuck in my mind,' said Joanna. 'Yet another Latin phrase. I wish I knew what was going on. "Be careful, you will soon be four" - what on earth could it mean?'

'Don't know, Mom,' said Peter, still sorting through the pile of CDs, 'and there was that other stuff she wrote about Dad meeting her on the other side.'

'And the other rubbish about Cheryl letting you down, Alan.'

'It's okay, Mom. It freaked me out because Frank Carter used the same words at school years ago.'

'Listen, boys, there's not much we can do but sit tight, and we must keep it from Dad. Agreed?'

'Yes, Mom,' they said in unison.

~

'Alan, where's your lecturer friend?'

'He should be here any time, Dad.'

Ben had seen Joanna and the boys talking. He'd noticed the whispers before. He tried to put it out of his mind, but he instinctively felt they were protecting him from something. He had seen the phrase written on the card at the graveyard. It matched the inscription on the Saint Christopher coin: *you must stay within the boundaries.*

Peter must have told his mom about our churchyard visit, Ben thought. *Jo, being Jo, will strive to keep things calm and put it all into perspective.*

Peter called his father to the phone.
'It's that lecturer bloke of Alan's. Wants to speak to you.'

17: Peter finds Cheryl's phone

'Mr Gil, we speak at last.'

'Oh, call me Don, please. Good to speak to you as well.'

'Are you coming today?'

'Sadly, something has come up and I won't be able to travel. I'm sure our paths will cross one day.'

'Of course, I understand. While we're on, how is that young son of mine doing?'

'Excellent! Ideal student. I've got to know both of them quite well.'

'Cheryl, you mean? Yes, she's lovely.'

'Fine girl, very thoughtful. Chatting at college recently she mentioned that your wife had been to the theatre in London.'

'Why do you mention that?'

'Such a coincidence. I saw *The Caretaker* at the Old Vic myself a few weeks ago. Anyway, Ben, must go. Sorry again, speak to you soon.'

Hardly having time to reply, Ben stuttered a 'what day did you go' that barely registered in his mobile phone's microphone. He can't remember saying goodbye to Don, and the conversation was cut short, but he was soon distracted by demands from Alan for more beers, sausages and rolls.

'Some barbeque if we run out of food, Dad!'

'Come on, help me bring it out from the kitchen.'

Ben didn't forget the conversation but tried to convince himself of its lack of consequence. In the days and weeks that followed, the familiarity of the voice he heard on the phone became more evident.

~

'You're welcome to stay. And Keith. Peter's set up a couple of camp beds in the conservatory. We can chat over breakfast tomorrow.'

'Thanks, Jo, if you're sure you don't mind,' said Liz.

'Pleasure. Nice to have some female company. I'm always surrounded by men.'

'You shouldn't complain, Jo. I wouldn't mind changing places.'

'Not complaining, but you know what I mean.'

'Liz, I've just realised something,' said Keith. 'You sound just like Joanna.'

'What do you mean?'

'Very similar accent, same tone of voice.'

'We might be sisters,' joked Joanna.

'Wonder what my new brother-in-law will say,' joked Liz.

Keith reached for his mobile. Joanna and Liz could not help leaning forward to catch whatever snippets were there to be picked up. He sighed as he turned to Liz to say he'd been called back to work. Liz had never explained to Joanna what Keith did for a living. 'He travels a lot' was the most she gleaned from their snatched conversations about him. Joanna had intended to find time to talk to Keith over the weekend, but now the chance evaporated. Just one last comment before he picked up his keys.

'Slave drivers are they, Keith?'

'That's how it is. Job's got to be done. Liz, do you mind packing my stuff and bringing it back tomorrow? I've got everything I need for the next few days at the flat. See you on Wednesday.'

'Well...'

Liz didn't have time to question him as he kissed her forehead, apologised again to Joanna and left the room. She looked as stunned as Joanna felt.

'Don't say anything please, Jo. Sorry, but could we leave it for now?'

For the first time in months, Joanna had sympathy for her friend. The growing lack of trust evaporated. Liz was in a strange relationship; attracted to this man but unsure how that relationship might develop. Joanna let it go and decided there and then to be supportive towards her.

~

'You must be Hannah. We've not met before. I'm Peter's Great Aunt Carol. Now I've said it, "great aunt" sounds a bit formal.'

'No, it's fine, lovely to meet you.'

Hannah gave Carol her natural smile, with sparkling brown eyes that might cause anyone to return that smile. Auburn hair caressing her shoulders, set onto her tall, slim frame. Carol could see how she had attracted young Peter.

She gleaned from the conversation that Hannah was a language specialist. With French, German and Spanish under her belt, her job involved travel. She had secured a six-month contract with the Foreign Office – something Peter had not told his parents – and the possibility of a move to an EU department not beyond her reach. *Beauty and intelligence, someone with a future,* thought Carol. *Peter is a lucky boy.*

'Call me Carol – "Peter's great aunt" really sounds very middle class.'

'Carol, Peter's told me such a lot about you. I was so sorry about Graham.'

'Yes, it's not been easy, but I've got a lovely family. Ben and Jo have been marvellous, so supportive.'

'Here's Cheryl. You've met already, I assume?' asked Hannah.

'Of course,' replied Carol, turning to Cheryl. 'Is that young Alan looking after you?'

'He is, Auntie, but right now his highest priority is a sausage sandwich.'

'Takes after his dad,' said Carol with a smile. 'By the way, did Ben mention the old coin his Uncle Graham left him?'

'Alan did say something about it,' replied Cheryl.

'Did they make sense of the inscription?'

'Not sure what you mean, Auntie.'

'You must stay within the boundaries,' said Carol.

'What?'

'It's written in Latin, but that's what it says.'

'Oh, Peter mentioned that,' offered Hannah. 'I'm sure he's seen it somewhere else.'

Behind Carol's back, Cheryl waved a hand across her mouth. The signal hit home. Hannah quickly changed the subject, making an excuse about the cricket joke Peter made when Ben asked him about boundaries. Carol, seemingly unaffected by the possibility of her husband's bequest being somehow ridiculed, exchanged a few pleasantries with the girls and moved away. Cheryl touched Hannah's arm.

'Can we have a proper talk sometime?'

'Yes, coffee shop one of the mornings?' replied Hannah.

'Give me your number; it will be good to compare notes.'

'0734 ...' Hannah started the first few digits.

'Hold on,' said Cheryl. 'I can't find my phone. I'll give you my number so you can text me. If I can't find it, I'll ask you to ring the number. It's probably on a garden chair somewhere.'

Peter didn't recognise the mobile that someone had left next to the pile of CDs. Guests had been in and out of the room all day; some with requests for more Sinatra or Tom Jones, many with requests for less. Mumford and Sons, Stone Roses and Blur the order of the day. He picked up the phone. *It's not pin-protected,* he thought, *just a standard screen saver. Must be a Prince fan – the Purple Rain album cover.*

While not naturally inquisitive, he did want to find the owner of the phone. A recent text not only supplied him with that information but also shook him. Cheryl had received a text from Trevor Knight, a local hairdresser. The text was flagged as 'unread', so she hadn't yet seen that one, but it didn't take Peter long to find a string of texts, both received and sent. There was only one saving grace for Cheryl from Peter's perspective – she was currently batting away Trevor's most recent advances. Cheryl, however, had betrayed Peter's brother. His relief that she no longer wanted the errant stylist went some way to calming his mood. The phone rang - it was Hannah. It took him a few seconds to recognise the number.

'What are you doing answering Cheryl's phone?' Hannah asked.

'Long story, love.'

'I'm listening.'

'Tell her to come and fetch it, will you?' said Peter.

~

'Peter, what's wrong?' asked Cheryl.

'You left your mobile in the lounge. Sorry, I didn't mean to pry, but I wanted to find out who had lost their phone.'

'It *is* private, or should be.'

'I appreciate that, but it's done now. You're probably not aware of the latest text from some bloke called Trevor.'

Cheryl's face turned the colour of the Dover cliffs, the blood draining into her neck and chest. She took the phone from Peter, swiped away the Purple Rain screen saver, and stared at the latest entry to her inbox.

'You've read it then,' she said, as she jabbed the offending text with her forefinger.

'Yes, and I will admit to checking out the linked texts. Quite a lad, isn't he? What on earth would Alan make of it?'

'You're not going to tell him, are you?'

'For Alan's sake, not now. You don't deserve this, but if you promise to keep away from Mr Knight, I'll keep quiet.'

'Thank you, Pete. Should I tell Trevor to keep away and stop texting? You can see that I've already tried that.'

'Don't worry, I'll have a little word with Mr Knight. Delete all the texts and forget it. Stupid of you to leave them on your phone. Then you go and leave it lying around.'

'I'm so sorry, Peter.'

'Alright, but if I hear any more about this, you realise what will happen.'

~

'Do I have permission to dance with your husband?'

'Liz Atkins, when it comes to men, when have you ever asked permission before?'

'I know, but this is different.'

'He's yours!' Joanna said with a smile.

It didn't take Liz long to search out her prey. There was a moment when Joanna hesitated, concerned that Liz, outspoken by nature, might lean on Ben's shoulder and ask all the awkward questions. She might pass on information that Joanna preferred he didn't receive. *At least Keith is no longer around to fulfil the role of bearer of secrets,* Joanna thought.

'Apparently, you're mine for the time being, Mr Stone.'

'Really?'

'Permission granted from your good lady wife.'

'Dancing, I assume?'

'Of course, what else? I reckon two fast ones and then the slow, smoochy numbers.'

As Joanna danced with her father, two sons (taking turns on DJ duty), John Greggs and two of the girls when they decided to launch a very embarrassing Destiny's Child tribute, Liz dominated Ben's time. For a barbeque, it turned out to rival many seventies/eighties disco revivals, with Liz in her element. As the slow numbers arrived, she couldn't have held Ben any closer, particularly as Phyllis Nelson came to the fore, advising them to move closer.

'I've always hated that song,' he said.

'Don't spoil it, Ben, I'm having a great time.'

Thirty minutes loan of her husband was enough for Joanna. She rescued him, joking with Liz that she would have swapped him for Keith had he not been called to work.

'I would have liked that,' said Liz.

Joanna laughed as she missed the glint in Liz's eye. She had told Ben how lucky Joanna was to have him and she seemed to think he reciprocated her feelings as they moved across the patio in each other's arms.

Into the evening, guests offered their excuses and the numbers dwindled. Peter took his great-grandmother back to the home, staying for twenty minutes to settle her in.

'I've had a lovely time Peter, and your mom and dad look so happy.'

'That's right, Gran. I'll pop and see you next week.'

A successful day, and now Joanna implemented stage two of Operation Barbeque – sleeping arrangements. Liz retained the camp bed in the conservatory, the one meant to be alongside Keith. Alan bagged the large settee in the lounge, and while Hannah went in with Peter, Joanna's parents took Alan's room.

A complex shower rota was put in place. Liz had first go, complimenting her friend on the new bath towels. Ben agreed to go last, his main job being key holder and security man for the household. With everyone in bed, he checked the windows and doors and headed for the bathroom.

With shampoo in his eyes as he stepped out of the shower, he grabbed for the towel as he heard Joanna whisper 'let me in Ben' from the other side of the locked door. He fumbled for the latch and let her in assuming she needed the toilet.

'No need for that,' she said, as she pulled the towel away from him. He turned to face her, holding out his arms. It wasn't Joanna.

'Liz, for Christ sake, what are you doing?'

She gazed at him as he quickly replaced the towel.

'You'd better go. What about Joanna?'

'I'm so sorry, Ben, don't know what I was thinking.'

'Back downstairs. Now!'

Footsteps on the landing. The door opened.

'What the hell are you doing?'

'Joanna, I can explain,' said Ben, as Liz pushed past him.

He gathered pyjamas and a dressing gown from the bedroom as the two women left him. Liz, first to reach the conservatory, was crying as she sat down.

'Jo, I am so very sorry.'

'What are you up to, Liz?'

'It's not what you think. I meant it as a joke after Keith said how much I sounded like you. Ben had no way of knowing. I feel stupid now.'

'You've embarrassed Ben. We'll be lucky to get past this. Liz, are you sure it was just a joke?'

As Ben closed the conservatory door behind him, trying not to wake Alan in the next room, Liz was sobbing.

'Is everything okay between you and Keith?'

'Not really, Jo. He can be cruel, and he's always away at short notice. The holiday in Mexico was fantastic, and he was so romantic. He's changed since then. Something else; he's always asking about Ben.'

'Where does Ben come into this from your point of view?' asked Joanna.

'He's so kind and thoughtful,' Liz replied, not realising that Ben was standing across the room, looking through the large windows with a view of the patio.

'You're so lucky, Jo. I wanted a man like Ben, but this isn't the way. What can I do?'

'Forget it, Liz,' Ben said as he joined the two women.

Liz's eyes once again filled with tears.

'Ben...'

'Let's put it behind us, but from what I've heard so far, you should dump Keith.'

18: Stay within the boundaries

Monday morning, and Ben was relieved to be on his way to the office. The barbeque and a host of conversations and relationship issues behind him, his current preoccupation Ziggy Stardust and the Spiders from Mars. RDS chipped in to tell him traffic was backing up on the A448 between Bromsgrove and Redditch. The local station was also giving him the latest odds on the Remain / Leave debate. *Leave me alone,* he pleaded, preferring the company of David Bowie to a bunch of talking heads, albeit on the radio. His attention wandering, the image of Liz pinged into his mind. Unable to remember the last time two women simultaneously displayed an interest in Ben Stone, he was flattered but recalled his blind panic as Liz impersonated Joanna. Flitting back to his dreams, he fixed his attention on his wife in London. What was it Don Gil said? He'd seen the same play. She had been out with 'two or three friends' that weekend. *No,* he reminded himself, *how can you be sure Don was there at the same time?* He had never met Don, but nonetheless recalled the conversation, catching a nuance in the voice from the telephone call. Alan described him – tall, thin, slightly gaunt. Yes, the description matched the voice. What would Joanna see in him? He reminded himself that since the day he met her, the doubts chipped away at his own confidence. He considered the possibility of Joanna having met Don Gil. *What are the chances?*

~

'I'm sorry Joanna, we are duty-bound to follow this through.'

'But Headmaster, you are aware of his behaviour, and his family were never bothered about his education. Nothing but trouble.'

'If an official complaint is made, it has to be dealt with. It's red tape, but the council expect the protocol to be followed and all the forms filled in.'

'You're right of course. I'm sorry if I've caused you any grief.'

'I'm on your side, Jo. One thing, I will stand my ground if someone suggests suspension. You've not been accused of physical assault. The letter from Mrs Enright states discrimination.'

'Oh? On what grounds?'

'The family think that because they are working class...'

'Working class?' interrupted Joanna. 'None of them worked until the cousin took him on to do some of his dirty work.'

'As I said, because of that, and as they consider James is seen as different to the other students, they claim you have singled him out.'

'Best I don't comment just yet, Headmaster. You might think less of me. I'll reserve my explosion for when I get home. Ben is used to me.'

~

'Jo, can you wait until I get home tonight?'

Waiting for the sales manager and warehouse supervisor to join him for the weekly review, Ben enjoyed the position of his desk at the Redditch office. A feeling of peace infused him within minutes of sitting alone in the south-facing office he used one day a week. The neighbouring farmland swept down to the village of Studley, leading to the Cotswolds. *If we moved house*, he considered, *we would live here*.

'I was going to wait, but the thought of that family complaining to the headmaster...'

'I'm really sorry Jo, but you say he's not going to suspend you?'

'He doesn't want to, but you know how the LEA view things. The Enright family have a history of going to the local press. The editor of Leeford News loves this sort of stuff. They'll make me sound like an axe murderer.'

'Jo, try to keep this in perspective. You've done nothing wrong, although that little berk deserves it. Anyway, I'll try to get away early.'

'Alright, love, I know you're busy. Thanks for listening anyway. See you tonight.'

Joanna had let it slip that Terry Hickens was James's cousin. As the meeting started, Ben's mind veered from pallet-racking organisation to Peter's run-in with Hickens. *Was there a connection? Now that James is working with Terry, he will pass anything back that would help the Enright family to find ways of hurting Joanna.*

As the morning progressed, Ben became more convinced that the attack on Peter was related to Joanna's relationship as a teacher with James Enright. She had intended to keep quiet about Terry, but in the circumstances couldn't help herself.

~

That evening, Peter overheard his mother giving Ben the latest news. Realising that James Enright had interesting family connections, Peter's first instinct was to search him out and deal with the matter himself. He was not afraid of Terry Hickens but considered he would make the situation worse for Joanna if he intervened. He resisted for now. Back at work after the weekend barbeque, he had taken time to visit Trevor Knight at the salon on the way to the gym.
'We've never met, Mr Knight, but you need to understand something. Cheryl no longer wants you. Do you get it? She is with my brother, and I don't want that spoilt. You've done enough damage. No need to explain, no excuses. If you agree now and stick to it, you'll have no trouble from me.'

After leaving the salon, he phoned Cheryl.
'Cheryl, it's Peter. If Knight gets in touch, please tell me straight away. Otherwise, as far as I'm concerned, that's the end of the matter. Okay?'

'Peter, thank you. I promise it will be different from now on. I love Alan and don't want to let him down. In some ways, I'm glad you read the texts. At least you can be sure I have finished with Trevor.'

~

Joanna could only repeat the facts she had relayed earlier in the day. They agreed not to dwell on the issue, and Ben even gave in too easily to an evening dominated by soaps. He didn't mind, displaying the mock displeasure that always made Joanna giggle. An early night resulted in both falling asleep within minutes of climbing into bed, Ben's last thoughts before conceding defeat to aching tiredness returning to his journey home. From the Redditch office back to Leeford there are four straight roads and three awkward right turns. Sometimes Ben shuddered when unable to remember taking those right turns. The radio, CDs, idle thoughts or all of these can conspire to throw one's concentration. Today, it was not his concentration lacking but the stupidity of another driver causing the shudder.

From the M5 junction near Bromsgrove, through Belbroughton village, the A491 took him past Clent and Hagley onto the B-roads he favoured that cut across country to the A449 leading straight into Leeford Village. The hills bordering the vast areas of farmland eventually led to one of Ben's awkward right turns. A busy main road, and to the left a sharp bend and a sixty limit capable of fooling a less experienced driver. Indicating right, he saw a Fiat Panda travelling at no more than forty approaching from his right. Clear to the left, he decided to make his move. At that instant, the driver of an Audi A4 decided enough was enough and seared past the Panda. Ben could almost smell the sweat on the tightened brow of the A4 driver as he sped past, missing Ben by a few feet. Fortunately, the Panda slowed down as Ben had already slammed his foot to the floor. 'Half a second from death' the expression going through his mind. He hadn't told Joanna. She was asleep anyway and he soon followed her.

His father approached him first.

'Not your time yet, son. They've tried before, but it's not your time. You still have much to do.'

'But Dad, what do you mean? Who are they?'

Jack moved back, away from Ben. His lips were moving but Ben sensed a controlling force, someone or something stopping Jack from saying any more, stopping him from being too helpful. It was as though a rule had been made that Ben should find his own way. As the image of his father faded into the shadows, from those same shadows he watched the faint outline of a woman moving towards him. When the image cleared, she had not aged from the day of the accident.

'Say no, Ben, say no.'

'Why, Mom? What do you mean?'

'You will know when the time comes, when it is time to say "no". Stay within the boundaries.'

'Mom, what boundaries? Can you help me?'

Again, he perceived a presence, a controlling force. Lucy smiled as she faded into the background. He felt a sense of peace but was still puzzled by the phrase he had first seen on the St Christopher coin - *Vos autem sedate in terminis*. He didn't understand but sensed that one day it would become clear. Graham couldn't get through to him, he assumed, but the gift was the message. The emotional bond between the young boy and his parents remained. Thirty-two years on, he still treasured that bond.

Three-fifteen. Shifting his gaze from the clock, he observed Joanna lying to his right. She was restless, mumbling. Still recovering from his own experience, feeling that he had stumbled unwillingly into his own dream, and people say dreams can seem so real. He was comforted by seeing his parents, albeit for a moment, albeit in his disrupted sleep.

'That was lovely. Hold me in your arms,' Joanna mumbled.
Ben drew closer to her, fighting the temptation to touch her shoulder, to wake her.
'No, it's not fair to Ben. It's been great, but we can't do this again. I'd never leave him.'
She paused as if waiting for a reply, or listening to the sound of another voice only received by Joanna. Not accessible to Ben. Her face contorted, he witnessed her internal struggle.

'No Don, we can't. Stay away from me, from my family. You've done enough damage already.'

He saw a single tear working its way down her left cheek. A gentle mountain stream winding through the crevices, her pale skin the landscape. He stroked the back of his hand against her face and drew back her hair. As she woke, guilt etched in her features, pain in her eyes.

'Ben, I've been dreaming.'
'I know, you were talking.'
'Was I?'
'You were with Don, in London.'
'What do you mean?'
'The play, and at the hotel.'
'No, you're wrong.'
'Why should you talk to him about me then? Were you with him?'
'With someone. In the dream.'
'Why did you say the name "Don"?'
'Ben, I've never met him. But, since Alan went to Manchester, he's talked about him a lot, then he phoned you to cancel his visit.'
'Are you sure? Just a dream?'
'Of course. I've heard you talk about old girlfriends in your dreams, and why would I need anyone but you? Anyway, your escapade in the bathroom with Liz wasn't a dream. You let her whip off your towel.'
'I thought it was *you*,' said Ben, pausing as Joanna glared at him.
'So, you wouldn't think of leaving me?' he continued.
'What?'

'In your dream, you said you would never leave me.'

'Ben, that is one part of the dream I will accept is true. Why Don came into it I don't know, but I can imagine saying that.'

'So, you still love me?'

'I don't need a dream to prove that.'

~

'Right, today we're going to launch a new range of antiperspirants. There will be four products in the range, and your task is to use the names agreed by the board. You were not part of the discussions, but as marketing manager, it is your job to take the name and do something with it.'

Several hands went up.

'Simon.'

'Mr Gil, do we all have to use the four products, or can we choose the one we like?'

'That's up to you. Work in teams of four if possible, and maybe have a product each.'

'What are they called?'

'I'm coming to that. The range is called "Devil May Care". There are four products in the range – Golem, Grendel, Wyvern and Lamia. You decide which of them is deodorant or antiperspirant, spray or roll-on. Create your range, then work on the labelling and marketing policy.'

Alan looked straight at Don and gave a flick of his hand. Eye contact would have been enough, and Don knew what Alan was about to say. He smiled, ready with the answer as Alan spoke.

'What do the four names represent?'

'You can do your own research, but I'll give you a starter. Golem means dumb or helpless in modern Hebrew. In Jewish folklore, the Golem is an animated being, created magically from inanimate matter.'

'Why not use modern names?' another student asked.

'Research has shown us that mythology creates interest. After Harry Potter and The Lord of the Rings, anything like this captures the imagination.'

'The other three names, Mr Gil?'

'Yes, Grendel was magically disguised as a normal-looking human, but having the ability to transform into a white, giant-like creature at will, resembling the giant in Beowulf. Wyvern was a legendary creature with a dragon's head and wings, two legs and a tail. Finally, Lamia – the mistress of the God, Zeus.'

Don paused, waiting for any final questions.

'Right, hope that helps. Make a start, and we'll review your initial findings next week.'

~

Alan spotted Don in the canteen after the late morning lecture. Intrigued why Don should choose such a strange subject for study, he made his way to the table.

'Do you mind if I sit here?'

'Of course, Alan. We haven't had a chat for a while.'

'The latest project...'

'I knew you would be interested,' Don interrupted. 'Have you heard these names before, Alan?'

'No, why do you ask?'

'There are ways of aligning characters in mythology to the present day. Take Lamia, for example. Now she reminds me of the lovely Cheryl.'

'What?'

'No offence, please don't take it the wrong way, but we can all be compared to characters in myth and legend. I see you as a young Arthur.'

'What, the Knights of the Round Table and all that?'

'That's it.'

'But Don, why on earth is Cheryl like Lamia?'

'Only a passing remark, Alan, as you were taking an interest. Nothing specific.'

'I'm puzzled why you mentioned it.'

'Nothing for you to fret about, Alan. Forget I said anything, but you could always do your own research.'

'What, because of your comment about Cheryl?'

'No, no, but with any project like this, just remember that the devil is in the detail.'

Alan made his excuses, heading for his room. He soon had a WikiMyth database entry on his laptop: 'Lamia – the mistress of Zeus; causing Zeus's wife, Hera, to kill all of Lamia's children. Lamia loses her mind from grief and despair, starts stealing children from other families out of envy, the repeated monstrosity of which transforms her into a monster.' Not knowing what to make of it, he also recalled Greta's comments 'you will soon be four' and 'she will let you down.'

~

'Hi, Cheryl.'

'Lovely to see you again, Hannah.'

Cheryl appeared on edge. As she took her seat at her favourite table at Jilly's Cafe, Hannah noticed her hand shaking. She stared at Hannah with eyes that betrayed her thoughts and emotions, the lines of her face seemingly of an older woman, the skin of her cheeks pale and lifeless.

'Are you okay, Cheryl?'

'I've been a bit low just lately, but I was so grateful to Peter for the way he dealt with the texts. I assume he's told you everything.'

'Yes, but it stays with us. He didn't like what happened, but he's convinced that you will stay loyal to his brother. He thinks the world of him.'

'I realise that, and I do love Alan so much. I've been stupid, and I need this fresh start.'

'Will you ever tell Alan that you slept with another man?'

'Not sure. Do you think there's any point?' asked Cheryl.

'Not at this stage. But if you both decide to have a long-term future, it might be for the best.'

'I'll find it difficult to say the words. What if Alan doesn't forgive me?'

'That's the risk you'll have to take. He's worth it, isn't he?'

'He is. I'm so lucky. I constantly worry that something will happen and spoil what we have.'

19: Paradox of Free Will

'Heard anything this week, Mom?' asked Peter.

'The official complaint has been submitted. The headmaster has already written to the LEA, refusing to suspend me if it were suggested.'

'Can he do that?'

'He's respected within the authority, and he says there have been previous cases like this. If a complaint is not concerning violence or any sort of abuse, and the student has left the school, the teacher can stay in post at the discretion of the head.'

'You must be relieved.'

'I'll be more relieved when it's finished. The Enright family are out for blood.'

'Mom - something I'd like to discuss if you don't mind.'

'What is it, Peter?'

He took his coffee in both hands as if warming them on a winter morning. He assured Joanna she did not need to worry, but when chatting to Alan he had discovered something interesting.

'Y'know, might be nothing, but Don Gil is more than a bit weird.'

'What makes you say that?' asked Joanna.

'In itself, it's not much, but Alan told me about the notes Don has left on his project folders. You know, the grade and the usual tutor comments.'

'Go on.'

'Well, at first, various Latin phrases. Innocuous in themselves, but remember Greta? Not sure if I can prove a connection with all this stuff, but we have spotted something in Don's spelling of certain words.'

'Like what?'

'For some reason, he's mentioned to Alan a couple of times the Pied Piper of Hamelin. The name of the town in Saxony is spelt with an "e". In German it's spelt "Hameln".'

'What's the significance?'

'Don Gil spelt it "Hamlin".'

'You've lost me, Peter.'

'Mom, the place in the States where Nan and Grandad travelled past that day. The place was called "Hamlin".'

'A coincidence surely.'

'Might be, but one thing Alan knows about Don - he's a pedant when it comes to spelling, place names, mythology and history. Not the type of thing he gets wrong - feels sort of... significant.'

'In what way?' enquired Joanna.

'A message, I reckon.'

'Who to?'

'To Dad.'

~

Later, Peter's mobile rang with the unmistakable sound of the Simpsons' theme – the ringtone he had selected for his younger brother.

'Hi Alan, Cheryl okay?'

'What makes you ask that?'

'Nothing specific, but when I saw her at the barbeque, she seemed... distant.'

'You're my big brother, but you're not the fount of all knowledge.'

'I was only saying...'

'Peter, she's fine, just concerned with all the crap at the care home. She worries about me. And Dad – does he know anything?'

'No, we've not mentioned Greta and all that stuff - someone letting you down.'

'You told me he saw the Latin inscription on the coin from Uncle Graham and then at the graveyard...'

'I'd rather not go on about that. Thought you didn't know.'

'Sorry Peter, but are you making sense of it?'

'I talked to Mom about the Pied Piper nonsense and my opinion of your lecturer.'

'You're being a bit unfair. He's strange, I'll grant you, but Cheryl seems to like him.'

'Are you sure?'

'Admittedly, she's not mentioned him recently. Come to think of it, after being at his house in April, but she's never criticised him.'

'Going back to Greta Armitage – any more theories on "soon you will be four"?'

'No idea. Cheryl was spooked when I told her, and I'm glad I never mentioned the "she will let you down" thing.'

'Not much we can do, Alan. When are you back down here?'

'Next couple of weeks. Cheryl's with us for the weekend. Hope things have settled by then.'

~

Joanna would use her free period to visit Lydia and tell no one what she was about to do. Particularly Ben. Lydia agreed to meet her informally – no séance – simply to discuss the previous revelations and to ask for advice. Joanna, agonising over this for many weeks, accepted that it was probably a complete waste of time. After being persuaded by Liz to attend the last séance, she now listened to the tiny voice in her head telling her to give Lydia a chance. Nothing to lose. If Joanna thought that Lydia was talking rubbish, she would walk out and put it behind her.

Joanna forced herself to keep any preconceived ideas out of her mind - Ben was likely to be furious if he knew. 'Load of rubbish' would be the start of his first sentence. If Lydia came up with something interesting, what would she do with it? She had no idea.

Lydia opened the door, smiled and grasped Joanna's hand.
'Nice to see you again, Joanna.'
'Yes, good to see you too.'
Lydia led her into the front room. Joanna recognised the table that had been used for the séances. Lydia gestured towards the nearest chair.
'How can I help you?'
'At the last séance, you mentioned the names "Peter" and "Jodie". Do you remember?'
'Vaguely. It was some time ago.'

'But do you remember anything about the session?' asked Joanna.

'I have seen hundreds of people since then and been through many experiences, but I remember the expression on your face when the name "Peter" came through. Your son, I believe?'

'Yes.'

'Did you know someone called Jodie?' Lydia asked.

'Not at the time, but a few years later, my son met a lovely girl with that name.'

'What happened?'

'Sadly, she died,' said Joanna, her eyes cast downwards.

'I am so sorry Joanna. I'm not sure how I can help – unless you want to contact her.'

'No, at least not at the moment. If I'm honest, Lydia, I'm not comfortable with all this. Séances I mean, as a Christian.'

'I respect that, but how can I help?'

'Members of my family have received messages, some quite disturbing, and I'd like to make sense of them.'

Joanna explained about Ben, his parents, Peter, Alan and Cheryl, and the various messages. She pressed Lydia on her thoughts concerning Jodie. Was it a coincidence, or had Peter been destined to meet her? She also focussed on the comments by Greta Armitage that Alan and Cheryl would 'become four'.

'You may not believe me, Joanna, but there was a genuine link between Peter and Jodie. I'm not saying I'm certain that we're talking about your son, but there was definitely a connection with someone in the room that day.'

'I'm not sure where to go with this. Please say what you think it might mean.'

'Have you heard of the Paradox of Free Will?' asked Lydia.

'No, does this help at all?'

'There are many theories, but philosophers over the years have argued about free will and determination. If we believe that events in the world occur according to fixed laws, then you could argue everything that happens is determined by events that have gone before, and so the decisions we make are determined by preceding events. Most of us are convinced we have free will, making day-to-day decisions in relationships and careers, but many consider this to be an illusion and that the path we take in life is set out in advance.'

Joanna frowned and leant forward.

'Why is this relevant?'

'If our lives are pre-determined, it means, for example, it was decreed that one day Peter would meet a young lady called Jodie...'

'And that she would die?'

'Precisely,' replied Lydia.

'What happens if things don't go quite to plan?'

'What do you mean?'

Joanna told her the story of Ben's life, in particular the tragedy of his parents' death. Not just the unfairness of what happened but questioning whether it was the end of the matter.

'I don't know everything,' said Lydia, 'but, sometimes, even a pre-determined path can have delays.'

'What on earth do you mean?' said Joanna, quizzically.

'Different people meeting at specific times in their lives, other events crossing over. Sometimes, the plan can go astray.'

'Can it be changed permanently?'

'I can't tell you that, but, if it is true, one day everything falls into place. For good or bad.'

'A depressing thought in some ways.'

'Sorry, Joanna, these are only my opinions, and how I see the world.'

'What about Alan and Cheryl?'

'This thing about them becoming four. Could there be another couple in their lives? Could they be having other relationships?'

Joanna stood up, walked to the window and noticed two young mothers pushing prams past the house.

'I'd not considered that.'

'I'm sure one day it will become clear. You say that the old lady in Manchester also made comments concerning your husband?'

'Yes, something about "meeting her on the other side". He has also received messages saying, "stay within the boundaries".'

'I don't know what's going on here, Joanna. There may be conflicting forces at work, or simply a series of coincidences. If what happens to us is pre-determined, there's nothing you can do. Just live your lives.'

'I'd not thought about pre-determination. My faith doesn't allow it, or at least the subject is never discussed.'

'Is there anything else?'

'I'm confused, Lydia, but I am very grateful for your thoughts.'

Joanna would never see Lydia again. Disturbed by the possibilities, the Stone family did indeed have to get on with their lives. 'Whatever will be will be' might be a fair motto, but she was determined to protect the people she loved, whatever happened.

~

'Cheryl, are you sure?' asked Alan.

'If something doesn't happen soon, I will have missed two periods.'

'Why didn't you say something before?'

'Not sure how you would react.'

'It's not how we planned things, but you must know how I feel.'

'So you're pleased?'

'Come here.'

Alan held her, surprised at the level of emotion rising within him, taking in the enormity of the news. With this girl that he held in his arms, they would become three. Despite his previous differences with Ben, he always admired the ethos by which his parents ran their lives, proud to follow on his father's belief in family, and in home. He even surprised himself with the maturity of his reactions and approach. He considered the issues, any possible negatives. No, despite his degree studies and his chosen career path, this was the best news.

Not possessing the faith so important to his mother, he nonetheless sent his thanks beyond the two people who had brought him into the world and cared for him. Gratitude to someone or something with an element of control, or at least a monitoring force on the side of right, on the side of good. He didn't think of that entity as 'God'. He made connections back to people he had never met. He knew their names – Jack and Lucy. The realisation of how important they were to his father brought home the love he in turn felt for Ben and Joanna. The creation of another life, from within him and Cheryl, strengthened the feelings he had for his parents. Cheryl, for her part, had changed his life. She had already given him everything he had asked for, so this was greater than the hopes and wishes of his dreams.

'Are you alright, Alan?' asked Cheryl.
'Sure.'
'You've not said much.'
'The only thing I can come up with is ... thank you.'
'Let's not get carried away. This is what I want as well, but it's very early. I've booked an appointment with Doctor Ellison for the back end of next week.'
'What about one of those testing kits?'
'Too unreliable, and I want to be sure.'

~

'Cheryl that's wonderful news!' said Hannah, as she placed the tray on their usual table.

'It is.'

'What's wrong? It's what you want isn't it?'

'Of course, and Alan is so pleased, even though we haven't had it confirmed yet.'

Cheryl's eyes stayed fixed on the coffee she had not yet started, avoiding Hannah's gaze.

'There's something else, isn't there?' enquired Hannah.

'Please promise that you won't repeat this, not even to Peter. Especially not to Peter.'

'You're worrying me now, Cheryl.'

'I told you that I went to Don Gil's house to collect Alan's phone.'

'Yes.'

'You remember that I fell asleep, fainted, whatever.'

'You said that Don was very kind and helped you. He called Alan and he came straight away to collect you.'

'There's more to it than that.'

'What is it, Cheryl? You need to tell someone. I can see that it's upsetting you.'

'I can't be sure, but I said at the time the top two buttons of my blouse were undone. Don said he loosened them to help me get my breath.'

'You don't think...'

'I've not repeated this to anyone, but something didn't feel right. When Alan arrived and they helped me out of the chair, I was still a bit woozy. Thing is, I felt a sensation, you know, and my underwear didn't feel right.'

'Like they had been pulled back on?'

As Hannah touched her hand, she saw that Cheryl was shaking. Tears filled her eyes and she stared at Hannah.

'Are you saying you might have been raped?'

'I can't prove it, but I was unconscious for an hour according to Don. The more I think about it, the more convinced I am that he drugged me. He insisted on me having a drink.'

'My God, Cheryl, you really should do something about this.'

'I can't. I'm so scared and I have no proof. Alan thinks Don has been so kind. He might be right. But, Hannah, you know that feeling, the physical feeling... and the dream.'

'What dream?'

'After I had the drink and fell asleep, I dreamt I was in another room. I was naked and a man violated me. I didn't stop him.'

'Was it...'

'Looked like Don Gil, and the other men watched. I didn't recognise them, but it was disgusting. When I came round, I tried not to think about it.'

'I understand, and I'm so sorry. In your heart, you knew it happened, but you didn't want to believe it at the time. This was mid-April? When's your next period?'

'I've just missed two.'

'Could the baby still be Alan's?'

'Of course, and I desperately want it to be. The alternative makes me feel sick.'

They sat quietly for over ten minutes. Hannah ordered two more coffees and again touched Cheryl's hand and reinforced the bond they shared, both women very much in love with the Stone brothers. One full of sympathy for the younger woman, the other full of dread and guilt, although, on this occasion, completely innocent.

20: Enright

He gazed at her, half-asleep and half-awake. As she stirred, her blond hair fell over her eyes. He gently used his forefinger to reveal the eyes barely capable of opening in the early minutes of the day. Mumbling something incomprehensible, she turned over and encouraged him to snuggle up for those precious moments they shared each morning. After two children and nearly twenty-five years of marriage, it would not be unusual if the passion did not burn as brightly. For Ben and Joanna, the flame still burned, but neither deemed it necessary to demonstrate it constantly. Out of bed first, Joanna invariably took the lead in the Stone household in those early hours. It was a rare occasion when either Peter or Ben initiated the regular sequence of events in the kitchen. Ben lay there for a few minutes, watching her as he always did, even finding the act of her draping a dressing gown over her slim shoulders pleasing to the eye. Refusing his offer to join her in the shower with a sharp 'we haven't got time, Ben', she compensated with a ruffle of his hair and a delicate kiss on his forehead.

Joanna considered her plans for the day. An important day. John Sellars, assistant director at the LEA, was due to meet both Joanna and the headmaster to discuss the Enright case. She had nothing specifically to fear, but it was a major inconvenience. *Get this out of the way,* she decided, *and the family can settle down. No more James Enright, no more Lydia and all that stuff. Encourage*

Peter and Alan to ignore the so-called messages and concentrate on keeping Ben happy.

'Toast or cereals?'
'Both,' replied Ben.
'Greedy. You're as bad as Peter.'
'My name being taken in vain?' as he entered the kitchen.
'Just feeding the five thousand, or at least it feels like it.'
'Toast and coffee will do me, Mom.'
'Enright today, love?' enquired Ben.
'Preliminary discussions. If the assistant director is going to recommend suspension, it will be today.'
Ben nodded in agreement as his son muttered 'bloody ridiculous'. They sat in silence over breakfast, after which Ben raced Peter to the bathroom.
'Me first. Getting in early today. Monthly meeting.'
By the time Ben had finished his shower, Joanna was dressed and ready to leave. He gave her a gentle hug.
'I'll try to finish early today. Good luck at school.'

~

'No decision will be taken today,' said the headmaster. 'I've worked with John in the past, and he plays it straight. He will carry out an objective assessment that is fair to both you and James Enright.'
'I could resign.'
'No way, Jo. I'm backing you all the way and I don't want to lose you. I can understand if you say it's not

worth the stress, but we know what James is like. Fortunately, he's not at the school now, although technically he's still registered as a student until the end of term.'

'I appreciate your support, Simon. I agree, let's see what John Sellars comes up with.'

Simon Hill sat down, took his coffee in one hand, the initial report in the other. He sighed as Joanna shut his office door to return to her classroom. She had arrived before 8am. Many of the staff were still to arrive. In preparation for her first lesson, she took the storeroom key from her desk drawer and unlocked the door. Joanna's classroom was one of the few with its own storeroom. Reserved for senior staff, this afforded them the luxury of not having to share cupboards and smaller storerooms dotted around the building. Switching the light on, she paused as the door closed behind her. *Now*, she mused, *As You Like It or Merchant of Venice? Most of the kids struggle with Shakespeare, but they do respond to a clever plot.* 'As You Like It' would be fine for today, one of her personal favourites. With her back to the door, she was at first aware of a slight breeze on the back of her neck.

A warm start to a beautiful summer morning had encouraged her to open the classroom windows. The door opened slightly, and the air ushered itself towards her. As she turned, the light went out. She felt herself being pushed towards a filing cabinet and a hand was clasped over her mouth. A rough hand, and the aura of a familiar character.

'Mrs Stone. Nice to see you again. Don't scream, please don't, or you will regret it.'

Something sharp pressed into her back.

'James.'

'Your career is finished, but this is just a little reminder. You and your rich family make me sick. Son at university, another one playing the guitar and messing around with other women. Your husband hasn't done a hard day's work in his life...'

'What do you want James? You must be aware the council are going through the correct procedure.'

'Yes, we all know that you lot stick together, don't we?'

'It's not like that.'

'What *is* it like?' he asked, as he gripped her arm.

She tried to wriggle free and managed to push Enright against the side wall. He wasn't carrying a knife, but a stick sharpened to a point. Joanna reasoned that he would be in less trouble if caught.

'Your family is a mess, Mrs Stone. Your husband is neurotic - we know his history. You think you're God's gift. Your sons have no idea.'

'What on earth do you mean by that?'

'For one thing, your future daughter-in-law will cause you nothing but trouble.'

As Joanna attempted to ask what he meant by his last remark, Enright again grabbed her arm, twisting it behind her back. She stumbled forwards, crying out in pain. The door opened.

'What the hell do you think you're doing?'

Simon Hill switched on the light and moved towards him. Enright released his grip on Joanna and shoved her to the floor. He pushed past the headmaster and ran out of the room.

'Jo, are you alright?'

'Fine, just a bit shaken.'

'I'd just come to tell you that Mr Sellars has arrived. He needs to be told about this.'

'Thank you, Simon, I'm so glad you turned up when you did. Oh, sorry Headmaster...'

'Don't worry, first names are acceptable in circumstances such as this. One of the supply teachers called me "Si" in front of the kids in the corridor last week. We can't have that can we?'

Joanna smiled, and Simon realised that humour and a few kind words had suppressed her tears. He thought it best to get on with the meeting without delay. After organising cover for Joanna for the first lesson, they sat down with the assistant director. Simon Hill, in Joanna's eyes, had become more human, less business-like, in those few minutes. She would not take advantage but realised that the headmaster was truly on her side. It did not take long for John Sellars to reach a conclusion.

'I will be writing to Mrs Enright. Joanna, you have no case to answer. It is obvious from the records and James's behaviour today that you've done nothing wrong. He has intimidated you. I am very sorry that you have suffered so much stress. I will leave it with you to decide if the police are to be contacted. As Mr Hill has explained, he witnessed an assault against you by James Enright and has confirmed he will appear as a witness if that is what you want. I will inform your union so the incident will be on file.'

~

'Both of you sit down. I want to tell you something.'

'Please don't say you've been suspended,' said Ben.

'I wish Alan were here, but we won't see him until the weekend, so I'll tell you the news. The case has been dropped.'

'Mom, that's great!'

'Peter and Ben, you have to promise me you won't react and do something stupid when I tell you what happened at school.'

Joanna recounted the events of the day. She watched Peter's knuckles whiten and expand as he gripped the arm of the chair. Although angry, Ben was happy to follow Joanna's line and let it go. Peter wanted revenge, and it took much persuading from his parents to make him promise to stay away from James Enright. The secondary shock he experienced was the news of the family connection of which James boasted – Terry Hickens. Joanna explained how she had visited the house, at first shouted down by Mrs Enright then introduced to James's cousin and employer.

She approached the police the next day with Simon Hill. James would receive a caution, and to avoid a charge of assault, he committed to staying away from the school and the Stone family.

As Joanna later explained to Ben and Peter, the caution would stay on James's record, and although not technically a conviction, cautions are taken very seriously and can affect an individual's future job prospects. It would certainly be considered if he transgressed again. James had also been warned that if Terry Hickens or any of his associates approached any member of the Stone family, the police would be paying James a visit.

'It ends now,' insisted Joanna.

'But, Mom...'

'Never mind "but Mom",' she interrupted. 'A constant stream of violence and revenge won't solve anything. Pete, you must tell me if you are approached by that family. You must promise me not to do anything silly.'

'Fair enough.'

'Ben?'

'You know me, Jo, a quiet life is all I ask for.'

Joanna smiled and said, 'that's settled then. Let's try and get on with our lives.'

~

'Do you want me to come in with you?' asked Alan.

'I'd rather you stay in reception if you don't mind.'

'Whatever you want.'

The receptionist called Cheryl's name. 'Doctor Ellison, room nine.' She turned to give Alan one last look, their world changing. She couldn't help the sword of guilt running through her; the possibility of this young man, the man she loves, not being part of her future. Cheryl had considered telling him everything. Trevor Knight, Ralph Clements, even her first affair, with Roger Timmings. What should she say about Don Gil? She walked towards room nine gathering a swirl of uncertainties in her mind. Ashamed of her behaviour while at the same time developing a loving relationship with Alan, the only excuse she offered herself now inadequate. Making sure Alan was the right man for her, getting others out of her system, an inherent weakness in her character. The demons continued to patrol, chipping away in her head.

'Cheryl, good morning, take a seat.'

The examination and the urine test completed, Ellison confirmed Cheryl's assertion. Approximately eight weeks, a scan suggested at twenty weeks. Questions regarding the father elicited no greater response from Cheryl than 'my boyfriend is in reception.'

She thanked the doctor and closed the door, struggling with her conflicting emotions, forcing herself to be convinced that the boyfriend in reception was the man responsible. She wanted him to be that man.

'You okay?'
'Wait until we're in the car.'

Alan held her hand as they passed by rows of patients waiting their turn. A smile from the receptionist. As if practising for what Ben used to call 'dad mode', he closed the passenger door gently, walked round the car and sat next to her. Silence for over a minute, then she spoke as he squeezed her hand.

'Mid-January, fifteenth probably, but it can be a couple of weeks either side. It's only an estimate.'

'April' was all Alan could say.

'When do you want to tell your parents?' asked Cheryl.

'Tomorrow? I told Mom there were no lectures today, so we came back early, said we were doing some shopping. I'd like it to sink in tonight first. They will be so pleased.'

'I'd love to make them happy. Make you happy.'

~

Alan delivered the glass of water Cheryl had requested. Not for reasons of sickness – she had not yet succumbed to the early morning variety – but to give her hands something to do. Rising early when the sun is shining has, for most of us, the advantage of setting up the day. A quiet, positive, healthy start to the day. Sitting in the conservatory, waiting for Ben and Joanna, Cheryl reflected on the events of recent months. She wanted so much for Alan's parents to celebrate the news, and she wanted to celebrate with them. Joanna would have started her Saturday morning an hour earlier had she known the plan.

'They're coming,' said Alan, sitting nearest the window.

Joanna entered first, sat down next to Cheryl and kissed her.

'What is it?' asked Joanna, sensing the atmosphere.

'Hang on, Mom. Sit down, Dad.'

'What's wrong, Alan?'

'Will you tell them, or shall I?' asked Alan.

Cheryl leant forward and said 'Joanna, Ben, you're going to be grandparents.'

The Football Pools or NS&I could not have provided Joanna with a better start to her Saturday morning. She hugged Cheryl and cried openly. Ben was first to speak.

'We couldn't be more pleased. When, and what are your plans?'

'Oh Ben, let them sort themselves out in their own time!'

'No, it's fine, Mom. We thought you'd be pleased and, yes, we will get married before the baby is born. Mind you, it will have to be a small affair. Registry Office.'

'I understand,' said Joanna.

'Thought you would insist on church?'

'No. If it's not right for you, it wouldn't be right. I've always been aware of your views, and you must do what is right for you.'

'I can't believe you're being so understanding.'

'As your dad says – when?'

'Should be around 15th January,' answered Cheryl.

'My father's birthday. A proud great-grandad,' added Joanna.

~

Later, after they had caught up with Peter, Cheryl and Alan relaxed in the garden. Peter found his mother in the kitchen.

'Where's Dad?'

'Sorting out the garage. You know, his annual spring clean. Gives him thinking space, he claims.'

'Bit late for spring.'

'What do you think of the news, Peter?'

'Brilliant, really pleased. I'm going to be an uncle! Wonder if it's twins?'

'What makes you say that?'

'The Greta Armitage thing. "One day you will become four." That's what she said.'

'Don't repeat that in front of your dad.'

'I know, but do you agree?' asked Peter.

'Cheryl will have to wait for the first scan. Anyway, you know I don't hold with all that fortune-telling stuff.'

'You're the one who went to a séance, Mom.'

'I'd rather not talk about that. But, if they're not having twins, your theory is out of the window, isn't it?'

'Maybe it means something else.'

'Sometimes you are just like your dad, overthinking everything. Just let it happen, wish them the best and let them get on with it. We'll help them whenever they need it.'

'I do hope you're right, Mom. We couldn't tell Dad all that stuff. He's worse than me. You're probably right, I'm reading too much into what has been said.'

'It's not about being right, Peter. All I've ever wanted is to care for my family, and that now includes Cheryl and Hannah. I would do anything to protect you. Each of you. One day you will have a family of your own and you'll understand what I mean.'

'I do understand, Mom. Thank you for including Hannah. She's very fond of you and Dad.'

'You love her, don't you?' she asked.

'I've never been able to hide anything from you.'

21: Confession

The end of the summer term once again brought the family together. After completing his first-year exams, Alan was back home until the end of September. Joanna was grateful for the fortuitous timing, giving her the opportunity to spend time with her future daughter-in-law. Peter, growing ever closer to Hannah, was well-practised in fending off his mother's suggestions regarding marital harmony. Ben, for his part, did what every well-behaved middle-class father did best – continued to earn a crust, and dutifully arranged for time off to take his wife for a week with her parents in Scotland.

Cheryl had not yet given the merest hint that Alan might not be the proud father. Through the summer months, Hannah kept her promise and avoided any mention of the day in April that could change Cheryl's life. All their lives. In blissful ignorance, Alan watched Cheryl's every move, only being beaten to the draw by his mother whenever Cheryl needed a drink, sandwich, even a footstool to rest her swollen ankles. Pregnancy took its toll on the expectant mother, and, in the bosom of the Stone family, she wanted for nothing. Alan now had time to think. He considered the odd events of the past few months and ran back through the comments from his lecturer. Up to now, he had developed the greatest of respect for the man, while considering him to be eccentric. However, for the first time he began to wonder if his motives were as pure as they should be towards

Cheryl. What Alan didn't realise was that during the week that Ben and Joanna stayed in Scotland, Cheryl planned to finally tell him the truth. At least part of the truth.

'What do you mean I've not been the only one?'
'There have been other men.'
'I know, I'm not stupid. You were so much more experienced than me, even on the day we met.'
'No, Alan, I mean recently.'
'How recently?'
'Earlier in the year.'
'Christ, Cheryl, is the baby mine?'
'Of course it is.'
'How can you be so sure? Back in April, I was so busy. You spent time with Don Gil.'
'Spent time? What do you mean?'
'Coffee shop at uni, that day at his house...'
'To collect your phone...'
'Are you having an affair with him?'
'No.'
'Were you? Back then?'
'Alan, I'm trying to be straight with you. I did see two men a few months ago, but not Don. I couldn't. He gives me the creeps.'

She panicked but forced herself to stay calm. *Alan might finish with me now*, she thought. She was telling the truth but holding back the nagging fear that she had been raped. A dream that felt so real, and yet Don had been calm that day, so helpful, contacting Alan to ask him to collect her.

'Are you sure there's nothing else, Cheryl?'

'Alan, I am so sorry. I do love you, and I finished with the man who kept texting me months ago. Peter will tell you...'

'What the hell has Peter got to do with this?'

'I didn't mean to tell you about that. He found my phone at the barbeque. He read the texts and threatened to tell you if I let you down again.'

'So not only my girlfriend, who is having my baby, is disloyal, my bloody brother as well!'

'No, Alan, it's not like that. Please don't blame Peter. It was all my doing. Ditch me if you like, but I promise you everything has changed. I am having your baby. Please forgive me...'

'You must realise what you've done.'

Knowing how difficult this would be, Cheryl confessed early in the week. The house to themselves during the day, Peter and Hannah at work, she had all week to bring Alan round. Even Cheryl didn't realise how much he loved her. She had hurt him and begged him to give her another chance. He spat back his answer.

'Shove it. I'm going back to Manchester where I might be appreciated.'

'What does that mean?' Cheryl asked.

'You'll find out.'

He grabbed a bag, wallet and keys. Cheryl took his arm, avoided saying any more but tried to kiss him.

'You've ruined this, Cheryl. You're on your own.'

As he slammed the door and pressed the fob to open the car, Cheryl slumped to the floor in the hallway. She agreed with him - she had ruined their relationship. By the time she returned to the lounge to consider her position, Alan was already approaching the motorway junction.

During the two-hour journey to Manchester, Alan had still not calmed down. His first instinct was revenge. During the last semester, he had rebuffed the advances of Jenny Sammonds, a student on his course. They chatted over coffee between lessons, and he liked her. If not for Cheryl, he would have pursued her. Jenny made it obvious she wanted him. *If Cheryl wants other men, I'll have Jenny*, he thought. As he approached the student block car park, he made his mind up to find Jenny. *I'll make Cheryl realise what she's done.* In one movement, he opened the door of his room and threw his bag onto the bed. Jenny was in college that week, staying in the adjoining block. Within five minutes he was at her door.

'Alan, are you alright?'
'I need to talk to you, Jen.'
'What is it?'
Alan grabbed her around the waist, moved close to her and kissed her on the lips.
'Stop, Alan! Not like this!'
She sensed his anger through the passion.
'Sit down and talk to me. Something has happened, hasn't it? Cheryl?'

He told her everything, and Jenny realised that his only motive was revenge. She had enough self-respect to turn him down. She liked Alan, but it wouldn't work like this.

'Think it through, Alan. You have so much to lose. Do you love Cheryl?'

He had calmed down enough to know that whatever he decided, he must take time, on his own. The answer to Jenny's question was yes, he adored Cheryl and didn't want to lose her. He kissed Jenny on the cheek.

'Sorry.'

'What for?'

'Taking you for granted, and I was going to use you.'

'I understand.'

They sat for an hour, and then Alan returned to his room. He phoned Cheryl.

'I'm not going to ask anything of you, Alan, I don't deserve it.'

'I'll come back tomorrow, and we'll talk. But, one thing, Cheryl...'

'What's that?'

'Mom and Dad must never know.'

Alan returned home the following day, still hurting, but he would not stop loving Cheryl. They agreed they would hide their problems from Ben and Joanna.

'There's Peter and Hannah. They both know, and it's not their fault,' Cheryl reminded him.

'We'll talk to them tonight. I hate the secrets we keep in this family. It was bad enough hiding the issue of

Greta. You know, Cheryl, there is one thing I have to confess.'

'What is it, Alan?'

'Greta said, "she'll let you down". She was right, wasn't she?'

'What do you expect me to say? I would do anything to put things right. You must accept I'm being honest now.'

'I think I do. We'll see how it goes. The baby is what's important now.'

'Thank you, Alan. I can't believe how understanding you are.' She kissed him and then left him alone with his thoughts.

~

'I remember that day, Jo. It was a Tuesday. We had Bryan Adams singing at the reception...'

'Ben, you do exaggerate. Bryan Adams didn't sing at our wedding.'

'Well, we played his record, and I still stand by the title of the song today.'

'So, everything you do is for me?'

'Course it is.'

'You old softy.'

'What are we going to do for our twenty-fifth? Party, concert, meal?'

'We're definitely not having a party. I remember the last one with your friends from work. Not again thanks. What about a nice family meal?'

'Not just the two of us?'

'No, I'd like to include Alan, Cheryl, Peter and Hannah.'

'Sounds nice. Only three months away. Shall I book a table at The Swan?'

'Lovely idea. Table for six.'

'It's a deal.'

Through August and September, the Stone family were together. Not just physically close. They had shared a lot in a short time, and each of them appreciated the support they received from the others. The summer months passed with no repetition of the hassle and intimidation suffered by Joanna and Peter in particular. No one considered the collective state of mind to be a false sense of security. However, on 4th October, a seemingly innocuous event changed that. The event was a text. Not in itself significant because it appeared on Peter's phone, but due to the apparent identity of the sender.

22: The Text

'What made you two get married on Bonfire Night?' asked Peter.

'The wedding itself was during the day,' Ben replied.

'You know what I mean, Dad. Mind you, it drops nicely this year on a Saturday.'

'You are so perceptive,' said Joanna.

'You always were the brains of the family,' added Ben.

'Cheeky, but don't forget Alan is the one at university.'

The banter continued as Peter finished his breakfast. Alan and Cheryl were still in bed. Ben grabbed his keys and set off for the office. Joanna loved having all the family together, but she cherished her quiet chats with Peter. He smiled at her as she took his dish to be washed up, then settled in the living room with the local free paper. A contented moment for Joanna about to be shattered. She heard him cry out.

'Peter, what's wrong?'

'Mom, it's Jodie...'

'What do you mean?'

'Look at this...'

He passed her the mobile phone. She stared at the text, highlighted in luminous green, and turned her head towards him. A number that neither of them recognised, but the content and the sender's name caused similar feelings in both of them.

```
Peter, hope you're okay. Sorry I've not
been in touch. I've missed you so much and
I will always love you. Hope to see you
again one day. I've been told that your
dad will be joining me soon. All my love,
Jodie  x.
```

Joanna held Peter's hand and drew him close. His face drained of colour. His eyes filled with tears. For a few minutes, they did not speak - couldn't speak. She grabbed the phone, searching for the delete function.

'No, Mom! Leave it.'

'But it must be a prank, someone's sick joke.'

'I'll have to see if they send any more. For a moment I thought...'

'I know love, who would be so cruel, so sick-minded to do this. Are you alright?'

'Yes, but if I ever find the bastard who sent this...'

'We must keep this to ourselves.'

'I've already thought about that. We can't tell Dad, and there's no point asking the phone company. They're useless anyway, and it's bound to be a non-traceable pay-as-you-go. Criminals do that all the time.'

'Please don't tell Alan and Cheryl.'

'I wasn't going to. The fewer people get to hear about this the better. If we rise to it and make a fuss, they've beaten us.'

'Peter, are you going to the grave today?'

'Of course, it's 4th October. It's something I do.'

'Do you want me to go with you?'

'That would be nice. We'll pick up the flowers on the way.'

They had almost an hour to collect their thoughts and calm down before Alan and Cheryl surfaced. Alan, three days growth and badly in need of a haircut, Cheryl now showing prominently at six months. Joanna moved a chair for her to sit at the breakfast table. Alan noticed something between his mother and brother.

'What is it you two? What are you cooking up?' he asked.

'Nothing little brother, just wondering if you pair are aiming for the Lennon and Yoko Ono record.'

'What?'

'When they stayed in bed for a week. Peace and love and all that.'

'You're joking,' said Alan.

'Oh sorry,' said Cheryl. 'Was she the one who married that Beatle?'

'Yeh, that's the one,' answered Peter with a grimace, relieved to have deflected the young couple from the obvious atmosphere. He went on to say he was taking Joanna shopping, but Alan had remembered the date.

'It's today, you know, when you go...'

'Yes mate, it's today.'

~

'Those are nice, Peter.'

'Jodie's favourites.'

'Do you want me to wait in the car?'

'No. I'd rather not be on my own today.'

Joanna always knew the right thing to say, the right thing to do. She held Peter's arm as they worked their way through the rows of older graves, past the huge oak so familiar to him. A woman walked past, headscarf covering her face. Peter stopped. They turned. She had gone, out of sight, past the oak.

'What is it, Peter?'

'That scent, do you recognise it?'

'Very faint, but yes I know it.'

'The one I bought Jodie for her last birthday.'

As they approached the grave, they saw a single rose. At first, they didn't spot the small card attached.

'PETER, I STILL LOVE YOU.'

'Jodie would never write like that. Who the hell would do this?'

'Twisted minds,' replied Joanna, sensing the anger in his voice.

'Do you think it's the Enrights?'

'Not sure, Peter, but we'll have to get past this.'

'That woman, earlier. I didn't take any notice at first. Just a stranger visiting a churchyard, but the smell of that perfume. Jodie's favourite.'

'One of the assistants at school uses it, Liz sometimes wears it...'

Joanna tried to put the thought out of her mind. *Keith and Liz maybe, or Mrs Enright?* She decided to keep her thoughts to herself and persuade Peter to let it go. A sick joke - an extremely sick joke.

~

Later that day, Peter and Hannah met for coffee. He was surprised by her news.

'That's great, but when do you go?' Peter asked.

'End of the month.'

'You'll miss Mom and Dad's anniversary.'

'Sorry, Peter.'

'No, it's fine, your career is important. What's your new title?'

'Senior Linguist - I'll be working in the European Parliament.'

'Will I ever see you?'

'Of course. I can come home at weekends, and I get five days off every six weeks.'

'Sounds good, but I'll miss you.'

'I'll miss you too, but I'll have a flat of my own. Once I'm settled, you'll be able to come out.'

'It will be like visiting a dignitary.'

'Don't be silly, I'm only a translator.'

'Translate this.'

He held her close and kissed her. Disappointed, naturally, but so proud of her. If his life had taken a different course, he could have pursued a similar career. He loved Hannah, but recent events now threatened to place Jodie at the front of his mind. He'd said nothing to Hannah, but he missed Jodie more than ever. Now, he was destined for a part-time relationship with Hannah.

~

Two days before the anniversary meal, Cheryl's doctor advised her to rest. Due in two months, she was suffering severe cramps and felt tired most of the time. Another casualty for the celebrations.

'Lads, you'll both be able to make it, won't you?'

'No problem, Dad,' replied Peter, and there was a nod from Alan.

~

A few years had passed since the four members of the Stone family travelled together. Holidays in Scotland, the Lake District and Wales are a distant memory. Saturday 5th November 2016, the day when they were again together, travelling in the same car, towards the village.

23:   Towards the Village

'Shame the girls couldn't come tonight.'
'At least we've got our boys with us,' said Joanna.
'We're not twelve, Mom. Mind you, it does make a change.'
'Now lads, children's portions tonight?'
'Always the comedian, Dad,' replied Alan.

A mile from the village, Ben reflected on his life with Joanna and their two sons. He had been protected from the worst of the strange events of the past six months, but he still considered it to be a difficult year. The loss of his uncle and two friends from work, and the problems Peter had encountered. That was enough for Ben. Now they were putting those difficult times behind them and he would celebrate the happiest twenty-five years anyone could hope for.

~

It was unusual for John Backley to work Saturdays. The call came through just after four.
'Are you able to collect a package this evening?'
'Is it urgent?'
'It's my grandmother's birthday today and I haven't been able to get down to the Midlands this week. A relative has bought something on my behalf and I said I would arrange delivery.'
'Right. Where do I collect it from?'

'Thirty Beasley Road, Leeford, on the Wolverhampton side of the village. About quarter past seven, this evening?'

'No problem, Sir.'

John would never understand what compelled him to take the job. He mainly did trade deliveries, rarely dealing with the public. Small deliveries of the odd parcel were not economic. Somehow, he felt he had to do this one. Driving through the village, the Swan on his left, he was unaware that the Stone family had a table booked for four waiting for them.

~

'What time is it booked for, Dad?' asked Peter.
'Half-seven. Are you hungry?'
'Is he hungry? Silly question,' remarked Alan.

Twenty-five past seven. John Backley's transit approached the church. He grabbed the wheel tight as a child stepped off the pavement, the van lurching to the middle of the road.

Ben didn't see the white transit van. Joanna reminded him that Sunday's service was early that week. A minibus slowed down without indicating and pulled towards the gutter. Ben glanced in the mirror, indicated and pulled into the path of the oncoming transit. Someone screamed. A flash of light. The smell of petrol. Blackness...

24:   Crisis

I can't see anything. Total darkness, but I know a main road is only feet away. Traffic is going by. The scent of trees to my left, the edge of the pavement to my right. One foot in front of the other, paving slabs beneath my feet. Stand still for a moment. Is anyone here to help me? A bird's wing, flapping near a tree. I can sense the branches swaying, the wind gently brushing past. The rustle of grass, an animal, a squirrel. I'm in the middle of the pavement - safe there. A few steps, not too far, get your bearings. I'm on the left side of the road walking in the direction of the traffic passing close to the kerb. Standing now near a car park. A building to my left, a large building, shops, a clinic? Sit down now. Tired, dizzy. Need to sleep.

Walking through the village. The church, the Swan Inn, garage, optician's, baker's. Two hundred yards to the crossroads. I can see now. All my senses in overdrive. Shopkeepers opening shutters, the sound of an ambulance, the smell of fruit, exhaust fumes. Days pass, in and out of sleep. Pain sears through the side of my head.

The sounds and smells of the village change. I remember the aroma from the bakery first thing in the morning; that wonderful smell of freshly baked bread evoking memories of home, childhood. Good memories. I remember the fruit on the market. I remember the old man's cigarette smoke, and the sounds of the shutters rattling and creaking as shops open, ready for business. Ready to start another day. I recall an ambulance rushing by, cars pulling over. No longer a sumptuous aroma of freshly baked bread, no tangy taste of exotic fruit. No cigarette smoke.

No creaking shutters. Cars glide soundlessly past, ambulance sirens on silent. No smells, no sounds, nothing. The sounds, smells, tastes, the senses that sparked in my dream, if it was a dream, have left me with a strange reality.

No one notices me, no one speaks. Not even Uncle Graham or my friends, Joe and Teresa. I remember I have a family. We were happy. There is a voice, maybe my own thoughts. It's all I have now. Something, someone is telling me I'll never go back. Where is this coming from? There is a threshold, a boundary, a window of time. I don't want to walk towards The Cross. I've never seen anyone return from there. He is imploring me to move on, cross the threshold. Do I know this voice or is it my imagination? I am so confused, and consumed with grief, grieving the loss of my family. I sense they are well, but they can't reach me.

The voice in my head is getting louder. He wants me to go to The Cross, go over The Cross, over the threshold. Someone else is trying to talk to me, but the man's voice, yes, I'm sure it's a man's voice, is controlling everything. I think he is the reason I am here. I force myself to walk away from The Cross. I am in the park again. Peaceful, serene, I forget how long I've been sitting on the bench. Another day must have passed. There is a note. It wasn't there when I sat down:

'Keep away from him. Don't go to him. You still have a chance to get back. A friend.'

This from someone who has tried to speak to me, trying to get through. I walk back to the village. At the crossroads, the boundary to my right, I turn left to find the familiar village high street. Still no sounds. Still the people rush past as if I'm not there. They can't see me. I don't know if I exist in this place, but I need to get back to the church, where it started.

Can't remember what happened. I can see the church, but I am held back. Pain in my head and neck again. A bright light hurts my eyes, a strong wind holds me back. I am not strong enough to move forward. He is talking to me again.
'Turn around, you must go through the village. Cross the threshold.'

A woman's voice. I don't recognise this voice, but she sounds old, so it's not Joanna. That's right, Joanna. I must hold on to the life I used to know. Joanna, Peter and Alan. Where are they? This woman's voice, it's not my mother. She's speaking clearly now.
'I said we would meet on the other side. Do what he says. Cross the threshold, walk over the boundary. Then you will be with us.'

'No!'
Someone is shouting, screaming.

It takes a moment until I realise the voice is mine. Some fight left in me. She sounded kind, but I sense she is being used. The man's voice appears again, this time not just in my head. He's close. He wants to meet.
'All you have to do is take just a few short steps.'

I've heard this voice before, but he sounds so... self-assured, speaking with authority. This is his domain. He controls where we go. I want to see him. Slowly, I turn round. The effort, or the movement, makes me dizzy. A faint outline of a man. Tall, dark-haired, but I can't make out his features. He is close now, his hands on my shoulders. His unpleasant breath floats towards me. I can taste evil. He gently pushes me, encouraging me to step towards the threshold.
'Not far now, Ben. Just two more steps. You'll be with your parents and your uncle...'
'Liar!' someone shouts from a distance, as I stumble to the ground. Feeling faint again, vision failing, a huge force surges through my chest. Thrown upwards, I then crash to the ground. My own heart is thumping, pushing against my ribcage, pulsing with blood. I cry out Joanna's name. For the first time since I arrived in the village, I can hear her voice. As if carried by the wind from the church end of the village, her words reach me and give me hope.
'Ben, we all love you. Please stay with us.'

I manage to get to my feet. He is behind me, pushing me ever closer to the threshold. For a second I think it would be easier to give in. Now there are voices on the other side, imploring me to join them. It's easier to concede defeat. How much more of this can I take? I am so tired. I have never seen anyone return from the threshold. No one seems able to return from this point. His hands in the small of my back, as he makes one last effort to push me into oblivion. To join those other voices. Then I hear another woman's voice. Again, it's familiar.

'Do not cross the boundary! There is no way back once you have crossed over. You are not ready yet.'

Someone, not sure if it's the woman speaking to me, gently takes my hands and pulls me back. The man roars obscenities at her, commanding her to leave, but she holds on. I am tempted, for an instant, to concede. I dare not believe who the woman might be. I just accept that she is on my side. My instinct now tells me there is a way back to the life I had before.

I am at the church. I can see Joanna, Peter and Alan in the distance. They are calling for me. I must make one last effort. A blinding light, someone is holding my hand. Every part of my body aches, and as I make one final step away from the village, I take one last look. I can see him now. Without the help I received, he would have driven me into another life.

25: Lost days

'Ben, can you hear me?'
The consultant checked Ben's pulse and nodded to the nurse.
'They can come in now.'

Joanna, Peter and Alan were led into the room by the nurse who had kept them informed throughout the crisis. Ben had been in a coma for over two weeks and his consultant warned Joanna that brain damage was a possibility. If he pulled through. He'd taken the full force of the impact in the accident, sustaining a serious head injury. He also had eight broken ribs, a fractured collar bone and both legs were broken. His right knee shattered, Ben expected a succession of operations in the coming months. He was lucky to be alive, but ironically his condition worsened as he came out of the coma. The crash team were called minutes after his eyes flickered for the first time. The doctors sent for Joanna and then Ben stopped breathing. All vital signs at zero, Joanna was ushered out of the room as the defibrillator shocked Ben back into life.

'This sometimes happens,' the doctor explained to Joanna. 'His brain has been recovering from the trauma. As he came round, his body went into shock. I think we have seen the worst.'
'Can we talk to him?'
'Yes, that's the best thing for him now. Just take it steady. You've been through a lot.'

When the transit van hit the front of their car, Joanna was thrown forwards, breaking her left arm. Alan and Peter, both badly shaken, walked away relatively unscathed. The angle of impact had spun the back of the car round so only the driver's side took the full impact. Alan, sitting behind his father, was particularly lucky. The van had sliced away the front of the car, but behind Ben's seat there was relatively little damage. They will never know how Ben survived.

'Ben, it's Jo, can you hear me?'

She could barely recognise him. His right eye was badly swollen and every part of his face and upper body covered in bruises. His eyelids flickered, and he managed to open his left eye. The nurse held his shoulders gently, easing him forwards for his first drink.

'Steady now, Ben.'

Joanna kissed him lightly on the back of his hand.

'We'll leave you to rest,' she said, as Ben succumbed to the painkillers, but this time drifted into a soothing sleep.

~

'I'm not going with you. I want to be with my family...'

As Ben came round, Joanna held his hand and smiled.

'We're here, how are you feeling?'

'Joanna... thought I'd lost you.'

'I'm going nowhere without you Mr Stone.'

'He wanted to take me.'
'Who wanted to take you?'
'Don't know his name, but he sounded familiar.'
'Rest now love, you're in hospital.'
'What happened?'
'We had a crash. Do you remember, our anniversary meal?'
'Yes, that's the last thing I remember. Jo, what's the date?'
'Twenty-sixth of November.'
'I've lost twenty-one days.'
'Don't worry, we'll make up for lost time. Just rest now, I want to get you home.'
'Jo, your arm – the crash?'
'Yes, but it's fine, the plaster will be off in six weeks.'
'I'm sorry, Jo. Were the lads hurt?'
'No, just a bit shaken, but they're fine.'
'That's a relief.'

The consultant broke the news to Ben that an early exit from the hospital was unlikely. However, thanks to his rapid recovery from the head injury, surgery on his damaged knee could now go ahead, the doctors considering it too dangerous in the first three weeks after the accident. Little chance of being home for Christmas. The impact of this was softened by the news brought to him by Alan and Cheryl. They had arranged a registry office wedding two weeks before Christmas. Ben would be taken in a wheelchair by nursing staff to the ceremony. Alan had discussed the situation with the consultant before making the final decision.

The baby was due in mid-January and the Christmas holiday made arrangements difficult, but he didn't want his father to miss the occasion. They would have a delayed reception combined with a homecoming for Ben as soon as possible in the New Year. Ben's private health insurance gave him some control over the care he received and the timings of surgery. The neck brace was to be removed before the wedding, but Ben would be using a wheelchair for at least a month. He surprised himself with his own demeanour. Survival brought relief. Being reunited with his family gave him more than that. Between visiting times, he went over the events of the two weeks that he was in a coma, convinced that something had actually happened but unable to bring himself to tell Joanna everything. There was so much his family had kept from him - he was unable to make the links.

Joanna had been told that a young man visited Ben on the one evening in the first two weeks that she didn't visit. From the description the nurse provided, Alan was able to identify the visitor.

'Frank Carter.'

'The lad from school?' asked Joanna.

'Yes, a few years ago now. What the hell was he doing visiting Dad?'

'If I see him, he'll regret it,' Peter added.

'Let's not be hasty. Dad's going to be okay, but I'll have a word with the sister. No visitors without my agreement.'

'Good idea, Mom.'

~

Joanna had not seen Liz since the summer. From her tone, she knew it was important. Liz, distraught when hearing about Ben, needed to speak to Joanna.

'I don't want to do this over the phone.'

'Coffee shop, tomorrow morning?' said Joanna. 'On my way to the hospital.'

Liz agreed to collect Joanna and take her to see Ben. On the way, they had an hour to catch up. Joanna could see that Liz needed to unburden herself.

'I'm so glad that Ben is going to be alright.'

'He's disappointed he won't be home for Christmas, but at least he can get out for the wedding.'

'Another operation the following day?'

'Yes, but he should be home in time for the baby.'

'You must be so excited, even considering what you've been through.'

'Of course, but Liz, what is it? There's something wrong, isn't there?'

'Do you know that I haven't heard from Keith since he left months ago?'

'I'm sorry it didn't work out.'

'No, it's not that. I needed to tell you. For months before the barbeque, he was always asking about Ben. He knew stuff as well.'

'What do you mean, "he knew stuff"?'

'Someone had been giving him information about all of you, but particularly Ben, and he seemed to want confirmation.'

'About what?'

'Where Ben was working, times of meetings, when he was having a day off, appointments and...'

'Come on, Liz.'

'Well, for instance, the date of your anniversary and what you were planning to do.'

'Are you sure?'

'Jo, I've been worried about this for months. After what's happened, I wish I'd spoken to you earlier.'

'It's not your fault, Liz. And anyway, it was an accident.'

'There is something else. I heard him on the phone a few times. A couple of days before the barbeque he spoke to a man and said his name. I think you're in for a shock.'

'What was his name?'

'Don.'

Whatever she did now, Jo knew she couldn't tell Ben. He needed to stay calm and have chance to recover. She wanted to act quickly. *Speak to Alan and Peter*, she thought. *All the stuff Liz has said, it must be the same man - Don Gil.*

~

26:   Hannah

'No, Mom. Hannah's not phoned for over a week,' said Peter.

'But she knows about the accident.'

'Of course, she asked about you and Dad. She sounded really upset. I've left loads of messages.'

Joanna sighed.

'Have you got a works number for Hannah in Brussels?'

'No, just a mobile.'

'Do you know her manager's name?'

'She never mentioned details, but I've got the name of the hotel she's staying in.'

'Perhaps give them a ring.'

'Thanks, Mom, you've got a lot on your plate what with Dad, and the wedding.'

'I care about all of you. Hannah is family now.'

Peter did not have the opportunity to reply, as Alan and Cheryl came into the living room. Joanna sensed that something was wrong.

'Alan?' said Joanna.

'It's weird. No reply from Don. I submitted my assignment weeks ago.'

'Maybe he's busy,' suggested Peter.

'He's usually on the ball with marking. Here's the thing. I just phoned the uni office. No one has seen him for over a week.'

'Is he ill?' asked Peter.

'That's where it gets peculiar. I spoke to Jack, a mate at college. He's on the same course. Someone went round to Don's house. They peered through the front window. No curtains. It's empty, and the house is up for sale.'

'What does this mean?' asked Joanna.

'He's gone. No trace. He's cleared all his stuff from his office. No one has a clue what's happened, but of course, the staff don't really want to discuss it.'

~

After years of thinking he could never love anyone else after Jodie, Peter had decided that he wanted to be with Hannah for the rest of his life – the dream about to be shattered. He spent most of the day contacting hotels, hospitals and various EU departments in Brussels. The nightmare began. No one had heard of Hannah. No one of that name (or anyone fitting her description) had been employed as a linguist.

'I'll have to go out there.'

'I'm so sorry Peter, but what will that achieve?' asked Joanna.

'I've got to do something.'

'I have an idea. Simon Hill is a friend of our local MP. I'll ring him now and, hopefully, he can do some digging.'

'Thanks, Mom. What the hell has happened?'

Peter tried to contact Hannah's parents. Number unobtainable. He had met them a few times at their house and stayed over on one occasion after returning from a concert with Hannah in the early hours of the morning. Joanna offered to go with him to see them.

'What are they like?'
'They're nice. I got on well with them.'
'Is it far?'
'Just the other side of town,' replied Peter, grabbing his keys from the coffee table.

~

In less than twenty minutes they were outside Hannah's parents' house. Peter opened the car door and helped his mother onto the pavement. No car on the drive, and Joanna noticed at once – no curtains. She walked up to the main front window.

'Peter, I can hardly believe this. The front room is completely empty. It's as if they never lived here.'

'I saw them a few days before the accident. I've just realised – the anniversary card they sent to give to you is still in my room.'

There was nothing else they could do at the house. Peter didn't want to involve the police, so they agreed to wait for the MP to get back to Simon, or maybe directly to Joanna. Simon Hill, the headmaster at Joanna's school, phoned the following morning.

~

'Jo, this is a real puzzle. John Bifford contacted a couple of MEPs in his party and an official he knows in Brussels. Hannah has never applied for a job as a linguist at the EU let alone started working for them. No one has heard of her.'

'What do you suggest?'

'You mentioned James Enright and his cousin. Why don't you ask Mrs Enright? A long shot, I admit, but it's all very strange.'

'Thanks, Headmaster. Sorry to trouble you. I'll pop into school in the next few days. I'd love to get back to work.'

'Jo, leave it until after Christmas now. We've arranged cover. Get yourself right and look after that husband of yours.'

Joanna and Peter wasted no time in driving over to the Enright house. A shock awaited them. Mrs Enright hadn't seen James for over a week. He'd packed an overnight bag, telling his mother he was working away for a few days. Terry Hickens came to collect him, and James tried to persuade his mother to stay inside. Before the car pulled away, she spotted two women in the car. One, a middle-aged woman with blond hair, the other, a woman in her early twenties.

'Pretty girl. Long, auburn hair.'
'Have you seen either of them before?' asked Peter.
'No, I've never seen Terry or James with girls before.'
Peter nudged Joanna.
'That was Hannah. No idea who the other woman is.'

They got back to the house, Joanna surprised by how calmly Peter was taking it. This would soon change. Hannah had left a few personal belongings in Peter's room, but he didn't expect to find her mobile.

'Mom, check this out.'

'She didn't take her phone, did she, Peter? Are you going to check the texts and calls?'

'Hang on, this isn't Hannah's usual phone. It's a pay-as-you-go. What the...'

Peter now reached the stage when he knew he would never see Hannah again. In the *Sent* box, he saw his own name. As Joanna watched, he clicked 'open text'.

```
Peter, hope you are okay. Sorry I've not
been in touch. I've missed you so much and
I will always love you. Hope to see you
again one day. I've been told that your
dad will be joining me soon. All my love,
Jodie   x.
```

Tears filled Peter's eyes and Joanna held him, understanding immediately what Hannah had done.

'I can't believe that a person could be so cruel. You've got to forget her, Peter. I think this is all about your dad.'

'She used me.'

'She used all of us, with the help of James and Terry.'

Alan and Cheryl had arrived back from Manchester and heard most of the conversation.

'I can't believe she would do this to you,' said Alan.

He asked Peter to describe the other woman in the car. It may have been third hand (via Mrs Enright), but he recognised her at once from that description.

'I wondered when she would re-appear. Melanie Crowther...'

~

A small room at the registry office, holding no more than fifteen, provided the setting for a fresh start for Alan and Cheryl. She had told him everything about her life except for the one thing she couldn't bear to repeat – the hour she spent at Don Gil's house. Something Cheryl didn't realise was that Alan had received an anonymous text from the phone Hannah used. He was aware of the incident with Don. Unable to establish if she had been dreaming, he wouldn't blame Cheryl anyway if Don had abused her. He knew everything and he was prepared to tell Cheryl that one day. For now, they would concentrate on starting a new life together – with the baby. Joanna had organised a buffet back at the house, giving everyone time to catch up with each other. Alan approached his brother, asking if he knew about Don and Cheryl.

'Sorry I didn't tell you, mate. When I was with Hannah, I trusted her completely. She told me not to tell you.'

'I found out anyway.'

'I'm sorry, Alan, but it does explain what Greta Armitage meant.'

'You mean "you will become four"?'

'I suppose that meant you, Cheryl, the baby and... Don Gil.'

'I hope that Don is out of our lives now.'

'So do I, Alan.'

~

Joanna sat quietly by herself in the conservatory, mulling over the events of the last few months. When James Enright had said 'your future daughter-in-law will cause you nothing but trouble', she was now convinced he meant Hannah, not Cheryl. Hannah had left Peter at the point where he had allowed her into his heart. Not *instead* of Jodie, but alongside her. Joanna, relieved that her son seemed capable of starting again, considered if she could bring herself to put Ben in the picture. As she turned towards the window overlooking the garden, she realised that Ben was sitting beside her.

'I didn't see you come in.'

'Sorry, love, you were in a world of your own. You okay? Are you happy about Alan and Cheryl?'

'Yes, of course. I couldn't be happier.'

She told Ben about James Enright – the things he had said – and found herself unloading the burden made up of six months of secrets. Surprised that he already knew some of the story, she nonetheless told him every detail: Terry Hickens, Peter, Alan, Cheryl, Greta Armitage, Melanie Crowther, Frank Carter, and of course, Don Gil. It was now clear that Liz had been an innocent victim all along. She had genuinely tried to help by accompanying Joanna to the séance, then found herself used by Keith, evidently an associate of Don Gil. The remaining mystery in Joanna's mind was *why*.

'This Don Gil character. How far does his influence spread do you think?'

'Ben, I'm not sure. Let's hope this is the end of the matter. We've all been hurt in different ways, and we nearly lost you.'

'I'll never leave you, Jo. Not if I can help it.'

'Ben...'

She hesitated, and he smiled as he realised what was coming next.

'In the hospital, you said that someone wanted to take you. Was that in a dream as you came out of the coma?'

'Must have been. Let's try to forget it.'

'If we can...'

Joanna had levelled with Ben, but he was unable to bring himself to tell her about his time in the village. Something that felt so real, so personal, but he forced himself to dismiss it as Joanna had described it – a dream. This would continue as he recovered through the Christmas period and into January with the birth of their first grandchild.

27:   Don Gil

'Dad, I'm so pleased you're here,' said Alan, as he met his parents in the corridor.

'How could I miss this? I'm so proud of you. How are they?'

'You and Mom can come through soon. Cheryl's fine, just very tired. Joshua is doing great.'

Joanna put her arms around Alan and squeezed until he forced his way out of the embrace.

'Mom, you're crushing me,' he joked.

The nurse beckoned to them. The proud father first into the room, followed by the proud grandparents.

'Oh Alan, he's beautiful,' Joanna said, not even trying to hold back her tears.

'How are you, Cheryl?' asked Ben.

'Exhausted, but very happy. Thanks, Ben.'

The following weeks provided no respite for the Stone family. Joanna had a particularly busy time, admirably fulfilling the role of helpful grandmother at the same time as returning to work.

The supply teacher's contract finished at Christmas and Joanna didn't want to take advantage of Simon Hill's good nature. Still recovering, Ben was nonetheless capable of filling and heating bottles and even retrieved his nappy-changing skills. Alan stayed at home, travelling two days each week for important lectures. Cheryl was grateful for the support of three people dedicated to both her and Joshua.

After the accident, no one heard from Don Gil or his associates. It was clear that he had been assisted throughout by people who betrayed the trust of the Stone family. James and Terry virtually terrorised Joanna and Peter, Keith used Liz to gain access to the family, Melanie Crowther manipulated Alan at the care home, and Hannah almost destroyed Peter. Ben was unable to talk about his own experiences. Joanna realised that all the events were related, the common factor being Ben, and no doubt linked to the death of his parents. Beyond that, she did not understand why the family should be persecuted. She told Ben about the séances and Lydia's theories on predestination. Ben possessed no deep religious faith. He did not believe that their lives were set out and controlled from the start. In truth, he did not know what to believe, but his pragmatic nature enabled him to live from day to day. The family as united and happy as it had been for many years, except for Peter's situation.

Three months passed. Ben had returned to work but arranged for a day working at home. The phone call he received changed everything.

'Who is this?' he asked.

'I think you know, but for now, I just want you to listen...'

'What the hell do you want?' he interrupted.

'What I have to say cannot be challenged. You were fortunate that other forces delayed the inevitable.

However, you will hear what I have to say. If not today, it will be tomorrow or the next day...'

Again, Ben interrupted, but he knew it was not going to help. He recognised the voice - he had a picture of a grey, gaunt face in his mind. No one, not even Joanna, had any idea what he had been through in the village, and even Ben could not be sure if it was reality. Images of his parents came into his mind. *This is what it's about*, he thought. *I will listen to him. I have no choice.*

'It was written that you would die with your parents. It was your destiny, and the mistake must be corrected.'

'I know who you are,' replied Ben. 'Leave my family in peace, and if that means I have to sacrifice myself, I am prepared to do that.'

'If only you had the power to decide your own fate, but you don't. You made a grave mistake. You should have crossed the boundary when I instructed you. You should not have gone back. You were warned. You will now suffer the consequences.'

'What do you mean? Why don't you have the guts to face me? I'm not afraid anymore.'

'Now is not your time, but you will live to regret your actions. And your friends cannot protect you forever.'

Ben took a deep breath before speaking again.

'What's going to happen?'

The line was quiet for a few seconds. Ben knew that he was still there, but he was not prepared for the final words from Don Gil. Before cutting the line, he said six words:

'My son will join me soon...'

Part Two

28: Honesty

Six months passed. Alan completed his second year at Manchester. No one at college mentioned Don Gil; his books gone, his house sold, the staff instructed not to speak his name. The closest they came to that might be 'your previous lecturer told you about...' and they moved on. No students were aware of what Alan and Cheryl endured. They had trusted Don, and he always intended to betray that trust.

There was no sign of Hannah, as if she never existed. Peter tried to trace her parents. Nothing. Ben was convinced they had been placed by Gil. The others, foot soldiers, did his bidding. From schooldays, Frank Carter bullied Alan. As he performed in his band, Peter encountered Terry Hickens. Terry's cousin, James Enright, tried to terrorise Joanna. She was made of sterner stuff – *he would never beat Mom*, thought Peter. They must have considered Alan the weak point in the family. Even as he took a part-time job in the care home, Greta Armitage, in her dying days, gave him strange messages for his father. Melanie Crowther was there to make sure life was difficult for both Alan and Peter, instrumental in the episodes at the graveside. Peter found it incredible that they even knew Jodie's favourite perfume and used that to unsettle him. Then there were the messages, supposedly from Jodie. Peter still loved her, and always would, even if he one day met someone else. Hannah was never going to replace Jodie, but he had loved her. From now on, he would find it difficult to trust another woman except for his mother.

Joshua, now eight months old, was a delight to his parents and grandparents. Alan believed that Joshua was truly his son, and even if Don Gil *had* violated Cheryl, Alan neither blamed Joshua nor Cheryl for that. He knew that she had been with several men, but he believed in his heart that they had drawn a line so the past, if not forgotten, could be filed away. Meanwhile, Ben held Joshua on his knee and gave thanks that the family is together and safe.

Ben's nightmares were less frequent, but still there. He and Joanna never discussed the phone call Ben received from Don Gil. He had preferred to keep it from Joanna, but she'd heard most of it.
'Ben, what did you mean when you said you'd sacrifice yourself?'
'Leave it with me, Jo, I'll deal with it.'
'What did he say at the end? You couldn't speak when you put the phone down.'
'Nothing Jo, he was just winding me up. I'd rather not talk about it just now.'

They were still not aware of the incident at Don Gil's house. His words had struck home, and Ben played them over in his mind constantly: 'my son will join me soon.'

Ben picked up bits and pieces when overhearing petty arguments between Alan and Cheryl. He concluded that

Cheryl must have had an affair with Don in Manchester, spending time alone there during April and May the previous year, as Alan carried out his work at The Meadows. Yes, The Meadows, aware of Greta Armitage in particular. Had he heard her voice in the village? He still hadn't levelled with Joanna over his terrifying experience. She still mentioned his 'dream' from time to time and Ben always responded in the same way.

'Yes, Jo, that's all it was – a dream,' trying to convince himself.

His lack of faith would still not allow him to believe that he had somehow crossed over to the other side, unable to use the phrase 'the next life' or 'another life'. *A transitional existence?* thought Ben. Jo told him that he 'died' for a few seconds. Could it be, like the way we experience dreams in a different timeframe to our woken state, that he had been close to the next life? Ben had read stories about near-death experiences – tunnels, bright lights, familiar voices – and up to now he had not believed a word. He still didn't accept the possibility but could not dismiss at the very least the many coincidences he had experienced. Don Gil was part of this, he knew that. He considered - *did Don Gil use hypnosis?* He seemed to have enormous power over several people, and, in their last conversation, Don used the connection with Alan and Cheryl, and, in particular, Ben's precious grandson.

~

'Time for a chat, just the three of us?' Ben said, aiming his question at Alan and Cheryl.

'Anything wrong, Dad?'

'No, just need to talk to you, son.'

Cheryl had grown close to both Joanna and Ben. She was getting used to their ways, and sometimes it just needed a look, a sigh, a sideways glance, and she could pick up the essence of the other person's mood. She sensed there was something. Alan squeezed her hand as they sat together on the two-seater sofa. Ben pulled up a dining chair, trying to avoid Cheryl's gaze for now. He wasn't going to find this particularly easy.

'Please don't be offended, and whatever you say stays with us. Cheryl, we've grown to love you and you know we adore young Josh.'

'Ben, what's wrong?' Cheryl asked, looking straight at him.

Ben surprised Alan by taking both of Cheryl's hands.

'When you were in Manchester,' he paused and breathed in. 'Did you see anyone else?'

'Dad, you can't ask that,' Alan said, raising his voice.

'It's alright, Alan,' said Cheryl, 'Ben deserves to know. Okay, Ben, I'm going to be honest with you.'

Tears filled her eyes as she told him the story of her trip to Don's house - the bus ride, the mobile phone, the drink he gave her and how she felt afterwards. Ben was silent for a while. He walked towards the French windows, trying to find something on which to focus, trying to keep calm. Cheryl hadn't mentioned the other men, but this had still opened up the possibility that Don was Joshua's father. A direct link in Ben's mind to his last conversation with Don still shocked him, even though he had half expected it. Cheryl was crying and Alan did not move. Ben crouched down and then knelt on the floor. Taking her hands once again, he kissed her on the cheek. Alan continued to stare at the floor, unable to contribute.

'I'm so sorry, Ben. What will Joanna think?'

'I'll find a way of telling her. Jo won't blame you and neither do I. We both love you and Josh. I'm glad we've talked. Are you alright, Alan?'

'Sorry, Dad. This is so difficult.'

~

'No, Ben, I won't accept it,' said Joanna. 'I can't believe that Cheryl even went to his house on her own.'

'I believe her, Jo. We can't prove it, but when you take into account everything that's happened, it makes sense.'

'How did Alan take it?'

'He's had more time to get used to it. He doesn't blame Cheryl – nor should he.'

'You're right, love, but it's such a shock. Anyway, is this all part of the family being honest with each other?'

'What do you mean, Jo?'

'You need to tell me, Ben. You need to tell me what you've been through. We've told you everything now, I think. But help me with this, please. Even if it *was* a dream, you must admit it's had a profound effect on you.'

Ben considered Joanna's words and decided she was right. He started with his first few moments in the village when he woke up to total darkness, then the experience of his senses changing and how he explored his environment.

'To me, it was real, and it took some time, but I started to remember you and the boys.'

'How long did you think you were there?'

'Seemed like weeks.'

Joanna, horrified when Ben described his battle near The Cross and the voices he heard, finally understood the trauma he had experienced. She was unable to bring herself to believe that he had placed one foot in the next life, even with her faith, but was convinced how real it had been to Ben.

'You should see our GP.'

'What for?'

'The stress you've been under has been horrific, especially after the head injury and being in a coma.'

'I'm fine now.'

'Ben...'

'I'll go if it gets worse. Anyway, you of all people should understand and believe this stuff.'

'What do you mean? That's not fair.'

'The next life and all that, and now I've told you exactly what Don said on the phone...'

'You mean about Josh?'

'If that's what he meant. Don't get me wrong, I'm not accepting everything was real, but I do have the feeling that Don is somehow trying to control my destiny – and yours.'

'You're scaring me now, Ben. What can we do?'

'Not much we can do except watch out for each other, and especially Josh.'

~

Joanna closed the living room door, taking the opportunity to have a conversation with Peter.

'I've booked your dad an appointment with Doctor Evans.'

'Is he okay?'

'Physically, almost back to normal, but the whole Don Gil business has shaken him.'

'Nightmares again? America?'

'Yes Peter, you know how it is.'

'How did you get him to agree?'

'He doesn't know yet. I asked him if he'd clear some time in his diary to take me shopping in Brum. But we're not going shopping.'

'Sneaky, Mom. You're braver than me.'

The sound of the front door opening and closing, followed by Ben's usual 'hi, love, I'm home' prompted Joanna to bring the conversation to an end.

'He's here now. Make yourself scarce and I'll break the news to him.'

Ben smiled as he opened the door. Whatever sort of day he's had, the sight of Joanna was the tonic he needed. She combined an advance apology with the explanation about Ben's upcoming doctor's appointment. The reaction was as she expected, but he gave in gracefully.

'No pills mind you. I'm not going to be a walking zombie.'

'Doctor Evans isn't like that.'

'A zombie?' asked Ben, with a grin.

'You know what I mean. He doesn't reach for the prescription pad as you step into his room.'

'I give in, Jo. I'm only doing it for you.'

~

'You should see a specialist or at least one of our counsellors.'

'Doctor, I've explained. All this has been done *to* me. I can't help my reaction.'

'Are you still having nightmares about losing your parents?'

'Sometimes. I wouldn't even call them nightmares. I'm just there, up to the point of the crash. Sometimes I wake up before the car flips over.'

'Are you able to control the dreams?'

'There's the strange thing. No, I don't think I can, but I always feel that someone else is.'

'Do you know who it is?'

'The man that caused most of this.'

'Ben, I know this sounds strange, but have you considered talking to the police?'

'They can't do anything. For a start, we have to prove that he's broken any laws, and it would pile on the stress for Jo and the lads.'

'Just a thought. Anyway, will you consider seeing a counsellor?'

'I'll think about it...'

~

Ben had a good team around him at National Flooring, much of his work being delegated. His friends and colleagues, not aware of the distress he had suffered, assumed the physical injuries were gradually healing. A terrible accident, but an accident just the same. On that basis, his fellow directors took on most of his duties, and it was, fortunately, a quiet period in terms of system developments and company restructuring. As financial director, Ben was responsible for such functions. The company had been through a few takeovers in recent years. Ben was grateful that, to some extent, treading water for a while was a viable option. He would never neglect the business, but he needed a period of calm and stability. His family and business colleagues afforded him such freedom.

Travelling to the office three days a week gave him a few days at home with Joanna and Joshua – Cheryl incredibly grateful for that. On the journeys to his Cotswold office, he used the time to think back to the people involved in the past year - the strangest of his life. Even though 1984 had been the most stressful. He had always been aware that one student at school brought out feelings of hatred from Joanna completely against her usual nature. Relieved he had left their lives, Ben nonetheless felt guilty that he failed to support his wife more at the time, being under the impression that Joanna could handle anyone – she usually did – but James Enright presented a different challenge. After it transpired he was the cousin of Terry Hickens, it made Ben feel even worse. Terry, responsible for the beatings meted out to Peter, supposedly over dalliances with Terry's girlfriend, seemed to be in the pocket of Don Gil. Why that should be, and what role Terry played now, remained a mystery to Ben.

Keith, a somewhat peripheral character, used Jo's friend Liz to get close to the family. Liz, good-hearted but naive, unwittingly fed him information that the Stone family would rather have kept private. She had no malicious intent, other than perhaps homing in on a possible romantic connection with Ben, even to the point of jeopardising her close friendship with Joanna. Ben could not help the glimmer of a smile pulling at the corner of his lips as he recalled the bathroom incident at the barbeque party. It had caused Joanna to doubt Liz's integrity, but she forgave her friend a single indiscretion after it became clear that Keith used Liz throughout their relationship, feeding information back to his master. Also, Liz revealed, it was Keith's suggestion that Ben might reciprocate her advances.

If needing further evidence that his battle with Don Gil was long-standing, Ben considered the relevance of Frank Carter. Had he known of the bullying at the time he would have dealt with it. Peter, it emerged, stepped in to protect his younger brother. Pride in his elder son, however, failed to override Ben's irritation with his own lack of awareness and inability to protect Alan. *My responsibility, I'm the father. Strange though, Frank Carter being involved at such an early stage, and words that he uttered back then being repeated five years later. How does all this work*, he mused. Melanie Crowther – obviously linked to Carter (mother, stepmother, aunt?) – managed to place herself in Alan's life. Too complicated to work out how she held a senior position at the care home where Alan applied for part-time work. *Coincidence? There are too many coincidences here,* thought Ben.

Greta Armitage sent Ben the message (one he didn't receive at the time): 'meet me on the other side'. *Did I hear her voice at The Cross in the village?* he thought. Again, a close connection with Crowther, Carter and, of course, Don Gil; Alan convinced that all three attended Greta's funeral, not appreciating the connection at the time. As Ben approached the long driveway at National Flooring, he thought of Hannah. How they had loved her, considering her to be the future for Peter. How Ben now hated Hannah for what she'd done. He felt in some way that Peter had come off worst of all, although his son would never accept that. He lost Jodie in tragic circumstances and fell in love with a girl who betrayed him, even to the extent of impersonating Jodie. Then she disappeared. *How will Peter ever recover*, he thought to himself, clicking the key fob and walking towards reception for at least a few hours of normality.

29: Ben's Research

Ben became obsessed with the notion of the afterlife and assumed that the threshold beyond The Cross in the village could not be described as heavenly. His agnostic leanings did not allow him any certainty regarding the existence of Heaven, but he was certain that if such a place existed it was not located beyond The Cross. In his own mind, he called it Hell. Out of curiosity and maybe in preparation (for what, he didn't know), Ben re-read texts from his youth. At school, he had flicked through Dante's Divine Comedy, and after revision quickly recalled the three realms of the dead – Inferno, Purgatory and Paradise. Upon death, the soul is apparently "lost in a dark wood, assailed by three beasts... unable to find the straight way". He read that the Christian soul views sin for what it really is, and the three beasts represent the three types of sinner: the self-indulgent, the violent and the malicious. In the poem, Dante and Virgil manage to escape Inferno, arriving on the Mountain of Purgatory. The mountain has seven terraces, corresponding to the seven deadly sins – wroth, envy, pride, sloth, lust, gluttony and greed. The number seven, if not the descriptions of each sin, brings to mind the seven people who directly helped Don Gil. Ben tried to dismiss the idea, forcing himself to accept (as he often told Joanna) that we can make ourselves believe anything, that we can also apply any theory to our personal situation if we try hard enough. In his reading, he was reminded that the virtuous can travel on to Paradise.

Internet searches led Ben to theories built into neuroscience and even quantum physics. He admitted to himself that he had taken this too far but was unable to stop. He read articles by scientists who discussed the boundary between life and death. *That word 'boundary' again*, thought Ben.

In their articles, scientists consider that to be alive or dead may just be the visible signs of a 'process of universal motion permeating every aspect of our universe', and that apoptosis (cell death) is just the final physical process in the body leading to its breakdown into the smallest particles known to science.

Ben considered whether being trapped in the village was the point at which his heart stopped. Being technically dead, albeit for no more than a minute, may have sparked a process deep in the brain, placing him in a transitional area. Those who would wish him ill might decide to entice him to join them. *Enough of this*, he told himself. *Joanna and Doctor Evans will have me in a straitjacket.*

~

The nightmares return every night now. Each night, the driver's face becomes clearer. The gaunt, thin face of his nemesis. Ben sees his mother and father in the car ahead of them. He used to turn away from him, but now Ben begs the driver to spare his parents.
'Tell them to stop, please!'

No initial response, and the driver's eyes bore into Ben. He shudders as the man's unblinking glare increases its intensity, the driver smiling as Ben imagines him peering into his mind, scanning his thoughts. The fourteen-year-old Ben strains to shut him out, but he also wants a reply. It comes.

'This was your destiny. You cannot stop what is about to happen. Your parents will die. They will join us on the other side of the threshold. Will you join us, Ben?'

Ben closes his eyes, but the image of his parents' car is etched in the circuitry of his mind, tearing at the synapses. He sees the car turn over, a scream, blackness, lifelessness, silence.

'Darling, I'm here.'

Joanna held him, stroking his hair. The fourteen-year-old boy, now a married forty-six-year-old man, sobbed as she pulled him to her chest.

'It's alright. You were dreaming again.'

'Jo, I'm sorry. He won't leave me alone.'

'Is it him, Ben? You've never met him.'

'I know his voice, and Alan has described him. You should have seen his face; like he was drinking in the torment and suffering, celebrating evil. Anyway, I saw him in the village...'

'Are you going to be alright, love?'

'Yes, just hold me. You make me feel better.'

~

Ben was not the only one to make the connection to mythology in the events of the past year. Peter, well-versed in the classics and feeling closer to his father than ever before, offered to help him. Peter could see the relevance of the number seven, and, although not convinced by any religious or supernatural backdrop, was sure that Don Gil surrounded himself with followers or helpers. Peter called them 'disciples'.

'Your mom's not going to be impressed. You're as bad as me.'

'Like father, like son. Seriously, Dad, there's been something weird about this from the start. I've been doing my own reading. Whatever the reality, Don Gil has definitely been influenced by someone or something in his quest or whatever it is.'

'Quest?'

'I don't know, but I found something interesting in the library.'

Neither man had any notion of believing the texts they found, but they wanted to understand what they were dealing with. Peter offered Ben the theory of Isis and the Seven Scorpions. Seven people have supported Don Gil, and in their many conversations during tutorials, Alan had heard Don mention his interest in the study of ancient Egyptian history, language, religion, literature and art.

Peter explained to Ben that Isis was married to Osiris. Her evil brother, Seth, murdered him. He then gave Isis seven scorpions with the promise that they would protect her and any children she had. She travelled to another town and was rejected at the house of a wealthy woman, but a peasant woman took her in. The seven scorpions decided to take revenge on the wealthy woman, and some believe that Seth directed them. One of the scorpions stung the woman's son, and as he lay dying, she begged Isis for help. Seth stood beside his sister and told the woman "I will save him if you give me your soul". She agreed, willing to do anything to save her son, and Seth condemned her to eternal damnation.

'Peter, what has this to do with our situation?'

'Not sure, Dad, but I can see the parallels. Don Gil has seven disciples if you can call them that. You need to be careful.'

'And Hannah is one of his disciples.'

Peter simply answered by providing Ben with another example of seven creatures from Greek mythology, likening them to each of Don's disciples, starting with Hannah. Typhon – a monstrous creature and the offspring of Gaea the mother Earth and Tartarus, a lower God of the underworld. The Sphinx (Keith Simmons) – a monster with the famous riddle; Echidna (Melanie Crowther) - half-woman, half-snake who mated with Typhon, creating creatures to bring terror and mischief to mankind. Those creatures were Orthrus (James Enright) - the two-headed dog; Cerberus (Terry Hickens) - three-headed dog, guard of the underworld; Chimera (Frank Carter) – an awful creature with the body of a goat, the tail of a snake and the head of a lion. Finally, there was Greta Armitage, likened by Peter to Harpies, snatcher of souls. Hiding in the dark corners of Purgatory or the gateway between this world and the next, she followed instructions from her master. Those instructions would include leading a newly departed soul over the boundary into hell.

'Peter, how do you know about this in such detail?'

'I've always studied mythology – you know that, Dad.'

'No, I mean the potential links to each of the disciples?'

'I wasn't going to mention this, but Hannah talked a lot about this subject. She studied it as well. I thought it was just to keep me happy.'

'She was an expert?'

'I didn't realise that at the time, and it's more than that. She's lived amongst them. She's part of it.'

'Part of what?'

'I can't explain it, but they are all linked, and they all point back to Don Gil.'

~

1984. Ben is back there again.

'I'm not bothered about Niagara Falls.'
'You'll like it when you get there.'
'We've got so much to get through, and I want to go to the zoo.'

Don Gil is there, in the guise of a waiter, and only Ben questions why he should join in the family's conversation.

'Young sir, you must see the Falls. If not, you'll regret it for the rest of your life.'

'What do you mean?' Ben snaps back.

'Don't be rude to the waiter, Ben. He's only doing his job.'

'What does he know?' mutters Ben under his breath.

Gil fires back at him: 'you should be with your parents,' the tone not being picked up by the adults.

Ben glares at him.

'Up to you, Ben,' says Lucy.

'No, I'll go to the Bronx with Aunt and Uncle. Is that alright?'

Don Gil retreats, muttering 'bide your time.'

'That's decided then,' says Jack. 'Niagara Falls for us, Bronx Zoo for you lot.'

Jack and Lucy brave the downpour to drive the 370 miles to Buffalo. They stay overnight and set off for Rochester the next day. Luckier with the weather at the Bronx, Ben, Graham and Carol are at the zoo.

'What's all that with the waiter, Uncle Graham?'

'He's just trying to help. You must come back to America one day and see the Falls. Your mom and dad will have a day they will never forget. Come back one day, maybe when you have children of your own.'

~

He is at the stern of the boat, watching his parents climb aboard. The leaflet floats into his hand.

'Jaw-dropping beauty...'

Some of the words are obliterated by the spray from the Falls.

'...Cupid to lovers, a muse to artists and a Pied Piper to millions of visitors each year.'

He can hear Jack and Lucy talking.

'Not sure we need Cupid, Jack.'

'Nor the Pied Piper of Hamlin.'

'We'll do the *Maid of the Mist* boat ride first, then the helicopter?'

'Whatever you want, Lucy.'

The boat finishes its regular circuit and they disembark on the other side of the Falls, climbing the steps to the hotel.

'Jack, can you see that man carrying the wine?'

'What, the tall thin guy?'

'Doesn't he look like that waiter in New York?'

'Can't be. Suppose he might have a brother.'

Don Gil catches Ben's eye as he places the bottle on the table.

'Mom, Dad, can you hear me?'

They can neither hear nor see him. Somehow Ben doesn't see them eating their meal, as if the scene he is witnessing has been edited. They are boarding the helicopter. Ben climbs in after his mother. She glances across to the hotel patio. Don Gil fixes his stare at her and smiles. She turns to tell Jack, pointing towards the waiter. Jack turns. Don is no longer there.

After an uneventful, though enjoyable helicopter ride over the top of the Falls, Ben is in the passenger seat of the car, following Jack and Lucy. He stares at Don Gil who refuses to take his eyes off his quarry – the car in front. He ignores Ben's pleas to stop. They are approaching the Devil's Nose headland. Jack is not speeding, just on the 55 limit. They reach the turn for the Hamlin Beach Park and Lucy points out the Devil's Nose. They reach the right-hand bend and Jack doesn't have time to reply. He will never reply. The front tyre bursts and the car leaves the road, hitting the kerb.

It flips over, landing on the marshland separating the two carriageways. Don Gil stops the car at the side of the road, some thirty yards short of the scene. Four other cars stop, and the drivers and passengers all run towards the stricken couple.
'Please help them!' Ben pleads.

The slanted smile on Don's face sickens the young boy who is unable to turn his face away from him. Not until Don points a long, bony finger towards the crash scene. The emergency services have arrived.

Fire crews work to free Ben's parents, and a doctor places his hand on the shoulder of a young, recently recruited paramedic. He shakes his head. They didn't stand a chance.

Ben is now peering through the windscreen. He cannot tell if Don is still with him, and he doesn't care. Someone is moving in the overturned car. A paramedic, fire officer? No, two people are walking away from the car towards Ben. The man's chest is crushed, and the woman's head is tipped to one side. They hold out their hands...

~

Ben lay on his back, his eyes open. He was alone in the room. *Jo must have got up early*, he thought. *I hope I didn't disturb her in the night. God, it's seven-thirty*, but his brain recovered sufficiently to remind him that on Saturday mornings he lies in. Joanna was already working in the kitchen. Before Ben contemplated getting dressed, he had made up his mind. He would go to the States to follow the route his parents took on their final day on this earth.

He had no idea if it would help but was determined to regain control of his life, even his own thoughts. He may never make sense of their fate or understand why he didn't die with them, but he had to try.

30: Back to 1984

Ben thought of the expression 'bury your demons', reflecting on events in 1984 and 2016. He wished he could bury his demons and promised himself that he would, at least, get to understand why the events centred on him. Not the kind of man who liked to be the centre of attention, but, nonetheless, resolved to take any necessary action to find the truth. With no idea what 'the truth' really meant, Ben considered his options. No clear plan came to mind until the annual Stone family tidy-up and clear-out placed Ben in the one room in the house he had to himself, and a place you would not find Joanna – the loft.

'George Orwell...' he said to himself, not realising he'd spoken out loud.

Jack and Lucy had given Ben a special edition of Orwell's famous dystopian novel on New Year's Day 1984. *Kids today don't realise – that inane programme on Channel 5 is based on the novel*, he thought. *If they'd only screened one series - interesting experiment, done to death now. Big Brother is watching you, and the Party wields total power over the inhabitants.* He smiled to himself. *You wouldn't get me stuck in that house with half a dozen daft celebrities - even worse, members of the public.* He read through the first few pages, amused by the circles, asterisks and underlining he'd inflicted upon the pages of the book. Certain quotes had stirred him at the time: 'who controls the past controls the future: who controls the present controls the past.' Thirty-three years on, he was still fascinated by the Party slogans: 'War is Peace', 'Freedom is Slavery', and 'Ignorance is Strength'. And, by the side of the third slogan, written in Latin: 'Ignorantia Virium'.

He compared the writing style with the other scribbling. *No, it's not my writing, nor Peter's*. He turned a few more pages: 'Alea iacta est', with the English translation, 'the die has been cast'. Again, not a writing style he recognised. He considered the expression. He knew it to mean a process that was past the point of no return. A line had been drawn to the white space at the bottom of the page. His name and another Latin expression.
'Ben Stone, 1984, requiescat in pace.'

He knew the meaning immediately, not needing his classics expert son to assist. He felt a shiver, and the cold air around the eaves of the loft surrounded him. He did not know if the phrase remained in his mind or if he spoke out loud:
'Ben Stone, 1984, R.I.P.'

~

Ben refused the kind and supportive offers from Joanne and Peter to accompany him on the trip to New York. Taking the same route as they did thirty-three years before, he remembered his uncle's BMW and the banter with his father and Uncle Graham. This was to be a much shorter trip, but he had allowed up to ten days, intending to only stay two or three. He booked the same hotel, the Algonquin on West 44th, and, as it turned out, the same car hire firm. Only when he entered the lobby did he consider whether Don Gil would present himself in some form.

The receptionist had no idea that Ben was returning to re-live, if only subconsciously, the events of his previous visit. She didn't realise that this middle-aged man standing in front of the desk was that young boy who arrived with four adults and returned home with two. Most of the staff were long retired, but the man in his early sixties standing behind the receptionist remembered the name.
'Hope you don't think I'm being rude, but let me introduce myself. George Laythorn, hotel manager.'
'Good morning.' Ben smiled at the man.
'You wouldn't recognise me Mr Stone, but when you last came here, I was a young porter. I've worked my way through the ranks, and all that time the name 'Stone' stuck in my mind. Are you the young lad who stayed with his family at the time of the Olympics?'
'Yes, how nice of you to remember.'
'I am so deeply sorry about what happened. Are you here on holiday or business?'
'Neither really, Mr Laythorn. Bit of a quest really.'

Laythorn did not push him for further details. He instinctively worked out the main reason for the visit.
'Is that a Yorkshire accent?' said Ben, changing the subject.

'Yes, I came over from Leeds as a student and never went back, apart from a couple of holidays to visit family.'

~

After a restless night and an uneventful breakfast, Ben wandered down the corridors of the hotel. The sports room – no table tennis these days, and the pool table had been replaced. Three large games machines tempted you with huge winnings as soon as you opened the door. Ben could never beat his father at pool. He didn't mind, especially as Jack had always been happy to be thrashed at table tennis. Ben still missed him. His mother was the first one to hug him tight and make him feel safe, but Jack provided the banter, development of skills, friendly competitiveness and jokes. His father had a great sense of humour. Between games, or out on a walk, they enjoyed people-watching. Not wanting to be cruel, but spotting someone with a Cleese-like silly walk (points out of ten on the 'Cleese Scale'), or a strange haircut, caused them both many fits of giggles. Lucy never worked out the joke but loved them both for it anyway.

'My boys, what are you like?' she would say.

Ben set off for Buffalo, having booked the same hotel as his parents, ready to head for Rochester the next day. He made the effort to find the Broad Street Bridge on the canal. He never found out if Jack had ticked that off his list. Arriving at the Falls, he thought about the leaflet in his recurring dream. There were leaflets, but nothing

matching the text in his dream. He stayed an extra day, however, after an attendant implored him:
'Don't leave the Falls before nightfall, Sir.'

At nightfall, he was relieved that he had heeded the attendant's advice.

At 10pm, Ben stood at the edge of the observation tower, marvelling at the Falls that were illuminated in a spectacular display of rainbow-coloured light. When the fireworks display started, he regretted visiting on his own. He needed time for reflection, but these were moments he imagined being shared with Joanna. As he closed his eyes, she was there beside him gazing with wonder at the lights and the crashing waters. But she was not with him, not at that moment.

The next day he emulated his position in the dream by standing at the stern of the *Maid of the Mist*, expecting something to happen. This wasn't a dream, but in reality where his parents spent time in their precious last few hours together. Jack and Lucy had been more than happy. Many couples lived their lives content, settled and happy, but they expected more from life. Ben considered how he viewed their relationship, describing it as 'complete'. Any deficiencies in their respective characters, and there were few, were compensated by the other's capacity to correct any shortcomings gently and diplomatically. Particularly in the case of Lucy. She occasionally glimpsed impatience in Jack's eyes, a flicker of anger. A slight touch of her hand on his shoulder brought him back to his usual demeanour. A kind, loving man, willing to help anyone, but there were times when the actions of others brought out his tougher, less patient side. Lucy, on the other hand, had limitless compassion, seeing the good in everyone.

'You'd lend a hand to the Devil if asked,' Jack would say.

'If he were in trouble, maybe I would,' was Lucy's reply.

Ben never understood that comment, but from the first few days he could remember, Lucy was the calming influence in the family, Jack the solid, dependable foundation. The couple shared a loving companionship as well as a passionate love, and, until their tragic demise, Ben had learnt by the age of twelve how that close bond filtered through to the rest of the family. Their demise shattered, for a considerable time, how Ben viewed family relationships. Joanna saved him, and only now, as he stood gazing up at the Falls, could he perceive the character traits she shared with his mother.

As the *Maid of the Mist* pulled away, he chided himself for expecting his parents to board the boat. How could they? The scene playing out in front of him was not a dream. There was a middle-aged couple, holding hands, kissing occasionally. He smiled, thinking how Jack and Lucy would do just the same. He so desperately wanted to be with them again, but accepted that, in this world, it was impossible. *Now they are studying the leaflet*, he thought. Jack would point out the various sights, offering

Lucy a special smile when she said 'I know Jack, I can read.' Dampness covered Ben's face, but not from the mist. He was crying, but smiling at the image he had created. They were there, in one way. Still with him and they still loved him.

As the spray of the Falls submerged the vessel, people screaming with delight, each relieved to have been issued with the standard waterproof poncho, the image of his parents faded. At the other side of the river, he left the boat with two couples, sightseers, the rest intending to complete the tour. Ben headed for his planned helicopter trip.

He followed Jack and Lucy's original path to the hotel on the other side of the river. There were three helipads now, his $116 flight booked as part of the package. As he boarded, glancing back across the hotel gardens, he focussed on the spot that Lucy's eyes had captured. No waiter looking up smiling. He didn't know whether to be relieved or disappointed.

He was soon on the coast road to Rochester and picked up a brochure about Lake Ontario at the first rest stop. Everything seemed different, although he wondered how it was possible to compare a place he had never visited. Ben felt he knew the stretch of road intimately, but the brochure mentioned places he had not heard of. As he drove, however, he soon spotted the signs for familiar places. Norway Heights, Hamlin Beach State Park, The Cottages of Troutburg.

He slowed down to forty and turned off to the Devil's Nose headland. They had not been there, but he wished he could go back in time, join them on the trip and turn off before that right-hand bend at Hamlin. After sitting for over an hour, looking out across the huge lake that is part of the USA's border with Canada, he told himself it was time. The physical act of turning the key to start the engine was difficult enough - having to drive towards that bend...

A convenient lay-by gave him the opportunity to take the flowers from the boot and lay them at the roadside. Impossible to cross the carriageway to the marshland, but in his mind, he had been there before, many times.

~

After Hamlin, he wanted nothing more than to get to Dartmouth House bed-and-breakfast in Rochester. He wanted to do that, but he remembered reading about the valiant efforts of the fire and ambulance services based in Brockport. Not a large town, but being only eight miles from Hamlin, on the Lake Road North, inland from Lake Ontario, it boasted several key departments in the Rochester area. The University of Rochester Medicine Imaging Department and Rochester Health Laboratories complemented well-respected emergency services. Before flying to the States, Ben had contacted the mayor's office in Brockport, discovering that paramedic Hank Smithson still worked for the department after thirty-four years' service. His name was listed as a member of the ambulance crew that night. He agreed to meet Ben, although not sure how he could help after thirty-three years. Now working in administration and due to retire in 2019, he waited for Ben at Brockport police station; the records for road accidents over the last fifty years were stored there - photographs, witness statements, officer reports. Hank felt that Ben should not see the official photographs, some of which were even more graphic than those contained in the original report Ben had seen as a young man.

When Ben arrived at the police station reception, Hank greeted him with a warm handshake and led him to an interview room. Ben gratefully accepted Hank's offer of a coffee.

'It's great to meet you, Hank. Thank you for giving me your time.'

'Of course, I didn't know your parents, but the experience stayed with me.'

'Why this particular case?'

'You would have read the original report, Ben. There was nothing we could do for your mother, but your father was still alive for about twenty minutes after the accident.'

'Yes, I read that. They tried to resuscitate...'

'It's not in the report, don't ask me why, but I was alone with him for a minute. I held his hand and cradled his head.'

Hank touched Ben's hand with the realisation that the young English boy who lost his parents in tragic circumstances now sat in front of him, and there was something he should be told. Ben's thoughts raced towards his dreams. He looked Hank straight in the eye and said:

'*A doctor places his hand on the shoulder of a young paramedic.* Was that you, Hank?'

'My God, how did you know about that?'

'I'm not sure - a dream.'

'Ben, I have to tell you, he spoke to me. Your dad spoke to me.'

Since the accident in Leeford Village over nine months before, Ben found it difficult to trust anyone. The hotel manager, the Falls attendant, and now Hank. Could he be part of Don's scheming? The doubts subsided as Ben peered into Hank's eyes, scanning for signs of deception. A sudden thought occurred to him – since being in the States he had not received any signs or messages in his dreams. Is something blocking the evil that followed him? No sign of deception in the man he is keen to listen to. Slowly, regaining composure, he asked what Jack had said.

'Your dad said, "don't try to follow us".'

'Are you sure?' Ben asked.

'Yes, then he said your name. He died soon afterwards.'

'It's the first I've heard of this.'

'I'm sorry Ben. I did tell a supervisor. Within weeks I was sent away on a training placement in New York. Six months I was there – I met my wife, Julia, and by the time we got back to Brockport, no one talked about it. I realise you will find this hard to take in, but your dad's words came back to me when your call came through to the office. I've often thought about your parents, but I think I'd blocked out that moment with your dad until you called.'

'Hank, it's not your fault. Did he say anything else?'

'It's a bit muddled, but when he said your name, I'm sure he said something like "stay that side".'

'Could it have been "stay on that side"?'

'Maybe, but he definitely said, "don't try to follow us".'

They sat in silence for a few minutes. Ben finished his coffee, then placed both of his hands around Hank's outstretched right hand.

'We'll probably never meet again, but I am so grateful for your help. I feel closer to them now.'

Ben left the station, heading for Dartmouth House in Rochester. One more night and he would return to New York for the flight home.

As he reached his room, before he had time to open his bags to unpack, reception put a call through. It was Joanna.

'Ben, are you coming home soon? We need you, something terrible has happened.'

'What is it, love?'

'Someone has taken Josh.'

31: Taken

'Why can't I use my phone during the flight? They do in the States.'

'Sorry sir, but they have different regulations for flights within the US. We don't allow calls to be made and received on transatlantic flights.'

'But this is an emergency.'

'I'm sorry, but the captain did ask everyone to set their mobiles to flight mode. You can use off-line apps such as games, that sort of thing.'

'Do I look like the kind of person who plays games on their phone for Christ sake?'

Seeing no point in continuing the argument, Ben conceded and set his phone as instructed. His last contact with Joanna, just before boarding, was no less fraught than the call at Dartmouth House.

'Jo, try not to upset yourself. I'll be back as soon as I can get on that damn plane. When I'm on my way, I'll ring you.'

'Alan and Cheryl are in a terrible state. They've left a policewoman with us in case there are any calls. They're setting up recording devices already.'

'Oh God, Jo, our little Josh.'

Peter came on the line, Joanna unable to reply.

'Dad, Mom's terribly upset. Are you okay?'

'Worried, son. I just want to get home.'

'It's that stinking bastard, isn't it?'

'Don't know Peter, but we'll find out. I have to go now. Speak to you later. Tell your mom I love her.'

'Will do.'

~

Thankful the flight to Heathrow was over, Ben found his car before contacting home. Peter answered again, and he could hear Alan in the background telling him to keep the line clear.

'It's Dad. He'll be back in two or three hours, depending on the motorway traffic.'

'Let me speak to him, Peter,' interrupted Joanna.

'Any news, Jo?'

'Just get home, Ben, I've missed you.'

The journey seemed to take much longer than the two hours from the airport to Leeford. Almost 9pm, ten miles from the motorway junction to the village along the A449 the last stage of his journey. As Ben approached Leeford Village, he found The Cross to be deserted. The lights on green and, as he passed through, his spine tingled. *That feeling again*, he thought. He muttered the cliché to himself, 'someone has walked over my grave'. The moment passed as he reached the church. It felt different to be back. He sensed that the dreams would return, but now everything had changed anyway, little Josh the most important part of their lives. Joanna was waiting for him on the drive as he stopped the engine, got out and locked the car door. She held onto him, sobbing into his shoulder.

'Let's go inside, Jo. We'll sit down and you can tell me what's happened.'

'Alan and Cheryl are frantic and I've never seen Peter so angry. He's threatened all sorts – the WPC had to tell him to calm down.'

As Ben lowered himself into his favourite armchair, Alan and Cheryl followed Joanna into the room. His face ashen and drawn, Alan stared at his father and, with an almost imperceptible nod, acknowledged his presence. He held onto Cheryl's hand as she sat next to him, facing Ben. Cheryl's face betrayed what looked like years of grief and stress. She had been crying, her eyelids red and the lines around her cheekbones adding many years to her young face. Her free hand shook as she spoke to Ben.

'We're so glad you're back home. What did Mom and Peter tell you?'

'All I know is that Josh has been taken.'

She couldn't continue. Joanna placed a soothing arm around her shoulders, leading her to the kitchen.

'It's him, isn't it, Dad?' asked Alan. 'Something to do with you.'

Ben's eyes widened as he looked at his son.

'How can you be sure?'

'After you phoned us to say you were setting off from the Falls to Rochester, I saw him sitting in a car in Blueberry Street.'

'That's only a few hundred yards from here. Did you approach him? Did he see you?'

'No. The thing is, Dad, I walked no more than fifty yards down the road, you know, by that One Stop shop, and crossed the road. I walked back towards his car on the other side of the road.'

'And?'

'He'd gone. The car didn't pass me, and it was pretty quiet at the time. I'm sure I would have heard an engine.'

'What happened then?' asked Ben.

'Didn't think too much about it, picked up a paper from the shop and walked home. It's only five minutes from the shop.' Struggling to compose himself, Alan took a deep breath and gripped Cheryl's hand, but nonetheless managed to continue. 'When I got home, Mom and Cheryl were running up and down the street shouting for Josh. Cheryl had left him in his chair in the conservatory.'

'Was the side gate locked?'

'Yes, and there was no sign of a break-in. Nothing. Someone must have climbed over.'

'And passed Josh over the gate to an accomplice?'

'The police think so,' said Alan. 'It's the only possible answer.'

~

The Victim Support Officer stayed with the family while the main meeting room began to fill with journalists and photographers. Detective Inspector Stanton explained to the couple how a television appeal works. Nothing he said reassured Cheryl. Alan thanked him, but essentially felt the same as his young wife. Not just the ordeal of sitting in front of the media and the public, but the thought of trying to appeal to the better nature of an evil man did not sit comfortably. Peter, advised by the police to stay out of the proceedings, declared that he'd cheerfully kill Don Gil, with no concrete proof he was behind the kidnapping. There was no trace of Gil or his friends, which convinced them even more. Peter knew, as did Ben - there was no doubt in their minds, but, for Joanna, Alan, and Cheryl, they tried to keep as calm as possible. WPC Nicole Jenkins, who had been with them since the first police car arrived at the house that night, tried to relieve the pressure.

'I'll be right beside you, Cheryl. DI Stanton is very good - he's done this many times.'

'Will we ever see Josh again?' Cheryl asked.

'I'm sure you will. They've no reason to harm him. After we've made the TV and radio appeals, we would expect some sort of demand.'

'Ransom?' asked Alan.

'Sometimes that happens, or it could be a protest. A grievance perhaps.'

'What do you mean, grievance?'

'If it's not about money, which it usually is, they could be the sort of people who have a problem with a member of the family. Maybe they're doing it to make someone suffer, but there should be no reason to hurt Josh.'

Cheryl closed her eyes, covering her face with both hands.

'Please tell me we'll get him back, Nicole.'

'We'll do all we can.'

The door opened. A young constable beckoned to WPC Jenkins, cupping his hand to whisper something to her as she approached.

'Cheryl, Alan, they're ready for us.'

WPC Jenkins led them from the small interview room to the largest room at the station. The lights dazzled their eyes as they sat between DI Stanton and Nicole. Stanton, a commanding figure, was ready to speak first. Nicole, virtually a member of the family now, held Cheryl's left hand.

'Thank you all for coming today,' began DI Stanton, as multiple flashes went off. 'As you are aware, a nine-month-old child, Joshua Stone, was taken from his pushchair at the family home of his parents, Cheryl and Alan. This happened around 3.30pm, on 31st October.'

Sitting together in the room next to the conservatory from which their grandson was taken, Ben and Joanna held each other as they watched the appeal.

'I'd not thought it before, Ben. He was taken on Halloween.'

Stanton handed over to Cheryl. Unable to hold back her tears, she sobbed her way through the prepared statement. Hardened journalists, noting down every word, had seen it all before. They could have written their reports before Cheryl opened her mouth. But, for these young parents, it was the first time. Hopefully, the only time in their lives when they had to appeal to the public to give the police any information – anything that might help to return Joshua to his loving parents.

Following the appeal, people tried to help, telling the police they had seen a car, a man and a woman, or someone hanging around the day before. After three days, there were still no firm leads, no demands for ransom or indeed any demand, until Ben's mobile rang one morning as he sat leafing through his morning paper. Everyone else still in bed, it was no coincidence that he was alone when the call came through, not on the landline that was monitored by the police every minute of the day, but on his new mobile number. Very few people outside the family and work colleagues knew the number, but, once again, Ben immediately recognised the voice.

32: The Demand

'What the hell have you done with my grandson?'

'This is not the time for you to speak. Listen to me, Ben, very carefully. If you do as I ask, you might save his life.'

'Alright, what do you want?'

'That's better. Answer me. What is the date today?'

'4th November. Why?' asked Ben.

'You remember a year ago tomorrow?'

'Not really thought about it, but yes, my wedding anniversary, and the day you tried to kill us.'

'Enough of this. You must follow my instructions. Tomorrow you will drive out to the old airport at Hillingdon. Got that?'

'Then what?'

'You will come alone – alone I tell you – and you will be given further instructions. Drive to the old tower. Be there at 5pm.'

'When do we see Josh?'

'That's out of your control, Ben. Just be there. Unfortunately, you will have to trust me.'

'You bastard,' Ben shouted, 'how can I trust you?'

'Careful, Ben. Remember, I have your grandson's life in my hands. I dictate the terms. I am in control. Come on your own, no police. Do not phone them and do not tell your family where you are going.'

'Okay, okay, but I want Josh.'

'You will see him, under my terms.'

~

Ben's first decision – whether to tell anyone. One word to Joanna and the police would be involved in minutes. *The state the kids are in*, he thought, *they wouldn't be able to think clearly*. Alan might follow him, bring the police in, anything. He decided – *Peter, I must confide in Peter. Ask him to trust me.*

~

'You should tell the police, Dad,' said Peter after Ben had told him about the telephone conversation.

'That's the logical thing to do, but they've no idea what we're dealing with here. I'm the only one who can fix this.'

'Why are you telling me and no one else?'

'Because I know you will support me. You are able to stay calm, and...'

'Because of Hannah?' asked Peter.

'That's part of it. You know she's with him, and you understand that I am at the centre of this mess.'

'Can you get Josh back?'

'Peter, it's all I care about right now. I must get him back, whatever it takes.'

'What do you want me to do?'

'I'll text you when I get there, but I'll have to hide the phone and switch it off. Gil has to believe that I've followed his instructions to the letter.'

Peter agreed to keep everything to himself. After the text from Ben, he would wait an hour then drive over towards Hillingdon, park half a mile from the airport and work his way to the rear entrance of the tower. Ben had taken Peter and Alan there many times to explore the grounds long after the last light aeroplane left the discontinued airstrip. Peter remembered from his childhood all the entrances, pathways and places to hide.

'Alright, Dad, I'll follow from a distance. No police unless something goes wrong. What if I can't pick up your trail?'

'I'll try to leave a note. Do you remember that cupboard in the airport reception area?'

'Yes, where Alan hid for over half an hour?'

'I'll leave a note on the floor – if it's clear where they want me to go,' said Ben.

'And if you get the opportunity. They'll be watching you.'

'Tell your mom I've gone to get her some flowers for our anniversary.'

'After an hour she'll start to worry. Then I'll be following you. What will she think?'

'If you say nothing, she'll have no idea where we are. If she phones the police, so be it. We're doing the right thing.'

'Okay, Dad. So you're going now?'

'Your mom's having a lie-down. She's not been bothered about our 26th. Josh is all that matters now.'

~

Ben arrived at Hillingdon twenty minutes later, the autumn sun fading behind the trees. He loved this time of year - this time of day - but it was not his concern for now. Seeing that there was no one near the tower, he approached the front door, finding it slightly ajar. The wind whistled past his neck as he stepped into the disused reception area. Dust covered every surface. No sign of life except for a Pepsi can, empty crisp packets and an old newspaper near the corner of the room. *Kids*, he assumed. He stood, listening for any sign of company. Nothing for a full five minutes. Then a faint voice, and footsteps, not coming to join him, but towards the back of the ground floor. He was sure the voice said, 'top floor, by the window.' Silence again, except for the wind and his own footsteps climbing the flight of stone steps to the observation room. As he opened the door, he saw it at once. The envelope sat on a shelf in the middle of the main observation window that scanned runway one. As he opened it, a bead of sweat trickled and twisted past his left eyebrow. He shivered. Ben didn't feel the cold, and it wasn't cold for the time of year. Fear gripped him, but not for himself.

Go to the trading estate behind the trees at the side of runway two. The main entrance is six hundred yards down the road past the airport main gate. As you go up the main entrance road, you will see a large warehouse, second building on the right. Be there at 5.30 pm. Wait outside.

As agreed with Peter, Ben sent him a quick text. He switched off his phone, wrote a short note and left them both on the floor in the ground floor cupboard. He had no idea that he was being watched.

~

'Do you all understand? We must not kill him. Stone must join us of his own free will.'

Don Gil's eyes scanned his group of followers, searching for assent on the face of each individual. Most of them offered a blank expression with an almost imperceptible nod of agreement. On the face of one, a glare returned to her leader indicating the need to speak.

'Well, Hannah?'

'The others. What about the others? Do you not want them dead? The crash should have finished them off.'

'Are you talking about Peter Stone? Were you not close?' asked Gil.

'Him especially. I did it for you,' said Hannah. 'I never enjoyed his romantic ways. Give me the word and he will suffer.'

'Not for now. We must concentrate on our target. He has escaped us for thirty-three years, and I have been aware of him much longer than that. We have his mother to thank for that.'

'Why can't we kill Ben Stone now?' asked Enright, sparking a venomous glare from Melanie Crowther.

'Don't you listen?' she snapped.

'He must cross the threshold willingly,' Gil reiterated. 'Otherwise, he is lost to us. His parents will fight for him as they did before, and the only way we can get him back to the village is in a comatose state – near death.'

The others nodded their understanding. They were all there – Terry Hickens, James Enright, Frank Carter, Keith Simmons, Hannah, and Melanie Crowther. Gil had disposed of Hannah's parents. They only worked with him under the false impression that Hannah could be saved. She had embraced evil as a child, targeted by Gil when he had worked as a teacher at her school. Gil, much older than he appeared, had taken a lover sixty years ago. Greta Armitage had succumbed to his advances, groomed for just one purpose many years later. She died to become the gatekeeper of the threshold, her fate dictated by Gil when the time was right.

'Your boyfriend was right, Hannah,' said Gil. 'He's clever, but you may well have led him to discover his theory about me.'
Hannah gazed at him, waiting for his next words, expecting to be punished.
'You discussed Egyptology and mythology. Even as you made love with Peter, you uttered the names of the gods.'
Even her level of devotion to him did not suppress Hannah's embarrassment at the thought of Gil being privy to her intimate relationships.
'I'm sorry, Don. I hated him, but I enjoyed the physical connection.'
'Until you join us completely one day, I accept that you are still a woman, flesh, blood and bone. No matter,

he did not discover my true identity, but you led him on the path towards the truth. Keith, do you have the box?' Gil asked, turning away from Hannah.

'Yes, it's ready as instructed.'

'Is the grave prepared?'

Two of the men nodded, one of them pointing to a dark corner of the warehouse. On an earlier visit, they had brought in equipment to break the concrete floor, enabling them to dig a pit four feet deep. Large enough for a man. Gil clicked his fingers, gesturing to Frank Carter.

'It is time.'

Frank left the warehouse, using a shortcut through the trees towards the Hillingdon tower. He watched Ben approach the front door, and through the window saw him open the cupboard near the reception desk. He waited a few minutes before triggering the recording Melanie Crowther had made. The button on the remote device caused her voice to echo gently through the deserted corridors of the building.

'Top floor, by the window.'

Frank crept into reception as Ben made his way slowly up the stairs. He hid behind the reception desk as his target returned to the cupboard to leave the messages for Peter. Once Ben had left, Frank opened the cupboard. He knew what he was searching for. The mobile safe in his pocket, he made his way back towards the trees. Frank didn't realise that when he opened the cupboard, the blast of air flung the notepaper into the opposite corner. He arrived back at the warehouse barely a minute before Ben approached the entrance.

'He's coming,' Frank told Gil and the others.

Don Gil addressed the group again.

'This is the time. We can now help Ben Stone reach his destiny.'

33:   Hell

As Ben approached the warehouse door, he had no idea that within minutes he would be humiliated, threatened, and filled with a terror he could not imagine. There were no lights and not a sound, other than his shoes crunching into the gravel path. He pushed at the door. It opened. As he stepped inside, the lock clicked. He sensed someone behind him, but he didn't turn round. He focussed on the shape of a man in the middle of the huge space of the warehouse. The shape appeared suddenly as the beam from a spotlight streaked across the floor reaching Ben's feet. He then became aware of other shapes as faint lights appeared from all directions, as if controlled by a dimmer switch. Ben counted six, maybe seven figures. He couldn't be sure. One of them, a female shape, faded into the background.

'We meet again, Mr Stone,' a voice boomed out. 'I will call you Ben, if you prefer,' he said more softly.

'Is Josh here?' asked Ben.

'Not yet. I need to know you are committed to helping us.'

'Helping you? How?'

'It is my job to see that your destiny is fulfilled.'

Ben's whole body shook as he responded.

'We had a deal. That's why I came.'

Don Gil ignored the comment, gesturing to the others to surround Ben, each of them holding a variety of weapons – iron bars, knives, hammers.

'Take off his coat and shirt, and his shoes and socks.'

At that, the whole building was awash with light. Ben had no time to struggle as the men held him while the two women tore at his clothes. They mocked him as Keith, James, Terry and Frank carried him towards the makeshift grave. Following the rehearsed routine, the men held him down in the filthy pit as Melanie and Hannah attached manacles to his bare ankles and wrists, placed thin stakes through holes in the manacles and hammered them into the ground. Immobile, humiliated and terrified, Ben screamed as Gil issued the next instruction.

'Let them go.'

Frank Carter's face almost split apart as he laughed and pointed to the victim. He picked up a basket, and, as he lifted the lid and tipped the basket, Ben winced. Six rats fell onto his chest. They squeaked, hissed, and seemed to chatter to each other, biting at Ben's chest hairs. He tried to keep still and could not help crying, and begged them to stop.

'You don't believe in Hell, do you, Ben?'

'I would rather die than talk to you. Please, please let Josh go.'

'Maybe, maybe. But, first, I'm going to show you what Hell is. Your own personal version of Hell. Hannah, come here.'

She walked to the side of the pit, peering down at the pathetic figure – the man once destined to be her father-in-law. Ben shivered. He wanted to urinate – he feared further humiliation. Don Gil continued.

'You were once close to his son, were you not?'

'Yes, Don,' replied Hannah.

'Would you say that you discovered much about Mr Ben Stone as his son fell in love with you?'

'Yes, quite a lot of secrets.'

'Did you discover anything particularly interesting about him?'

'Yes, I know his greatest fear, apart from death itself.'

Ben felt the rats' feet clawing at him and their fur rubbed against his chest and arms as Hannah stared directly at him. His face clammy, the feeling of a full bladder worse still, he recoiled as a rat slithered over his face. He clamped his mouth shut tight. *It can't get any worse*, he thought. But it did.

Gil spoke again. 'Hannah, please tell everyone what the phobia is that will strike absolute terror into his heart. He cannot move so he has no influence on what happens next.'

He knelt beside the pit and stared at Ben. The others closed in, grinning, waiting.

'Go on Hannah, tell us.'

Ben felt Hannah's eyes bore into his as she said:

'Frogs. He is terrified of frogs.'

'No, please don't!' cried Ben.

'Ben, tell me now, if I take you back to the village, will you cross the threshold?'

'No, never!'

'Bring it over!' shouted Gil.

Terry Hickens and James Enright carried an old tin bath towards the side of the pit. Half filled with dirty water, it contained at least two dozen frogs and toads. They slowly tipped the contents of the bath onto Ben's face and body. No one had ever considered Ben a coward, but this took him beyond anything he could endure. His whole body shaking, his tears flowed, he screamed for help, and he had the additional embarrassment of his obviously wet trousers. Everyone laughed and pointed. As the animals slithered over his body, some behind his head and between his legs, it became too much for him. Ben passed out as his heart rate soared and his brain could take no more.

'Cover him!'

Gil had planned each stage in detail. The stages of Ben's suffering. It became obvious, even to his followers, that he enjoyed seeing a human being suffer. He would inflict pain and humiliation on an innocent person for the sake of it. For the sake of evil. Simmons placed a pair of goggles, the type that might be used as DIY safety glasses, over Ben's face. Then, he placed a swimming snorkel into his mouth. The other men filled the pit with earth. Only the top of his air pipe and Ben's left foot sticking out from his makeshift grave now visible.

Gil plunged a needle into Ben's foot. Ben had now regained consciousness. The pain seared through his body. Gil passed the needle to Melanie Crowther, who took great pleasure in repeating the action every few minutes. They wanted to make sure he was breathing. He couldn't suffer if he were dead.

'We must keep him alive but take him to the brink of death. Keith, bring me the box you have prepared.'

Keith placed it at Gil's feet. As he did, Ben's body once again wretched in agony as Crowther plunged the needle into the light skin between his toes. Blood trickled amongst the dirt across his foot. Gil opened the box. Seven scorpions writhed about, their tails flashing left and right. He smiled.

'We are ready,' he said.

~

Peter pulled into the pot-holed driveway. The airport had been disused since 1952, but he remembered the games of hide-and-seek he played with his father and younger brother during his childhood, almost fifty years later. A few hundred yards to the tower. Few people visited anymore – the occasional evening courting couple, birdwatchers, but not too many 'hooligans' as Ben called them. Peter noticed that the graffiti on the walls of the tower presented something of an eighties atmosphere.

The door was open and Peter stepped into the reception area. He at once saw the cupboard where he expected to find his father's phone and a note. Ben had explained to him that they would no doubt search him, and the phone would be taken anyway. His plan was to get Josh, escape, and retrieve his phone. He would then phone the police with the whereabouts of the kidnappers.

Peter soon discovered that his father's plan had strayed from the script. *Nothing there apart from dust and spiders*, he thought. Then, as he grasped the door to close it, a light breeze blew the small piece of notepaper towards his foot. He read the note. *The warehouse, he's in the warehouse.* Any thoughts of protecting everyone from his father's dilemma left him. He decided that he needed Alan. No police, at least not yet. Josh was, after all, Alan's son, but he wanted to make sure that Alan's trauma and panic caused by the kidnapping didn't make things worse. First, find their father, then somehow get to Josh.

~

As Peter waited for his brother, Don Gil instructed Keith, Hannah and Melanie to put Ben in the van they had parked at the side of the warehouse.

'Melanie, do you have the antidote?'

'Yes, it's in the van – on the dashboard.'

Meanwhile, Terry Hickens and James Enright positioned petrol cans around the building, inside and out. Gil intended to cover his tracks. Once Ben had been placed on the stretcher they had placed in the back of the van, he told everyone to return to the warehouse and await final instructions. Ben, barely conscious, was now tied to the stretcher, arms and legs bound tight. Though immobilised, he was becoming increasingly aware of his surroundings, aware that he was alone with Don Gil.

'Why threaten to harm your own son if you really are the father of Cheryl's baby?'

'I have many sons,' Gil replied.

He smiled at Ben. The smile of a man in control. Ben saw it as the face of evil. Unable to move, but he strained every muscle as Gil placed his hand on Ben's bare forearm.

'You know about scorpions, do you, Ben?'

'Well, I suppose...'

'I will satisfy your curiosity,' Gil said as he placed the box on Ben's stomach, tipping it at an angle so Ben could view the contents.

'You can't scare me any more Gil, you bastard. Do your worst. Peter will find Josh, and the police will be on their way.'

'Let's focus on what is going to happen to you.'

Gil pulled a thick glove onto his right hand and selected one of the seven scorpions. As Ben saw him place the creature on his stomach, fear returned to him.

'At the end of its tail is the telson, a pair of venom glands. Soon the scorpion will inject its venom into you through the stinger. Before you ask, yes, it will hurt.'

'What's the point in killing me?'

'Oh, I don't intend to kill you. At least not yet.'

The scorpion's tail flapped around as if the creature wanted to taunt him.

'I have the anti-venom here, prepared in a syringe, but this is deadly venom,' explained Gil. 'An adult male of your weight could expect to go into anaphylactic shock in five minutes. Most types of scorpion give you a sting no worse than a bee or a wasp, but this is the deathstalker scorpion.'

'Why are you telling me this?'

'It's one of the deadliest in the world. Its venom is highly toxic. Before death, you will go into a coma.'

'How can you be sure?' Ben asked.

'Let's just say I've done some testing.'

'Who with?'

'I might as well tell you – Hannah's parents. They would not continue their cooperation once they knew what was happening.'

As the scorpion raised its tail to strike, Ben asked one more question.

'Why do you need me in a coma?'

'You will be near death, and you will once again approach the boundary. This time, you will cross, and join us forever.'

At that, the scorpion's barb sliced into Ben's skin. He screamed as the pain surged through his nervous system. The shock had an immediate effect. His heart pounded faster and faster. After thirty seconds he couldn't make out the features of Gil's face. Sweat poured down his face. His arms stiffened. He couldn't swallow. He lay there in agony for another few minutes. Breathing now a problem, Ben sucked in air but began to choke. Blackness descended.

~

'Follow my lead, Alan. Do you promise?'

'I trust you, Pete. Please help me get my son back.'

Alan had left a note for Cheryl. Semi-hidden on the kitchen table, he hoped she would find it but not straight away. His calculation proved correct - Joanna and Cheryl both spotted it as they offered the visiting WPC a cup of tea. The thirty-minute delay gave Alan enough time to join his brother at the airfield before police cars were despatched. They wanted the initial approach to the warehouse to be low-key.

As their father slipped into a coma, they peered through the window next to the warehouse main door. Gil's followers were all in there, plus one important addition. Hannah, standing nearest the door, gripped the pushchair handle.
'He looks fine, Alan.'
'We must go in now.'
'No, wait to see what the others are doing,' said Peter.

Except for Hannah, everyone busied themselves collecting evidence in black bin bags. The torn remains of Ben's clothes, mobile phones, anything that could either prove that Ben had been held there or help the police to identify them. Keith's next action prompted Alan to grab his brother's arm.
'He's pouring petrol round the building. I'm going in.'
'Okay, Alan. I'm with you.'

The lock didn't hold them, Peter hurting his shoulder as he crashed the door open. Hannah stepped to one side as they burst in to confront Gil's followers. Before Alan had time to turn round, she grabbed Josh and ran outside. The five remaining followers ran towards Peter, Alan already through the door after Hannah. As he backed out of the door, Peter spotted two pallets leaning against the outside wall. He blocked the exit just as Terry and James slammed their shoulders against the closed door.

'Peter, I can't see where she's gone!'

'We'll catch up with her, Alan. There's no vehicle parked nearby. She can't get far with Josh.'

'Christ, Pete, the smell of petrol.'

Peter didn't consider stopping his brother as Alan reached for his lighter. He had kept his smoking habit quiet, but Peter always knew. Alan spotted a brick on the ground. Within seconds he had smashed the window, flicked the lighter and hurled it into the building. Alan and Peter both jumped back as flames licked at the window. James Enright managed to open the window to the left of the door. As he climbed through, the fire engulfed him. Even his screams were eclipsed by those of his colleagues. The building was ablaze in minutes and neither of Ben's sons regretted their actions.

'They deserved it, after what they've put us through.' Peter's face glowed, partly from the heat of the flames. He showed no regret. They stepped back, scanning the area for movement.

'There she is!' shouted Alan, running across the field.

'Get Josh! She's mine!' yelled Peter.

It didn't take long to catch up with them. Hannah let go of the pushchair, knocking it sideways to the ground. Alan arrived seconds later, finding his son crying but otherwise uninjured. Hannah sprinted into the woods away from the airfield. Peter followed her, gaining ground fast as they heard the sirens. Three police cars bumped over the field towards the edge of the woods and Peter had Hannah in his sights. She tripped on a thick branch, falling heavily. Peter would show no mercy.

'Where is my father, bitch?'

'It's too late. Don has him.'

For the first time in his life, he punched a woman, hearing Hannah's jaw crack as she fell backwards.

'I'll ask you again, where is he?' Peter shouted, squeezing her jaw until she screamed, blood oozing across her chin.

'Blue van... cottage two miles down the Enville road... too late.'

Peter wanted to hit her again. Love turned to intense hatred. Four police officers raced towards them. He held his fist in check, pausing to pass on the information he had forced from his former lover.

'Leave her with us now, sir. We'll have a car at the cottage in a few minutes.'

'Take me with you. I need to see my dad.'

34: Final Visit

Back in the village. This time not by the church, the scene of the accident. This time Ben awoke to the sound of aeroplanes overhead. One after the other, Spitfires and Lancaster bombers filled the air with their customary whines and droning. He was lying against a large oak on the tree-lined road leading west out of Leeford towards the airfield. He understood this time that some of the imagery may have been caused by his mind playing tricks, but not everything was imagined. The pain across his forehead, like a chainsaw slicing through wood, made him physically sick. Hours seemed to pass as he gradually recovered. Maybe time, if not standing still, behaved differently in the village. The van, he thought, I was in the van. The scorpion, Don Gil, I'm in a coma...

Ben's concept of reality kept his emotions in check. Able to control the pain because of the realisation that his physical body was somehow in another dimension. He pinched his arm. He could see and speak and, on this occasion, smell the blossom of the trees. He was there, in the village, but not in the way a normal intelligent human would understand. Ben realised this was the gateway, and he knew what Don Gil wanted.

'You're here then, Ben.' The voice shook him. He forced himself to sit down. 'You'd better come with me.'

'No, I won't give in.'

Don Gil did not physically touch him, but, as he walked away, Ben felt compelled to follow.

'That's better,' said Gil.

They reached The Cross in less than a minute. Standing a few feet from Ben, with his back to the boundary, Gil pointed beyond Ben's shoulder.

'They're here. My friends are here.'

Ben dropped to his knees as the first one staggered past. Terry Hickens, his skin peeling from his face, most of his hair burnt off. He gestured to Ben, his smile painful. Gil tapped his shoulder as he crossed the threshold. As he did, a grey mist descended. The outline of his body glowed red and green as he slid into oblivion.

Next, James Enright, then Melanie Crowther, Keith Simmons, and Frank Carter. Each one scorched and scarred but somehow still moving. One by one, they received the lightest of touches from the man they followed. They would never see this life again.

'Your turn, Ben Stone.'
'Never!'

A strong wind forced him forwards. Now only feet from the boundary, feet from the end of his life. A woman appeared in front of him, an old woman.

'I said we would meet on the other side. Why don't you join us?'

Don Gil, like a snake slithering in the undergrowth, had made his move. Standing behind Ben, he whispered obscenities in his ear and without needing to physically touch him, forced Ben closer to his fate. Greta Armitage reached out to touch Ben's hand. He felt a warmth, not an unpleasant experience, that compelled him to shuffle towards her. His arms outstretched, he aimed to embrace her and finally concede...

'No!'

A female voice screamed from behind Don Gil.

'Leave him, he is not ready, and he will never join you in that place!'

The moment passed. Greta Armitage faded and Ben spun round to see his mother.

'Look at me, Ben.'

'Mom...' Emotionally, he was a child again.

'Get away from Gil. He only means you harm.'

'What can I do?'

'Nothing. I will take your place.'

'I don't understand.'

'This is my fault. One day you will understand. Mr Gil, take me, I started this with the pledge I gave you many years ago.'

No response from Gil, but Ben needed to speak to his mother. He had so many questions.

'But what about Dad? I thought you were with Dad!'

'He will wait for you. You will meet him again one day, but not yet. Not just yet.'

'Mom, you can't do this. I don't understand.'

His tears hurt his eyes. He was choking again, his head spinning. Don touched Lucy's shoulder and led her across the boundary. As she passed Ben, her hand glanced across his - a faint touch, but enough for his mind to accept a final message.

'Aunt Carol will explain. She doesn't know it yet, but she will have the answers.'

The mist descended to envelop Gil and Lucy. As they disappeared, Ben collapsed.

~

Alan, with his son safely in his arms, returned home with the help of the WPC. Cheryl did not cry as she saw Josh holding his father's hand. She threw open the front door and ran towards the car. She had no tears left, but as she held her baby boy, Alan's anger turned to tears. Joanna joined them on the driveway and held him tight.

'It's alright, Alan, you're back together again.'

'Mom... I'd thought we'd lost him,' sobbed Alan. 'Dad's in danger. Peter's gone with the police to find him. Gil has him.'

Joanna said nothing but squeezed Alan's hand as they went back into the house. They had waited long enough to be reunited with young Josh. They would have to trust Peter and wait again. This time for Ben.

~

It didn't take them long to reach the cottage on the Enville Road. Peter shouted out to the driver as he spotted the blue van parked at the side, partially covered by conifers that spread from the front garden to the rear of the cottage.

'Leave this to us, Mr Stone.'

Peter, ignoring the instruction, slammed the car door and raced towards the van. As he opened the back doors, he saw his father on his back. As he approached him, there was no movement, no obvious sign that he was breathing. Lying on the van floor, his face pale and strange as if the very life force had been sucked out of him, Ben, thankfully, showed at least minimal signs of life. Don Gil sat next to him, motionless, his eyes open. There was no response as a constable secured handcuffs. His trance-like state, however, did not concern Peter. An ambulance had already been called, and the paramedic expressed his concern about Ben.

'He's in a coma. Drugs possibly, or some sort of reaction.'

It was only then that Peter spotted the scorpion. As they moved Ben's arm to check his blood pressure, the creature crawled past Ben's knee. Peter had no hesitation in crushing it under his foot.

'Good God, look at these!' the officer exclaimed.

The remaining creatures writhed and clicked in their box. He gestured to a constable.

'Cover this box. Get it to a local zoo.'

The paramedic noticed the mark on Ben's arm.

'Scorpion venom. Luckily they've left the antidote in the front of the van.'

'Can you be sure it's safe?' asked Peter.

'Sorry son, but we have to try this. I've got the hospital on the line. We only have a few minutes. It's a risk, but if we do nothing, his heart will fail.'

Peter nodded his consent. It was his father. He'd take responsibility.

~

The village, now devoid of any sound or movement, appeared to be waiting for Ben. Waiting for what, he didn't know, but after the events involving his mother, Don Gil and his followers, his whole body ached. Beyond weary, he lay down on a bench just yards from The Cross. He had given up; there was no fight left. No longer scared, he nonetheless conceded that his past life was over. He would see his father, but the realisation that Lucy was lost to them forever hurt him more than anything. He waited for sleep and to drift away. No more pain. Peace might show its face at last. He heard a voice and tried to respond.

'Is that you, Dad? Have you come for me?'

A pause, then he felt a hand gently stroking his wrist. An arm around his shoulder helped him to sit up. Blurred vision and intense nausea prevented him from taking in his location.

'It's me, Dad. Peter.'
'Is my father here?'
'No, Grandad's not here. He's with Grandma.'
'No!'

'It's okay, you're back with us. You'll be fine.'

Gradually, Ben regained his awareness. He remembered the van, Don Gil, the scorpion.
With limited strength, he hugged his son and did not want to let go.

35: Lucy

Carol's dreams were always dominated by Graham, and she was consoled by the daily thought of meeting him again. Sometimes she forgot what he looked like and then saw him clearly, giving her that special smile - the one reserved only for her. This night was different. She could see Lucy, heavily pregnant, at home with Jack. Ben was not there, then Carol realised that Lucy was pregnant with him. Carol could hear them talking as if she was standing in the room with them. She called out, but no one heard.

'Try not to upset yourself, love.'

'But Jack, I'm only six months gone,' replied Lucy. 'I've had two weeks' bed rest and the bleeding has started again.'

'I've called the doctor. He's on his way.'

~

Lucy wanted this baby more than anything. In those days, ultrasound scans were used but they didn't reveal the sex of the child. That didn't matter to Lucy. She instinctively knew she was having a boy.

'We'll call him Ben,' she told Jack.

'What if it's a girl?'

'Unlikely. I have an instinct, but you choose.'

'Deborah, or Jackie?'

'Deborah, I think. Debbie sounds nice when they shorten it.'

'That's settled then - Ben or Deborah.'

~

The doctor arrived within an hour of Jack's call. He quickly decided to call for an ambulance.

'You'll have your baby today, Mrs Stone, probably by C-section.'

'I wanted a natural birth.'

'Best for the baby.'

'I suppose...'

Jack was down the stairs almost before they heard the bell ring. Two paramedics attended - one a woman about twenty-five, the other a man in his early thirties. The woman assessed Lucy, then stepped away to consult her colleague.

'I'll get the chair and the ramp ready. Could you stay with Mrs Stone?'

The man nodded, taking Lucy's hand.

'You'll be alright,' he said.

'I'll do anything to save my baby.'

'Anything?'

'I'd sell my soul to the devil if he could make things right.'

'You should be careful what you promise,' he whispered. Jack was just out of earshot on the landing.

Lucy gripped the man's hand.

'I don't care. If God deserts me, what do I have left?'

Jack heard the last comment. It hurt, but he shared his wife's desperation. The other paramedic returned to the bedroom, and they lifted Lucy carefully onto the chair.

'No problem, the chair will fit down these stairs. We've done this a hundred times.'

The female paramedic driving, the man stayed with Lucy in the back of the ambulance. Jack has decided to follow by car. The journey for Lucy was uncomfortable, but she was oddly reassured by the words of the man.
'Mrs Stone, if you meant what you said, we can save your baby. We will meet again one day. Your son will always be with you, even on the day you die.'
'My son, will I have a son?'
He didn't speak again until the ambulance doors were opened at the maternity entrance.
'Good luck, Mrs Stone, remember what you promised.'

~

'I hate talking to you about this, Ben.'
'It's okay, Aunt, you're helping me to understand everything that's happened.'
'I never told you that I used to dream about your Uncle Graham every night.'
'Used to?'
'For the last few weeks I've been scared to go to sleep. I've seen and heard things that are not possible. With all that's happened to you, I think my imagination has gone into overdrive.'
Ben held Carol's hand and tried to convince her that maybe not everything she dreamt was from the depths of her imagination.

'But Ben, these things don't happen in real life. Your mom and dad died in that terrible accident. We were with you. I don't know how you coped.'

'I know, Aunt, but please try to remember what Mom said to you.'

Reluctantly, Carol began to recount her dreams. She refused to believe that she was a messenger between a man and his deceased mother. A consolation for both Ben and Carol the realisation that even if they were 'just dreams', none of the information gleaned by Ben would be of any help to Don Gil.

'Just before you were born, there was a paramedic. Any opportunity to get Lucy on her own... well, the things he said...'

'Carry on, it's alright.'

'Lucy virtually promised her soul to him. Promised that at the point of her death, he would be allowed to take away from Lucy the eternal peace she believed we have when we die. I think Don Gil expected her to die in childbirth, but she survived until that terrible day in the States. He had been waiting for that moment, but something went wrong, and Lucy was somehow suspended between two worlds.'

'What about Dad?'

'I don't know. I think your mom only had the energy to talk about you and the reason you have been targeted by Gil - if that's his real name. '

Carol went on to explain that, in retribution, Don Gil initiated a plan to condemn her child, instead of Lucy. He was to be condemned to eternal damnation, but he had to go willingly. He had not agreed to give up his soul. His mother had made that commitment.

'I can't believe we're talking about this.'

'Aunt Carol, you don't know how helpful you've been. I'm not saying I believe all this, but it helps to explain why I've been targeted by Gil and his followers. They've used my family to get to me. The boys have unwittingly been involved throughout their lives.'

'What will you do?'

'Not sure there's much I can do,' said Ben. 'The police have Don Gil and Hannah, and the rest of the gang are dead. Somehow, we've got to move on from this. And, Aunt, I'm sorry you lost Uncle Graham – I mean in your dreams – I do hope you get him back soon.'

He would have preferred to put it behind him, but as he left Carol's house, Ben phoned Peter.

'Are you at home? Great. I want to see you. I'll be back in fifteen minutes.'

~

Peter heard the car pull onto the drive. As the front door opened, he was already in the hall waiting for his father.

'Still not sure I believe what's happened, Peter. It's clear that Gil planned this all along, and that those people, including Hannah, had been recruited – each for a specific purpose.'

'Dad, every time her name is mentioned...'

'Sorry, son,' said Ben, leading Peter into the lounge.

'No, Dad, don't worry. It's just that I don't think I've ever hated anyone so much. Not even when Terry Hickens and his gang beat me up.'

'It's understandable. You fell in love with Hannah. She's a beautiful girl, but she betrayed you. She deserves to be despised. Even your mom will never forgive her.'

'Even with her Christian beliefs?'

'There are limits.'

They returned to their discussion about Egyptology and Peter's theory of Isis and the Seven Scorpions. If nothing else, the irony of the scorpions was not lost on them. The creature had stung the boy in the story and his mother Isis begged for help. Seth, the brother of Isis, told the woman 'I will save him if you give me his soul.'

'So Don Gil is Seth,' concluded Peter.

'I don't know what to think,' said Ben.

Ben's weary eyes, betraying the fire that once burnt, now lacked vigour and the youthful spark he had retained into his forties. He was more than tired, possibly damaged forever, but he knew there was one final task to fulfil. Ben and Peter would go to the police station where Gil was being held. They both wanted to speak to him. The least he could do was offer a proper explanation.

'Will you want to see Hannah?'

'No way, Dad. She can rot in hell as far as I'm concerned.'

'She probably will.'

36:   Over

Peter called the police station to ask if DI Tromans had given permission for them to visit Don Gil.

'We can speak to him, Dad.'

'What did they say?'

'He won't tell them anything new, but he's admitted to a connection with our family. He's promised that he will explain everything to you.'

'You know, Peter, I wouldn't trust him as far as I could throw him, but we have to finish this.'

The journey to the police station took much longer than expected. Every set of lights on red. Hold-ups at every junction. Ben, sensitive to his son's feelings about Hannah, restricted comments to mundane matters except for a couple of derogatory stabs at Gil's character. Peter, reluctant to burden his father with his own continuing anguish, relived the sequence of events from early in 2016 to the point where he struck the girl he had fallen in love with. Her broken jaw a testament to the conclusion of that particular story.

He recalled the night he was beaten up by Terry Hickens for snogging Terry's girlfriend, Barbara. He savoured the feelings he had for Jodie in that wonderful year they spent together. A year that ended in tragedy. The family still only mention her name on 4th October each year. He thought about the secrets they had kept from Ben, the messages from Greta about 'meeting on the other side', his translations of the Latin phrases, and the troubles with Alan and Cheryl. They arrived at the station. He wouldn't see Hannah, but it was hard to get her out of his mind.

Ben thought about Joanna. Their life together encapsulated by the fun of shocking poor Mrs Granger at number 56 contrasted with the trouble caused by James Enright. 'You'll be sorry one day,' Enright had told Joanna. It took a long time for the links between Enright, Hickens, Gil and the rest to make any sense. Ben didn't know at the time, but Joanna had suspected Liz of betraying the family. She didn't know why, but after the séance, Keith appeared on the scene. Liz, albeit not involved in the conspiracy, could not be considered completely innocent after her move towards Ben. Joanna eventually forgave her, and always trusted Ben. The Latin phrase translated by Peter, 'unus dies vos cognoscetis' ('one day you will know') was now understood by Joanna. Someone knew that Peter was destined to meet Jodie. Someone knew he would lose his first love and meet Hannah.

Alan, bullied at school by Frank Carter, battled with another of Gil's accomplices, Melanie Crowther. He also had no idea that the old lady he looked after, Greta Armitage, had been given the role of 'gatekeeper'. She had never met Ben, but the long-standing promise his mother made to Gil had been common knowledge among the group of evil for years.

Cheryl had betrayed Alan more than once, but not with Don Gil. He had tricked her into his house and violated her body and her mind. She couldn't be sure of the identity of Joshua's father but desperately hoped it was Alan. Ben thought she would prefer not to know for sure. So much had happened, so much kept from him. No recriminations now. The family's priority was the safety of young Josh. Ben's train of thought was broken as Peter pulled into the parking space reserved for visitors.

Built as part of Banfield Civic Hall, the police station appeared grander to the first-time visitor than it deserved. A wide, sweeping drive led to an L-shaped block with an ornate reception area housing tall, Victorian-style windows. Ben and Peter had been there before. When Josh had been taken, the televised press conference had been carried out there.
'I'll do the talking, Peter.'

Ben wanted to control the situation now. Having been, it seems, controlled by Don Gil all his life, he wanted to wrestle the initiative back. He was to be disappointed, but at the same time reflect that their problems could be over.
'Inspector Tromans will see you in room six. I'll take you there.'

Ben and Peter followed the young WPC along the corridor like a pair of 12-year-olds being taken to the headmaster.

'Good morning. We haven't met, but I am fully aware of the case. Mr Stone, will you take a seat?' said the inspector.

'Call me Ben, and this is my son, Peter.'

'Well, Ben, I have some news for you. Just after your son called, Mr Gil died in his cell.'

'What? How?'

'The coroner will have to confirm it, but we are treating it as a possible suicide.'

'Christ,' gasped Ben.

'Peter...' The inspector paused as if waiting for a signal that it was alright to continue. 'Peter, I believe you had a serious relationship with Miss Brooks...'

'Different name, but yes, I went out with Hannah.'

'There's no easy way to say this, Peter, but it appears that Hannah has also taken her own life.'

'What?'

'...at the same time as Mr Gil. Precisely the same time and they had no means of contacting each other.'

Ben placed his hand on Peter's left shoulder.

'Son...'

'It's alright, Dad. It's just a shock.'

Ben pulled his thoughts together.

'Inspector, what was the cause of the two deaths?'

'As I said, it needs to be confirmed, but it's the strangest thing. In each of the cells, next to each body we found a live scorpion.'

'Deathstalker,' said Ben.

'Excuse me?'

'The deathstalker scorpion.'

'I won't ask how you know that,' said the inspector. 'We've collected them in a box. The expert from Banfield Zoo is on her way. Hopefully she will confirm your theory.'

'Most deadly in the world,' explained Ben. 'Maybe Gil thinks he's had the last word. I think it's poetic justice, but I did want to speak to him.'

'We found a note. Gil was holding it in his hand. It's for you, Ben.'

Tromans reached over to the table, taking the note that was addressed to 'Mr Ben Stone, Leeford Village'. Underneath were written three words in block capitals:

IT IS OVER

37:   Closure

'Ben, they look so happy. Is it going to stay this way?'
'Jo, in all the years we've been together, I've never made you a promise I can't keep.'
'You promised to keep us all safe, and you did that.'

Ben still found it hard to believe that it was finally all over. He never discussed the events with the young couple sitting on the living room floor playing with their young child. They had been through enough and he felt responsible. Jo understood that - so did Peter. They both managed to convince him that although Don Gil should never have been trusted, the man had finally given up. Ben's mother had triumphed over evil, saving her son and his family. For Ben, it wasn't so much concern that Gil would somehow return, but the unresolved issue of his parents. Were they at peace? He convinced himself there was no way of finding out.

~

'Ben, could you call in sometime for a chat? Nothing urgent.'
'No problem, Aunt. I can come over straight away if you like.'

Ben knew from her tone that the 'chat' was more significant than she described. The last time they sat down together, Carol had described the vivid dreams she had experienced. Dreams that felt so real. Ben still couldn't bring himself to believe that his mother had spoken to his aunt.

Within half an hour, Carol's doorbell rang and she greeted Ben with a kiss on the cheek.

'Sit down Ben, I have to tell you. Everything has changed.'

'Are you okay?'

'Of course, I'm fine. Graham is back.'

'You mean...'

'Yes, in my dreams, but they are so real.'

'Has Graham seen Mom and Dad?'

'It's not as simple as that. He is aware of them, but not in a physical sense. He just places thoughts in my mind. I find it so reassuring.'

'Aunt, I'm so happy for you.'

'Ben, there's something else. The Cross, the threshold. It's closing.'

'What does that mean?'

'I don't understand it any more than you,' said Carol, 'but I'm sure it means that your torment is finally over.'

'Mom and Dad...' Ben sighed.

'Lucy and Jack will let you know. Everything will be alright.'

The journey home from Carol's always took Ben over The Cross. He considered going the long way round, down the A449 and back the other way into Leeford Village, but something told him he should stick to his usual route. As he approached The Cross, Ben braced himself for the shudder down his spine that he had occasionally experienced. This time, a different feeling.

An inner calm, but he felt light-headed and had to pull into the side of the road.

He could hear his father's voice. His words were as clear as if he were sitting next to Ben in the car.
'This is the last time you'll hear from me, Ben. You know that Gil and Hannah died. We fought him at the threshold. Your mom had not quite crossed over - Gil had planted that in your mind. Lucy is with me now, and we're happy to stay together forever. Gil and the seven have no way back. The threshold will soon close forever, dividing good from evil.'

As Ben wiped away the streams of tears from his face, he heard a soft, female voice. Faint, but just audible.
'Goodbye Ben, we both love you. We'll be together again one day.'

Author Biography

Michael Braccia is a writer and musician living on the Staffordshire / West Midlands border. After working in I.T. for twenty-two years, part-time lecturing at the local college and running three small businesses, Michael retired early to look after his wife and son. He self-published two books in 2015 and went on to create the concept for a light drama / soap opera, Leeford Village.

After being widowed in January 2019, Michael formed a writing partnership with his friend and ex-colleague, Jon Markes. In September that year, through to mid-2024, the serial 'Leeford Village' was published by the regional newspaper the Express and Star, on their website. Michael and Jon went on to publish the first Leeford Village book in 2022.

In the spring of 2019, Michael began to visit folk clubs, initially to watch other performers. However, he was eventually persuaded to step onto the stage in front of more than fifty people to sing a few songs. At that club (The Woodman Folk Club), he met a lady who had been singing in folk clubs for many years. They formed the acoustic duo, *Second Chance,* became a couple, and eventually married in April 2024. Music and writing are now central to their lives, and while Michael is writing stories, he also co-writes songs with Lesley, and they published their first album, *'Did you think of me'*, in 2022.

At the time *Leeford Village* was created, Michael also planned to write a novel – very different to the soap opera serialised by the Express and Star newspaper. All of Michael's stories are based around the fictional village of Leeford, in the fictional town of Banfield.

Vision of Another Life is Michael's debut fictional novel.

www.michaelbraccia.co.uk

Printed in Great Britain
by Amazon